A Collection of Three Christmas Novellas

A GIFT for all TIME

Tonya B. Ashley
Jenny Carlisle
Ellen E. Withers

Scrivenings
PRESS
Quench your thirst for story.
www.ScriveningsPress.com

Published by Scrivenings Press LLC
15 Lucky Lane
Morrilton, Arkansas 72110
https://ScriveningsPress.com

Printed in the United States of America

Paperback ISBN 978-1-64917-334-8

eBook ISBN 978-1-64917-336-2

Editors: Amy R. Anguish and Linda Fulkerson

Cover design by Linda Fulkerson - www.bookmarketinggraphics.com

Once Lost now Found

Tonya B. Ashley

Keep the lamp lit!

Tonya B Ashley

To Papaw Bradford and Papaw Rebel, who cherished my words and saw something special in me.

1

December, 1845
Van Buren, Arkansas

The rough-hewn door of the blacksmith shop creaked open at Levi Snow's light touch, breaking the morning stillness. He needed no lamp to guide him through the pre-dawn darkness. As though part of his very being, he knew every rut in the dirt floor and the location of tree stump stools, work table, anvil, and tools.

Crossing to the sitting area, he paused before lighting a fire in the potbellied stove. A winter chill had settled in the workshop. He laid his hand atop the stove, the cold surface a rarity for someone who worked with hot metal every day. The temperature had dropped more than thirty degrees following the previous day's severe storms.

He tossed a match into the woodstove. *Whoosh*. The sound of the fire catching conjured images of churning clouds and fierce winds from the previous afternoon. What kind of losses had folks experienced up and down the river? What kind of help would they require? He pushed the thought away—no need to worry about that now. Someone would find him if he were needed.

Leaving the stove door open provided a little light. Levi started a pot of coffee and sat at the small, makeshift table near the stove. He hadn't wanted a sitting area in the smithy because it would encourage folks to drop by throughout the day. Sam Mooney agreed to take orders at the mercantile, which Levi picked up regularly. While collecting requests for new orders from Sam, Levi dropped off completed projects. However, customers with metalwork orders too large to deliver to the mercantile came to the forge, often too early. With no sitting area, they invaded his workspace with idle chatter. So, at Sam's suggestion, he provided two tree stumps, a table, and a deck of cards, which kept most occupied while preserving the peace and order he cherished.

Levi lit a stubby candle, providing a slight halo of warm light. Then, taking pieces of paper from his pocket, he unfolded them and spread them on the table. Stars, holly, wreaths, bows, candy canes, and Christmas trees. Though he had little regard for Christmas, he pulled these sketches out every December. This year, Sam requested Christmas-themed bells and the usual tree ornaments. Unfortunately, folks were too impatient to order catalog ornaments.

Levi closed his eyes, taking a deep breath. The cool winter air mingled with ribbons of heat from the stove. He preferred sitting with an idea before sketching a design to scale. He pulled a blank page free from the others and grabbed the sketching pencil tucked over his ear. The tip of the pencil slid through his calloused fingers to the paper. The door creaked. His hand slipped. The lead scrawled across the page. He pursed his lips, exhaled roughly, and dropped the pencil on the paper.

Mahala Hogue appeared in the doorway, her oil lamp

flooding the room with light. "Levi? Levi Snow? Are you at it already?"

Levi rubbed his palms over his face and shielded his eyes. "Yes, Mrs. Hogue. Up and at it before dawn, as usual."

Entering, she closed the door behind her. Lamplight exaggerated faint creases under her eyes and laugh lines framing her mouth. She fisted a crocheted shawl tightly at her neck.

"I have news—"

"Extinguish the light, please." Levi picked up the sketching pencil.

"The light?"

"I spend early morning hours in candlelight only." He waved a finger overhead, indicating the intrusion of light. He'd grown accustomed to the low light that allowed him to see the subtle details or flaws as he worked glowing hot metals. "Lamplight after coffee."

"Of course." With a nod, Mahala extinguished her lamp. "A young man brought news from the river. The *Resilient* didn't make shore before the storms hit. It's run aground on a sandbar."

Turning the paper over, Levi began to sketch again. "Survivors?"

Mahala joined him, setting the darkened lamp on the table. Pulling her shawl tighter around her shoulders, she rubbed her arms vigorously. "A rescue launched a while ago. The *Valiant* should be arriving with the passengers sometime this morning."

"Any word of Captain Cobb and the crew?"

"Nothing definite. The young man said they expect to bring in the *Resilient* later today. Can you go to the wharf to help?"

"I'll make time." His hand glided across the page with quick strokes. Levi habitually responded to a crisis because he often gained work from it. "Have someone send for me when you get word of the *Resilient's* arrival."

"You misunderstand. Help is needed now to prepare the landing to receive the rescue boat." She patted his hand. "I know you're just interested in the work, but your ability to think and act quickly is well known. This town can't have a crisis without Levi Snow to set it to order. I'll wake Justin. He can go with you."

"What about Mr. Hogue?" Levi asked, hoping he could gain a few hours in the forge. "He's every bit as good in a crisis as I am. Better, I'd say."

"Down in his back."

"No need to wake Justin." Levi rubbed a hand over his hair. "He's tending the horses. Should be here any minute to begin his apprenticeship work."

"Have him stop by the kitchen before you go. I'll gather some food for you."

He nodded, followed her to the door, and relit her lamp with his candle. Justin stepped out the stable door as Levi waited for her to disappear into the boardinghouse.

"Was that Ma? What is she doing out here so early?"

"Hitch up the wagon. We're going to the landing. Don't know how long we'll be there."

"Trouble from the storms?"

Levi nodded.

"Once the wagon is hitched, get the coffee off the stove and take it to your Ma so it doesn't go to waste. She'll have food for us." Levi paused, eyeing Justin. "Comb your hair, tuck in your shirt. Your Ma doesn't say anything but worries when she sees you looking unkempt. I've got a sketch to finish, and I'll start loading tools."

Justin nodded and went straight to work. Returning to the workshop, Levi resumed his sketching. Quick strokes completed the image of a bell with a border of holly leaves trimming the bottom. He collected the papers and placed them in the order box on his work table. Other designs would have to wait until he and Justin returned.

Levi gathered tools—handsaws, axes, rakes, hoes, whatever might be helpful. Justin reappeared with two flour sacks of food. Levi smiled and shook his head. "How long does your Ma think we'll be gone?"

Justin chuckled. "You know Ma."

"Yes, I do. Did she get her hug?"

He nodded. "She must be worried. I got a peck on the cheek too."

Levi knew Mahala Hogue would want to hug her son goodbye even though he was twenty-two and she saw him daily. Their relationship intrigued him. Mrs. Hogue wasn't intrusive but made time whenever Justin wanted to talk, and she never failed to greet him or send him off with warm affection. Would he have such a relationship with his mother if she hadn't died so young?

"Best get going." Levi climbed into the buckboard wagon, taking the reins. His coat, gloves, hat, and scarf lay on the seat. "Did you do this?"

Justin nodded as he climbed up. "I know you tolerate the cold until the forge gets heated, so I figured you might not think of these until we got down the road a piece."

Levi donned the winter garments. "Good man."

2

The old wagon slogged through the mud under the extra weight of the tools. Frequent interruptions to remove debris from the road made the trip from the boardinghouse to the waterfront tedious. Justin had taken to bouncing his knee in between stops.

"I've told you again and again."

"Sorry, Levi. I'm anxious to get there and get to work."

"We'll get there when we get there. Not a moment sooner. Quit that bouncing, or you'll walk the rest of the way." Levi flicked the reins, urging the horses to pick up speed. A futile gesture as the mud kept them trudging along. "Did you notice the window at Mrs. Grace's? We'll make a set of bars to cover it. This is the third time it's been broken out by that old tree."

"You know she can't afford that."

"It's our gift this Christmas." Levi clicked his tongue at the horses. "She doesn't have anyone to look after those things since Mr. Grace died. So, it's up to us to help her now."

Though the trip to the landing took almost a half-hour, three times longer than usual, the town looked in decent shape. It was still bleak and gray, with no sign of Christmas. A few structures had near misses with downed trees, some with broken windows, perhaps struck by debris caught in the wind. However, no trees had fallen on the road, only large limbs. The largest branches required both Levi and Justin to remove them from the roadway.

The landing, however, bustled with chaotic activity. As Levi's gaze roved the waterfront, he spied debris cluttering the wharf and river banks. It would require hard work, but it wasn't devastating. The *Coffee No. 7* and the *Agnes Toupe* were docked at the landing. The *No. 7* appeared all right, while the *Agnes Toupe* had signs of damage.

"Justin, take a look. What do you see?"

"A lot of hard work." He wiped his brow as if he'd already begun. "Hard work."

"Notice anything life-threatening? Anything truly destructive?"

"No." Justin tilted his head and relaxed his shoulders. "No, I don't."

"Either we're missing something, or they need someone to pull them together. They probably rode out the storm on the steamboats. Perhaps they're still shook."

Levi plodded down the slope toward the steamboats, calling men to him as he went. Justin stayed on his heels. When Levi had gathered several men, he stopped. The men wearing damp, disheveled clothing shivered and stamped their feet as they circled Levi and Justin.

"Crewmen from the *Coffee No. 7*?" Levi surveyed the ragtag group, and six men raised their hands. Levi nodded to the closest one. "How many in the crew of the *No. 7*?"

"Twenty-five, sir."

"All right, fine, then. You," Levi pointed to a smaller cluster of men, "from the *Agnes Toupe*?"

They nodded.

"Crew size?"

"Twenty-three."

"Where can I find Captain Horn and Captain Toupe?"

They all answered at once. Levi held up a hand. They quieted. He pointed again to the crewman from the *No. 7*. "Where is Captain Horn?"

"Captain Horn is aboard the *No. 7*."

Levi pointed to a crewman from the *Agnes Toupe*.

"No one has seen Captain Toupe, sir."

"Men from the *No. 7*, tell Captain Horn I need to speak with him. From the *Agnes Toupe*, gather all the crew members you can find and have them meet back here. Go on."

Levi turned to Justin. "Start bringing the tools from the wagon."

"What are you going to do?"

"I'm going to speak with Robert Horn and the men of the *Agnes Toupe*. Got to get everyone working together. Otherwise, the rescue boat won't be able to land." Levi patted Justin's back, sending him on his way.

Robert Horn approached with a growl. "What's the meaning of this, blacksmith?"

"We've done enough business, Horn. You know my name."

Levi extended his hand. Horn stared, not offering his hand. A sawed-off piece of work, eyes of stone, skin like a rough-cut, well-worn piece of dark rawhide, Horn intimidated many. Unfazed by Horn's rigid demeanor and unrelenting stare, Levi plowed a line straight to the point.

"Gather the men from the *No. 7*. We must get everyone working together. A rescue boat will arrive soon, and the *Resilient* is coming later."

"Get the townspeople to do it."

"Your men are here. Besides, I need to send Justin to have

townsfolk bring dry clothes, food for your crew, and wagons to transport passengers and cargo into town." Levi clapped his gloved hands together a couple of times to stave off the cold, anxious to get to work. "I found a third of your crew wandering about when I arrived. Better for your boat and the *Agnes Toupe* if we organize them."

"Let Toupe worry with his vessel, and I'll worry with mine."

"Captain Toupe is missing." Levi glanced at the wounded steamboat.

"Missing? What do you mean, *missing*?"

"No one has seen him."

"Fine. Fine. L.B. Toupe pulled me out of more than one scrape. I guess I owe him." Horn narrowed his eyes. "We'll do it your way—against my better judgment."

Assembling the crews, Levi took a headcount. There were seven unaccounted for—three from the *No. 7* and four from the *Agnes Toupe*, including the captain. He divided the men into groups and assigned them to specific tasks, prioritizing the cleanup of the wharf and riverfront. He designated a handful to attend to the injured and act as messengers. The remaining men formed two groups, one to work aboard the *Agnes Toupe* and one aboard the *No. 7*.

"Eight men to work the *No. 7*." Captain Horn snarled. "Out of a crew of twenty-five."

"The rest of your men will return to the boat as soon as the landing is cleared."

Horn scratched his head. He barked orders to the group returning to the *No. 7*. Then he turned to Levi. "I'm going aboard the *Agnes Toupe*. L.B. Toupe better not be lollygagging when I find him."

"I understand, Captain. I expect you'll let him have it when you find him."

With a nod, Captain Horn set off to find Toupe. Levi chuckled and shook his head, recognizing Horn's comment as the most profound expression of sentiment he'd ever seen from the man.

Levi scanned the area for Justin and, having spotted him, waved him over.

"Are the tools out of the wagon?"

"Yes. The men clearing the landing have all the tools they need." Justin shook his head. "That was something, watching you set all that in order."

"I like order. When things are set to order, you can get more done for more folks. Of course, it helps when folks are willing to work together. We're lucky Captain Horn agreed." Levi patted his cold cheeks. "I reckon it's got to be close to eight o'clock. Head up to the mercantile and tell Sam Mooney that we need dry clothes and food for crew members. Wagons for the passengers coming off the rescue boat. As much as the townspeople can provide."

Justin took a few steps, and Levi caught his shoulder and pulled him back.

"One more thing—see if you can find the doctor. If he's not available, bring the barber. Better yet, get them both."

"You think it's that bad?" Justin's eyebrows furrowed.

"So far, I've not seen anything life-threatening. A few injuries should be seen, but mostly bumps and scrapes. Problem is, we have no idea what we'll have when these boats come off the river, especially with Toupe still missing."

"I'll be back with help. Lots of it."

It wasn't long before a handful of townsfolk arrived. A few men brought tools and joined the crewmen clearing the landing. Some women organized food and clothing on Water Street. Someone brought a load of dry firewood and started a great fire. Levi had hoped more would come to help, but soon

14

both vessels' crews had a meal, a change of dry clothes, and a place to warm themselves. With their spirits lifted, the men cleared the landing in less than two hours.

Levi finished a conversation with Captain Horn as Justin walked up with Sam Mooney.

"I'm sorry we couldn't get more people to come," Justin said. "Most of them, like the barber, wanted to get their businesses open or their property cleaned up."

"At least the doctor came, and the others are hardworking."

"Any word on Captain Toupe?"

"Horn found him. Heavy cargo fell on him while he was checking on his men. His leg is broken, but Doc said he believes he can save it." Levi turned his attention to the mercantile owner. "Sam, don't you have a business to open?"

"Closed the store. My niece was due to arrive on the *Resilient*. When will the rescue boat arrive?"

The low moan of a steamboat whistle sounded. Men at the landing flew into a flurry of motion, preparing to land the vessel. Levi, Justin, and Sam ran to meet it. Despite the swift current, the landing went smoothly. As soon as it was in place, passengers swarmed the gangplank, pushing and shoving. Before the trio of men could shoulder their way through the crowd, pandemonium broke loose. Their shouted instructions were absorbed by the ruckus.

As Levi made it topside, a chilling scream split the air as a body plummeted over the side. Spying an empty barrel nearby, he began barking orders. "Justin, knock the bottom out. I'll find a rope."

3

Looking over the edge, Levi watched a slip of a girl in a lavender dress carried away by the current. He threaded the rope through the barrel and turned to Justin. "Hold the barrel here. I'll jump in holding the rope. When I reach her, slide the barrel down to help keep us afloat."

Throwing off his winter hat, gloves, scarf, and coat, Levi jumped in feet first. He fought the urge to gasp until he surfaced. The sensation of pinpricks peppered his body. Each breath took a concentrated effort to steady. Reaching the girl at an awkward angle, Levi struggled to gain control of her torso and head while maintaining his grip on the rope. Fighting the current, he pulled her to him.

Using his free hand, he tucked her limp body tightly into the crook of his arm. The rope tangled with her dress. Her head lolled, a mass of reddish-blonde hair covering her face. Waving his free hand, he motioned to Justin to release the barrel.

The rope slipped. Levi went under. Pushing the girl's body up, he wrangled the cord from her skirt. Resurfacing, he hoisted her body up onto the barrel. Slowly, they were pulled

16

toward the steamboat. He clapped his hand on her back a few times. Water spewed from her mouth. She sputtered and came to life, feet kicking and arms flailing.

Levi pinned one arm and whispered in her ear. "Easy now. I've got you. There's a warm fire waiting."

She shivered, closed her eyes, and hugged the barrel. Levi rested his head against the side of the barrel, exhausted and chilled to his core. When they reached the side of the *Valiant*, a second rope dropped. Levi encircled her waist with the rope, and she was hoisted aboard. He let the barrel slide free from the first rope and tied it around himself. His body bumped and scraped against the hull of the boat. Moments later, hands grabbed his belt and deposited him on the deck. Justin hovered over him.

"That was Sam Mooney's niece you saved."

"Tell him I promised her a warm fire." Levi closed his eyes.

It seemed his eyes had been closed only a few minutes when someone nudged Levi's shoulder.

"Have a good nap, Levi?"

Levi opened one eye. Justin loomed large, with a boyish grin and fine chin hairs. Levi pushed him away. "Too close. What do you mean nap?"

"You've been asleep a few hours."

He snapped awake. "A few hours?"

Justin offered a hand to help him sit up. "Sound as a new foal."

"I've been asleep? For hours?" He scanned the unfamiliar surroundings. "Where am I? What about my clothes?"

"Horn made a tent for the doctor. I guess he got you into dry clothes. Kept you and Mooney's niece for rest and observation."

Levi raised his head. "Where is she? Is she okay?"

Justin nodded across the tent. "Still sleeping."

Levi eyed the bed of crates piled with quilts, a plume of wavy, strawberry-blonde hair hanging from the end. "Where is Mooney?"

"The steamboat captains wanted him to gather supplies for repairs, so he returned to the store. I told him that we'd bring his niece home. Of course, I've loaded all the metalwork into our wagon." Justin sat next to Levi. "I'm about to check with Captain Horn to see if he needs us to do anything else before we go, but Doc says the two of you are free to leave. Once she wakes, of course."

"What about Captain Cobb?"

"He and his brother left for the boardinghouse as soon as his crew was taken care of. He'll get a good day's sleep and start fresh tomorrow. We might have more work from him later." Justin stood and handed Levi a pair of boots. "There's still a good fire going outside. Hot coffee too. Extra coats and winter wear in the corner."

"I'll be out momentarily." Levi stretched and raked his fingers through his beard. "You go ahead and talk to Horn."

"Holler if you need anything," Justin tossed over his shoulder as he left the tent.

Levi threw off layers of quilts, slipped on the boots, and breathed deeply. He was getting up when Horn pushed his way through the tent flap.

"Pretty clever taking a nap to avoid the hard work, blacksmith." Horn's lips curled into a smile.

Levi grasped Horn's elbow and ushered him out of the tent. "Sorry I missed all the fun."

"I'd say I'm the one who missed out. I hear you fished that pretty thing out of the river." Horn's voice boomed.

"*Shh*, hush. She's still sleeping." Levi patted the air. "I understand Justin has loaded some items needing repair."

"Be sure to put my repairs at the top of the list." Horn

cleared his throat and spit. "My boat makes the trip to Fort Coffee, Oklahoma, in seven days instead of the usual eight to ten. That's why I call her the *Coffee No. 7*. These repairs will put me behind schedule. I need to get going as quickly as possible."

"I'll do what I can."

"And I'll check your progress daily."

"I know you will." Levi ducked inside, patting his arms.

The form on the crates hadn't moved. Should he wake her? He hesitated, moved close to the makeshift cot, and reached out.

"I'm not asleep. Just cozy warm under these quilts." Her soft voice broke the silence. "I've been awake quite a while, listening."

Levi pulled his hand back. "Listening?"

"Trying to hear anything the doctor had to say. Men are more forthcoming with information when talking to other men."

"You think so? I don't guess I've noticed that."

"My mother's doctor knew she was dying. He told my father. Neither of them told me. They didn't think I could handle it." She cleared her throat, rolled over, and sat up. "I figure if I want to know my condition, it's better to pretend to be asleep and listen."

"I see. And how are you? I hope you didn't get too banged up when they hauled you up the side of the boat."

"I'm a little sore, but not bad. Coffee and a warm fire would be lovely. If memory serves, that's what you promised, a warm fire." Her blue eyes glimmered.

"Good memory." Levi sorted through the coats, finding one for each of them. "Now, forgive me because I don't recall your name."

"Time didn't allow for introductions." Her easy smile and

sparkling eyes caused his heart to skip a beat. She held out her hand. "Allie McLaughlin."

"Levi Snow." He shook her hand. "Join me for coffee?"

Allie nodded, donned the coat, grabbed a quilt around her shoulders, and followed him out of the tent. Noticing a box of blankets at the end of the woodpile near the fire, Levi took one and laid it over the close-by log. He motioned for her to sit and grabbed two tin cups from another box. Keeping one for himself, he handed the other to her. Next, he found the coffee pot and filled their cups. Then he leaned against the woodpile.

"I must look frightful." Allie wiped at the grime on the trousers. "The only clothes they could find for me belonged to some of the boys on the steamboat crews."

"It becomes you." Then, seeing her brow furrow, he tried again. "I mean to say that you were unconscious when I first saw you. So, it's good to see you walking and talking."

She grinned. "I owe you a great debt of gratitude. I wouldn't be here if you hadn't risked your life to save me."

"I'm thankful I was there. I'm curious, however. I didn't see what caused you to fall overboard." He shifted under the weight of her pointed gaze.

"When the boat docked, Captain Reed told us to disembark, and everyone began moving quickly. But, of course, it was overcrowded with double the passengers. I was being shoved toward the railing. A man beside me turned abruptly, striking me with a large burlap bag, and over I went."

"I'm glad I could spare Sam such a loss." Levi stared into his coffee cup. "Losing a loved one so close to Christmas is especially difficult."

"Did you lose someone?" Allie's voice was almost a whisper. "Close to Christmas?"

"My mother, Christmas Day."

"How did she die, if you don't mind my asking?"

Her mesmerizing eyes captured his gaze. Looking away, he rubbed the back of his neck. "Are you warm enough? I can grab another blanket from the box or add a log to the fire."

"I'm sorry. I've said too much." She thumbed the handle of the tin cup. "I'm notorious for going one step further than I ought."

"Hey, Levi."

Justin reappeared, and Levi was grateful for the interruption. "Yeah?"

"I'm going to leave this box here." He sat the box next to Levi. "Don't let me forget to take it with us when we leave."

"What is it? A hatbox?"

"No idea. Captain Horn found it on the road where passengers' belongings were unloaded. No one picked it up, and all the passengers have been carried into town except Miss Allie."

"Have we been introduced?" Allie tilted her head.

"Well, no, but your uncle wouldn't leave you in our care without telling me your name, would he?" Justin grinned, warming his hands over the fire and stamping his feet.

"I guess he wouldn't." Then, shaking her head, she smiled. She nodded toward the box. "It's not mine. I don't recognize it."

"That's okay." Levi patted the box. "We'll take it back to the boardinghouse and put it in the lost and found."

"You ought to see what's inside. It might give you a clue as to who the owner is." Allie lifted the coffee cup to her lips.

"Nah." Levi waved his hand at the smoke wafting toward him. "If it's missed, the owners will ask around, and someone will send them to the boardinghouse. Most of the town knows Clayburn Hogue's boardinghouse acts as lost and found for items left on the steamboats."

"The loft above the bunkroom is getting full. So, starting to locate owners isn't a bad idea." Justin clapped his hands together and rubbed his arms as he turned to go. "I've got a couple more things to do. Be back shortly."

"Well, I don't care what you say. I'm going to take a peek." Allie stifled a cough, moved from her perch, and knelt at the box next to Levi. "Look, the lid lifts right off, nothing securing it closed."

Levi leaned closer as she raised the lid, revealing handfuls of straw and scrap fabric. "Looks like nothing to see."

"Hold the lid." Allie shoved the box top into his hands and began to pull out a small handful of packing material. "What is that? A wooden propeller? Could it be a miniature windmill?"

"Could be an invention of some sort." Levi tried to put the lid back on the box. "Best to let it alone."

"Wait a minute." Allie pushed his hands back, filling the lid with straw and fabric. She pulled more material from the box, trying to free the object. A few wooden pieces tumbled out. Resting the cover on the ground, Levi picked up the pieces and rolled them around in his hand.

"What are those?" Allie pulled his hand close.

"Tiny carved figures. Looks like a man, woman, and child." He answered.

Allie pulled the larger object from the box. Several more figures balanced on a platform beneath the propeller. "Look, an angel, some animals. Those must be shepherds. And here— three kings." Her eyes danced. "You know what this is?"

"Not yours. Put it back."

"It's a nativity. I've never seen one like it. It's beautiful." Holding it with one hand, she ran her fingers along the smooth wood. "When we get to my uncle's, we should set it up to see what this propeller does and inspect it to see if there is anything to indicate who the owner is."

Levi furrowed his brow, rubbing his forehead. "Or Justin

and I could take it to the boardinghouse. Of course, someone is bound to show up at the lost and found inquiring about it."

"I like Miss Allie's idea." Justin reappeared. "We can head over to the store right now. Everything is taken care of here."

"Wouldn't it be fun? Trying to find the owners would be a grand adventure." Allie beamed. "It could help me learn my way around town."

Levi helped her pack the nativity pieces. "I would think you'd had your fill of grand adventures, Miss McLaughlin. Nearly drowning in the river. Besides, if this is so important, the owner will find us."

"But don't you see, it is important?" She clasped his hands in hers. "A nativity is the greatest symbol of hope next to the Easter cross. The skies were gray, and the journey was long and grueling even before the storms. What if the nativity is the last bit of hope the owner has, and it slips away right at Christmastime?"

"Levi doesn't hold much to the hope of Christmas." Justin took the box from Allie and helped her up.

"Is it because of your mother?" Allie's voice softened.

Justin's head snapped around. He looked at Levi wide-eyed, mouth agape.

"That's part of it." Levi swallowed hard and plodded ahead of them.

They walked up the hill to Water Street in silence. At the road, Justin put the box in the old buckboard and helped Allie into the wagon. Levi climbed in and took hold of the reins. He clicked his tongue, and the horses started down the road. Allie's warmth pressed to his side stirred something inside him, and his breath caught. He bit his lip. Relationships come at too high a price. He moved over a little. Then, from the corner of his eye, he saw her shiver. She scooted closer, but this time he didn't budge.

"Levi, can I at least show it to my uncle when we get to the store?"

Her voice was sweet, almost musical. Levi let it hang in the air between them a moment before answering.

"We'll see." He tugged slightly at the reins, slowing the horses. He needed time to think of a reason to hurry home after returning Allie to her uncle that would satisfy her and keep the nativity in its box.

4

"I can't wait to show the nativity to my uncle." Allie clutched Levi's forearm as they neared the mercantile. She snuggled close, trying to ward off the chill. Levi stiffened under her touch like a knight in a suit of armor.

"Listen, Miss McLaughlin. Perhaps we'd better head back to the boardinghouse." Levi took her hand and placed it back in her lap. "Mrs. Hogue is likely holding dinner for us, and I should get started on this metalwork for the steamboats."

Her body buzzed with excitement as she flashed a winsome smile. "It will only take a few minutes. Besides, Uncle Shadow hasn't been able to thank you properly yet for saving me."

"Uncle Shadow?" Justin chuckled.

"Yes, before he moved here, Uncle Shadow lived near us in Charleston. He followed me everywhere when I was little, checking to ensure I was all right. He was my shadow." She laid her hand over her heart and sighed. "I have missed him. Quickly now, let's go."

"But Miss McLaughlin —"

"C'mon, Levi." Justin clambered down from the wagon. "You know Ma has no idea when to expect us home. And every room except mine at the boardinghouse is full right now. She's not going to make them all wait. She'll let everyone eat and save us some." Justin offered his hand to Allie. "Miss Allie."

She took his hand with a slight curtsey and glanced back at Levi. "Why, thank you, Justin. How gentlemanly."

Levi pressed his lips together, his eyes narrowing at Justin. Then he picked up the box and tucked it under his arm. Offering Allie his elbow, Justin ushered her into Mooney's Mercantile.

Once inside, Allie rushed around the counter and threw her arms around her uncle. "Uncle Shadow, you always did give the best hugs."

Sam patted her back. "I've missed you, dear girl."

Turning her loose, he rounded the counter, placed a CLOSED sign in the window, and locked the door. Then, returning to Allie, he took hold of her hands. Rubbing them between his, he kissed her forehead. "Your hands are freezing. And what is this get-up you're wearing?"

"I'm afraid clothing choices were slim after I fell in the river."

"This has been a harrowing voyage for you, hasn't it?" He rubbed her arms vigorously from shoulders to elbows. "Levi, it's your act of bravery that brought her safely here. You have my deepest gratitude."

Levi cleared his throat. "You know I was only there for the metalwork, Sam."

"Metalwork, my eye." Sam chuckled. "This fella shows up anytime anyone needs help. Always says he's just there for the work. Of course, jumping into a river to save someone's life doesn't earn you extra work, does it?"

"If people trust me to do the right thing, they'll bring their work to me. What kind of man would I be if I saw someone with a dire need and did nothing?"

"Well, no one else jumped in that river today." Sam reached out and slapped Levi's back. "You're a hero, I tell ya!"

"He sure is!" Justin added a few more slaps on the back.

The slightest smile graced Levi's reddened face. He looked at the door. His brown eyes warmed. Was this a hint at what lay beneath the armor?

"Oh, Uncle, I want to show you what we found." She nodded to Levi. "It was separated from its owner when they took us off the *Resilient*, and we had to leave our things behind. No one came back for it."

Levi set the box on the counter. Then, like a giddy child, Allie yanked the lid off and tossed it aside. She pulled out handfuls of packing material, setting it next to the box.

Levi picked up bits of straw and fabric that had fallen to the floor. He pushed the material into a neat mound. "You're making a mess. This belongs to someone, Miss McLaughlin. Don't you think we ought to leave it alone?"

"*Pfft.* I want to show it to Uncle Shadow, and then we'll box it up. No harm done." Allie's breath caught as she carefully lifted a sizeable wooden piece out of the box. It had a round base of four stacked circles, the largest on the bottom and the smallest on top. Two curved columns rose from the third circle to create a dome-like shape. At the center of the platform was a Christmas tree. A thin metal rod protruded from the top of the tree through the intersection of the columns. Affixed to the top of the rod was a propeller. There were four small candle holders around the bottom.

Allie ran her fingers along one of the columns. Picking it up, she inspected it. Turning it this way and that and, finally, upside down. "Look—there is something on the bottom."

Levi, Sam, and Justin leaned close as she pointed to the letters stamped on the bottom.

"J. Zimmermann."

"Craftsmen often sign their work in some way." Levi took the piece from her and rubbed his thumb across the letters.

"Could it help us figure out who the owner is?" Allie covered her mouth as a cough escaped.

"You should have the doctor check that cough." Levi's eyes softened with concern.

"It's nothing to worry about. What do you think? Could it help us find the owner?"

"Doubtful." Levi placed the piece on the counter. "If it was sold or made for someone else, it will be difficult to track the owner. Most craftsmen don't keep a record of customers. The only way that might be helpful is if he kept it for himself. Made it for his own family or something."

Allie, heart thrumming, was lost in the joy of the moment. She raked her fingers through bits of scrap packing material, picking out the carved figures. "It's so precious. Here, help fit the pieces around it."

Levi hesitated. He glanced at the pieces and back at her. There it was again. That guarded look in his eyes. She bumped him with her shoulder. "Don't be a killjoy."

Justin placed shepherds and animal figures, a cow, a sheep, a donkey, and a camel, on the circle with the columns. Next, Levi put the wise men around one side of the tree. He held his hand out for more pieces.

Allie pulled her hands close to her chest, the remaining figures wrapped in her fingers. She smiled. "I'll set these in place."

Carefully, she placed each figure around the other side of the tree, a man, woman, and baby in a manger. "The holy family. Uncle, do you have some candles and matches?"

Sam pulled a box of matches from under the counter. Then he sidled down one of the aisles to grab a box of votives. "Been keeping all the matches under the counter since two young boys nearly burned down the store. When you're ready for it, there's a snuffer under there too."

Sam placed the candles around the base, and Allie struck a match to light them. The air warmed around them and drifted upward. Slowly, the propeller began to rotate. The small circle at the top of the platform turned. The Christmas tree, holy family, and wise men rotated, allowing the small audience to take in the scene. She smiled, her heart dancing.

An awed whisper escaped Allie's lips. "It's beautiful. Simply enchanting."

"It brings it to life, doesn't it?" Justin leaned his elbows on the counter, propping his chin on fisted hands.

Levi reached for the candle snuffer. Allie caught his hand, pulling it back. She diverted her attention from the nativity, setting her eyes on Levi. "Hope is patience with the lamp lit. Be patient, Mr. Snow, and leave the lamp lit a little longer."

Levi's face contorted. He snuffed out the candles and put the tiny figures back into the box. "You could use a little life in here, Sam. I'm surprised you haven't spruced up the place. Especially seeing how you've been hounding me for Christmas tree ornaments and bells."

"Bring the place to life, *hmm?*" Sam walked the length of the storefront windows. "I might do exactly that—a live display in the window. Business owners up and down Main Street will thrill at the idea. We could bring the whole street to life."

"What do you think, dear girl?" He turned to Allie. "I might need your help."

Allie joined Sam at the window, imagining all the windows on Main Street alive with charming scenes of Christmas. "I think it's a wonderful idea. Of course, Levi and I will search for the owners of the nativity, but I'm sure I can find time to help."

Levi's head whipped around.

"Now, wait a minute. I didn't agree to that." He pointed toward the door. "I've got a wagonload of work out there and more on the way. Plus, I had committed to Sam to make ornaments for the store before that storm rolled in. So, I've got no time to meander through town with this thing, especially when we don't know where to start looking."

He gave the box a shove as Justin put away the propellered platform.

"Levi, we have to find the owners." Allie crossed the room, taking his hands in hers.

Levi slipped free of her grasp. He studied his shoes. "I don't see why it's so important to find the owners of something that stays packed away in a box most of the year."

"Allie's things made it safely here, but some steamboat passengers lost everything." Sam rejoined them at the counter. "Captain Cobb brought back all he could, but his vessel was overloaded with soldiers and supplies bound for Fort Smith. So, when the sandbar appeared, they had to toss passenger cargo. Cobb felt terrible about it."

"This may be the only thing one of those passengers has left in the world. All their worldly possessions may have been tossed in the river except for this." Allie pulled the box close, a tear welling in the corner of her eye. She knew only too well what it was like to lose so much. "What if they lose all hope without it?"

Levi's voice was low and hoarse. "I can't promise anything. I've got to hold to the commitments I've already made. But maybe—if no one has come by the boardinghouse looking for it—we can ask around Monday."

Allie threw her arms around his neck, landing a peck on his

cheek. His warm, smoky scent chased away the chill she'd felt since falling into the river. "You won't regret it. I promise."

He pulled her arms free, redness rising above the dark line of his beard. Then, he turned to Justin. "C'mon. Your Ma is probably worried by now, and I'm starving."

As he and Justin went out the door, he paused. "If anyone turns up here looking for a replacement nativity, let me know. Better yet, send them to the boardinghouse. Everything lost and found on those old boats ends up there."

"Is that how you turned up there?" Allie grinned.

A hint of a smile crossed his lips. "As a matter of fact, it is."

5

The forge's heat offered welcome relief after a long day in the cold. Levi pumped the bellows a few times, fanning the flames. Finally, the door of the shop creaked open, and Justin entered.

"Feels toasty in here." He walked over, offered Levi a bowl, and placed a wadded napkin on the work table. "Ma sent this bowl of stew since you didn't come in. Cornbread in the napkin there."

"Thought I'd better get started on this work tonight. No sense waiting until tomorrow."

"Plenty of sense, I'd say." Justin rubbed his eyes. "I'm exhausted. Of course, you had that nap today."

Levi chuckled.

"I hate to duck out, but I'm headed to bed." He ruffled his wild, wavy hair. "Don't stay up too late. I can help you organize the work in the morning. You'll be sifting through the chaos tonight. We both know how you hate that."

"Listen, before you go, let's talk about the bars for Mrs. Grace's window."

"Shame she won't let anyone remove that tree."

"Mr. Grace loved that tree. She keeps it in memory of him."

Levi set the bowl on the table. "Trying to shutter that window herself when these storms pop up is too much for her. I think bars across that window will protect it well. We'll work eight to ten rods with a basic twist. Let's put that at the top of our to-do list."

"It's a good plan. I'm gonna hit the hay."

Levi waved him out the door. "I'll head that way shortly."

Levi envied Justin. The boy would be asleep before his head touched the pillow, not a care in the world. He ought to sleep like that after such a long day. But here he was, trying to establish order in chaos like he'd been doing since his father left when he was fifteen. Since the day his mother died. He would never understand why tragedy and loss struck so close to Christmas.

Levi unwrapped the cornbread, dipped it in the stew, and took a bite. Images of the nativity scene turning on its pedestal played through his mind. Slowly it turned, such a stillness about it. He recalled things he'd heard over the years. Peace on earth. God with us. Seemed more like a fairytale than reality to him.

Then there was Allie. She had lost her mother too. And where was her father? How did she keep her heart so open? Her bright eyes, vibrant nature, and willingness to embrace people awakened something inside him.

An uneasy feeling settled over him. The memory of Allie linked arm-in-arm with Justin as they entered the mercantile flashed in his mind. An unwelcome twinge reverberated through the pit of his stomach.

Levi placed a piece of metal in the fire, shifting it under layers of burning charcoal. Moments later, he pulled it out, put it on the anvil, and hammered it into shape. When cooled too much to be workable, he returned it to the fire, then back to the anvil. He repeated the process several times, turning and bending the metal to make a simple ornament. He drew the warm air deep into his lungs. This is where he brought order to the things in his life.

He had to keep the lid on the nativity and Allie beyond the door of his world.

6

Robert Horn sat at the makeshift table, drumming his fingers, a scowl on his leathery face. Levi's chest tightened. Sunday mornings brought a welcome change of pace for him. Justin and the rest of the Hogues spent the morning at church. Other boarders joined them for services or slept later than he did. He savored time alone in the smithy without interruption or noise from the outside world—with the crackling fire in the forge.

Levi sipped his coffee, then pulled a piece of metal from the fire as he eyed Horn from across the room.

"Got another cup?" Horn continued drumming his fingers.

"Nope."

"Got a table, cards, and a coffee pot, but no cup for customers?"

"That's right." Levi pounded the metal.

"Doesn't seem very hospitable."

"Not trying to be hospitable." Levi turned the piece and struck it again. "Just keeping folks out of my workspace."

"How do you drink your coffee?" Horn crossed the room to

the work table and anvil. The stench of gin oozed from Horn's pores, triggering mental images of Levi's father.

"Black."

"Just how I like it." Horn took Levi's coffee and topped it off. Then he took a sip and returned to the table with it. "How much longer? I'm two days overdue, and Fort Coffee is a mere two hours away. Makes me a might anxious sitting around waiting on repairs."

"Don't play games, Horn." Levi made a few passes over his work with a wire brush, knocking the scale off the piece. "You and I both know that you don't have any repairs. The damage to the *No. 7* was superficial. You loaded my wagon with maintenance work."

"Repairs, maintenance—either way, it's got to be done."

"Boat's not due for maintenance for another month. So, these repairs could wait until your return from Fort Coffee." Levi set his tools down and leaned closer, pressing fisted hands into the work table. "Better yet, you could have the blacksmith there do the repairs. I'm sure you've got no reason to hurry back this close to Christmas."

"I don't like his work."

"Then you'll wait. Patiently."

"What exactly am I waiting for, Snow?" Horn reached across the table and patted the box sitting there. "Sam Mooney tells me you're on a goose chase for the owner of this here thingamajig."

Levi's nostrils flared. He had asked Mahala Hogue to put the box in Justin's old upstairs bedroom since the loft above the bunkroom was overflowing with lost and found items. The invading thoughts about the nativity and Allie McLaughlin had been easier to push away in the absence of the wayward package. Distractions removed, he had made good progress on the storm projects until the box resurfaced on the table near the wood stove.

"That box is no concern of yours." Levi returned the metal to the fire. "The only thing slowing progress on your maintenance work is you. If you keep intruding, I'll move your work to last. How'd you like to change the name of your boat to the *Coffee No. 15*?"

Horn slammed down the coffee cup, sloshing its contents onto the tabletop and dirt floor. As he stood, the shop door opened, and Allie McLaughlin appeared. Horn shoved the chair, knocking it into Allie, causing her to stumble backward a few steps.

"I'll be back, Snow."

Levi covered the distance between them in a blink. Then, gripping Horn's arm, Levi shoved him out the door. "Learn some manners. And stay out of the bottle or don't come back."

He turned sharply, the heels of his boots grinding a new rut into the dirt floor as he returned to the work table. Levi took the piece of metal from the table and shoved it into the fire, sifting it through layers of burning coke. "What are you doing here, Miss McLaughlin?"

Allie cleared her throat. "I didn't mean to interrupt."

"What are you doing here?" His words carried more bite than he intended. He picked up the hammer and struck the anvil a few times, taking a deep breath with each strike. "You can't keep showing up like this. You can't barge into a man's life whenever you like."

"Barge in?" Allie folded her arms across her middle. "To a man's life? Is this not your place of business, open to the public?"

Levi removed the metal from the fire and returned to the anvil. Allie stepped closer. He struck the metal, sending red-hot bits of scale flying. Allie stopped short.

"Place of business, yes. Open to the public, not on Sundays."

"Well, for your information, Mrs. Hogue invited me to dinner after church. She asked me to let you know the meal is ready."

Levi looked her square in the eyes and struck the metal again.

"Where is the nativity?"

He pointed to the table beyond the woodstove. "There. Why?"

"I plan to show it to Mr. Hildesheim at the pastry shop this afternoon." Allie scooped the box from the table.

"He's a tenant here. Why don't you take it in and show it to him now?"

"The Hogues dropped him at the store on the way home. He planned to work on some new ideas today. For Christmas, I think."

"I thought we agreed to wait until Monday."

"I spoke with him at church. He said the design sounds familiar and would like to see it."

"Hildesheim went to church?" Levi paused, resting the hammer on the anvil. If Conrad Hildesheim attended church with the Hogues, how much longer would he be able to evade Mahala Hogue's efforts to get Levi there? What had she said or done to convince him to go?

"Is it uncommon for him to go?"

"Of all those staying at Hogue House, Hildesheim is the last person I ever expected would go."

"The way everyone gathered to him, I thought he attended regularly."

"He has a way with people despite his unusual accent. Some people are destined to be at the center of everything."

"Like you?"

"Me? You won't find me at the center of anything. The moment that happens, the whole town would fall apart."

"It didn't sound like that to me." Allie shifted the box to her hip. "Everyone was talking about how you showed up after this big storm and organized the cleanup at the waterfront. They said the rescue boat wouldn't have made it safely to shore without you. I certainly wouldn't have made it to shore without you."

"That's a bit of a stretch." Levi's cheeks warmed from more than the hot metal. "Someone would have taken charge at some point. Someone is bound to have jumped in after you if I hadn't been there."

"Justin says you do this sort of thing quite often. You leap into action whenever there is a threat or an emergency."

"I go because there is often work to be gained from it."

"Work like the bars for Mrs. Grace's window?"

Levi's head jerked up, and his hands stilled. "What do you know about Mrs. Grace and her window?"

"Justin told me you're creating a decorative grate for the window—as a gift. He said you do it every Christmas, whether there is a town calamity or not." Allie crossed to the vacant end of the work table and set down the box. "You make something for someone who has a need but can't afford to pay."

"Justin talks too much."

"I think it's wonderful and sweet."

"It's not sweet. It's what everyone ought to do." Levi moved to the forge, lengthening the distance between them. He stoked the fire and turned to Allie. "Mrs. Grace's husband died three months ago. This is her first Christmas without him. They have no children, so there is no one to help her with that window and other things around the house. She's going to need help from time to time."

"Perhaps it is what everyone ought to do, but it's still sweet."

Allie's blue eyes and gentle smile tugged at Levi. The light from the forge accentuated the gold in the strawberry-blonde hair gathered at her shoulder. When she cleared her throat and glanced away, Levi realized he'd been silent too long.

"Well, eh, yes." He turned quickly and fidgeted with the fire. "Mrs. Hogue won't hold the meal much longer. She'll be put out with us if we don't join them soon."

The door rattled open, and Justin appeared. "Hey, Old Man, are you eating with us?"

Levi bristled. Justin was only five years his junior. However, the weight of Levi's life experiences in contrast to Justin's often made him feel as though they were separated by decades. Levi shot a sidelong glance at Justin.

"Listen here, young whippersnapper, I've got grown folk things to do," Levi smirked. "I'll be in as soon as I adjust the gate on the forge. Otherwise, gas will build up and cause an explosion. That's the last thing I need right now."

"Make it quick. You know Ma." Justin stretched out a hand to Allie. "Miss Allie, may I escort you back inside?"

She smiled, taking his hand. "You may."

Levi's lips pressed flat. His muscles tightened. Justin had such a comfortable way with people, even women. Perhaps an advantage of growing up with six sisters. He gingerly rubbed his thumb across the tops of Allie's fingers. Levi's stomach clenched. Would she have so readily taken his hand had he dared to offer it?

"Oh, Levi, you won't be sitting in your usual seat at the table. Doc Ewing is here, so he's sitting next to Rebecca."

"Did your mother invite the whole town to dine with her today?"

Justin laughed. "It's only two people. But you'll sit between the twins, so keep your napkin handy."

All the life experience in the world hadn't prepared Levi for six-year-old twins, Ollie and Nellie. If there was anything he had learned about children in his time with the Hogues, he only had the patience and skills to deal with one child at a time, no matter their age. Levi dropped the fire shovel into its stand with a clang.

"Sitting between the twins? Where are you sitting?"

"Next to Miss Allie, of course." Justin patted her hand. "What sort of host would I be if I didn't give her my full attention?"

Of course, Justin would want to sit next to such a vision. Seeing as the Hogue family was hosting Allie, it was well within his right to do so. But surely, there was another sibling who could sit between the twins. Levi checked off the list. Ivajohn would be in and out of the kitchen. Cordelia, in a pretentious phase, would complain throughout the meal. Simon and Martie were inseparable. No way around it. He was stuck between the twins.

Levi's jaw clenched as he crossed his arms. "I don't know what sort of host you'd be. But you'd be the kind of man who helps his mother while *she's* entertaining guests."

"Don't you worry. I'll be helping Ma with baby Edie." Justin gave a wink as he ushered Allie through the door. He called over his shoulder, "See you at the table."

7

After dinner, Allie made her goodbyes, hugging every member of the Hogue family, except for Mr. Hogue, who was down in his back. Levi held her coat while she slipped her arms into the sleeves. He swept his forearm underneath her hair and freed it from her collar.

It reminded Allie of when he'd gently pulled little Nellie's hair back from her face while she ate her sweet potato pie. Nellie had picked up the entire piece of pie and plunged into it instead of cutting a bit off with her fork. Levi seemed uncomfortable when Justin announced he'd be sitting between the twins, but he had been patient and gracious through all their antics. More so than Allie could have been. A smile emerged before Allie could suppress it.

"Did I miss something?" Levi handed her a bonnet and a pair of gloves.

"I admire how you handled the twins during dinner."

Levi's cheeks reddened. "I've found a simple strategy is best with them."

"Oh, and what strategy might that be?" Allie tied the bonnet under her chin.

"Divide and conquer." He grinned. "Divide and conquer."

Allie giggled and donned her gloves. She picked up the nativity box. "Mr. Hildesheim is waiting. Shall we go?"

"After you." Levi opened the door and made a sweeping motion with his arm. He followed her out the door, then took the nativity box. "It's a short walk to the pastry shop."

They walked for a few moments in silence. Allie relished the calm. She hadn't experienced much quiet since the steamboat accident. Uncle Shadow had been over-attentive since her arrival. He kept urging her to eat more at supper and popping in to check on her before bed. She enjoyed the peacefulness of walking with Levi, but curiosity gnawed at her.

"You have difficulty taking a compliment, don't you?"

He continued in silence, raking his fingers through his short, dark beard. Allie allowed the long pause to settle between them. Finally, he spoke. "I don't know that I do anything to warrant a compliment."

"*Hmm.*" Allie hugged herself tightly as a stiff winter wind blew up the hill. "I heard so many stories this morning about the difference you've made in this town."

"Nonsense. I go through life looking for work. That's all." Levi shifted the box to one side. "How long will you be visiting Sam?"

She smiled. "That didn't take long."

"What?"

"For you to change the subject." Allie tugged her scarf up to meet the edge of the bonnet. "You do that quite a bit. You're not comfortable talking to people, are you?"

"I'm talking to you. I'm inquiring about your stay."

"Perhaps you're not comfortable talking about yourself. Or you're avoiding conversations that go deeper."

"If you don't want to tell me about your stay, fine." He squared his jaw, and they walked a short distance farther in silence.

"Honestly, I don't know how long I'll be with Uncle Shadow." Allie cleared her throat. "Life has proved uncertain since my mother died. I don't know what is coming next or where God means for me to be."

Levi took a deep breath. His eyes trained on his feet. "You've mentioned your mother a couple of times, but what of your father? Where is he?"

A lump caught in Allie's throat, and she swallowed hard. "He married Julianna, a woman only seven years older than me. They set out to explore the West."

"You didn't want to go with them?"

"Father didn't want me to go."

"Why wouldn't he take you with him? Was there tension between you and his new bride?"

Allie stopped. Her eyes narrowed as she turned to face Levi. Tilting her head, she looked him up and down quizzically.

"What?"

"You don't strike me as the sort of man who asks many questions about others." She started walking again. "I expect you enter a conversation looking for a way out of it."

"You're not wrong." Levi jogged a couple of steps to catch up. "But you're unusual."

She shot him a warning glance. "I'm not a sideshow, Levi."

"I didn't mean—" Levi stammered. He pulled his collar up around his ears. "There's just something about you—"

Allie's cheeks warmed. "Then I'll employ your tactic of avoiding the question and leave you with a mystery to unravel. How much farther to Mr. Hildesheim's shop?"

Levi pointed in front of them. "It's here, at the end of the road."

The door of the pastry shop scraped the floor as Allie and Levi entered. Levi grimaced. "Looks like Conrad might need new hinges."

"Are you offering to supply them? With all the work you already have on your plate?" Allie grinned. She couldn't resist the playful jab.

He half-smiled. "Conrad? You here?"

"Levi, is zat you?" Conrad ducked through the blue curtain dividing the shop from the ovens in the back room. He motioned for them to join him behind the counter at the work table.

"What is that smell?" Levi sniffed the air. "It's wonderful."

Conrad picked up a tray of dark brown cookies with a light swath of icing across the top. "Gingersnaps. Mother's olt recipe. She woult make zees close to zee holiday. Please, try."

Levi and Allie took a cookie. Snapping hers in two, Allie took a bite. The hint of sugary sweet icing complimented the sharp punch of ginger. "This is delicious. Such a nice snap when you bite into it and slightly softer inside."

"Zey are special to me." Conrad placed the cookies on the end of the table. "I'm glad you like it."

"Miss McLaughlin mentioned she met you at church today. I'm curious about what you were doing there. Aren't you Jewish?" Levi took a bite of his cookie.

"*Ja*, I am. But I hafe my eyes set on Clara Watson. She is not Jewish." Conrad winked. "I vant to earn her family's trust. Perhaps they vill get to know me if I visit the church. Hafe you brought zee natifity?"

Allie held up the box, her heart pitter-pattering like a child on Christmas morning.

"Goot. Sit, sit." Conrad brought a couple of extra wooden stools to the table. "Let's take a look."

Levi helped Allie free the pieces from the packing material.

They displayed it as they had at the mercantile. Allie handed the final pieces to Levi. Momentary disappointment pinged in her heart when he unceremoniously plunked down mother and child.

"Well, Mr. Hildesheim, what do you think?" Allie leaned close, holding her breath in anticipation.

"Zis is as I expected." Conrad gave the propeller a light turn. "It is a German Christmas pyramid, zough I hafe never seen one vith such elegant lines. Most have one to three tiers and straight supports. I like how zey hafe incorporated zee Christmas tree, my favorite tradition. You said zere is somezing on zee bottom?"

Allie scooted the figures to the side, and Levi lifted the platform to show Conrad the stamp. Allie pointed. "See, here it is. J. Zimmermann."

"Ah, ja, I see. Zimmermann is carpenter." Conrad took the piece from Levi.

Allie's heart sank. "Oh. Zimmermann is the German word for carpenter. I guess that doesn't help us any, does it?"

"Nein, you misunderstand. Zimmermann is family name for carpenter." Conrad picked up a muffin tin and patted the side of it. "My mother's family name is Becker, which is baker. I follow in zee footsteps of her family."

"So, you think the person who created this uses the family name of Zimmermann?" Levi popped the last bite of the cookie into his mouth. "And holds the occupation of carpenter."

"Jawohl, perhaps. I also zink zis is zee first of its kind. See zee number one scratched beside zee name?"

"How can you be sure that's a number and not a mark made accidentally?" Allie wiped the crumbs from her hands.

"I cannot be completely certain, but rarely hafe I seen a Christmas pyramid one-tier. It is usually two tiers or more." Conrad returned the display piece to its upright position. His hands followed the curves of the arched supports. "Never have I seen curved platform, always straight. It is unique. Very beautiful."

"It doesn't help us, though." Allie looked at Levi. "What can we do?"

"Hold on a minute." Levi rubbed her back. "There is some useful information here. This is a piece the craftsman can be proud of, and, being the first of its kind, he may have kept it for himself. If so, we can ask Captain Cobb if there were any German emigrants named Zimmermann on the *Resilient*. He should be able to look at the passenger manifest and tell us."

"That still won't help us figure out where they are now."

"But it narrows it, doesn't it?" A broad smile edged across Levi's face. "The owner is here in Van Buren. So, if the name Zimmermann is on the manifest, we can limit our search to German emigrants. That should allow us to find the owner rather quickly."

"Ven I first arrived here, I vent to courthouse to inquire about land." Conrad rose from the table and collected ingredients from a nearby shelf. He began measuring flour, ginger, and cinnamon. "I stopped zere every day for weeks. Is good place to continue your search, *nein?*"

"Yes, thank you." Levi shook Conrad's hand and then packed up the nativity. "What are you making now? More gingersnaps?"

"*Nein,* gingerbread. It is a little different." Conrad finished adding dry ingredients and set the bowl aside. He creamed butter and sugar together in another bowl. "Baking helps me zink. I hope to zink of a vay to make Clara Watson notice me."

"Isn't gingerbread used to make houses?" Levi picked up another gingersnap, and Conrad nodded. "May I? Perhaps you could make her a Christmas house."

"Ah, zis Christmas pyramid gives me an idea. Christmas is

not my custom. I vill make gingerbread natifity scene to display in zee vindow. Hanukkah is passed, but I vill also put gingerbread menorah in zee vindow. Perhaps she vill enjoy to learn about me if she sees I enjoy to learn about her."

"You're a wise man, my friend."

Levi stood and patted Allie's shoulder. "We'd better get you home before your uncle gets worried." He turned to Conrad. "I'll come by soon with new hinges and rehang that door for you."

"I appreciate zee offer, but I cannot pay."

"I can spare a few hinges. Consider it a gift."

"You are too kind." Conrad handed Levi two tins of gingersnap cookies, one for each of them. Allie scooped up the nativity box, and they followed Conrad to the front of the pastry shop, where he opened the door for them.

"Mr. Hildesheim, how do you say 'thank you' in German?" Allie wrapped a scarf around her neck.

"Ve say *danke*." Conrad smiled. "*Danke* for sharing vith me. It has been an honor."

"*Danke*, Mr. Hildesheim. You've made it possible to continue this search." Allie hugged his neck. Hope fluttered in her heart as Levi closed the door behind them. "So, off to see Captain Cobb next?"

A tickle in her throat set off a coughing spell.

"That's a *no*." Levi eyed her warily. "We'd better get you home to rest."

8

"When can we talk to Captain Cobb?" Allie tucked the nativity box under her arm.

"I might be able to catch him at the boardinghouse this evening. He overnights shipside if the *Resilient* needs work or he has an early departure the next day." Levi guided Allie through the muddy, rutted street to the boardwalk opposite the pastry shop. Mindful of her stylish navy boots with plaid uppers, he avoided areas that might bog them down. "But Cobb will spend Christmas with the Hogues, so he's not leaving until early next week. There's a good chance he'll take time to relax in the evenings through the holiday."

The spark in Allie's eyes dimmed. "Oh. I hoped we would speak to him together."

"I guess we could, but I thought it might speed things along if I ask him when I get back." The disappointment in her eyes left a bitter taste in his mouth. "Perhaps I could wait until tomorrow. I need to get some work done early, but I could pick you up around mid-morning. Then we could visit the courthouse later."

"I would so appreciate that." A grin lit up her face. "I want to be there for every moment of this journey. I get the feeling that something wonderful is bound to happen."

Levi never understood what others found so remarkable about Christmas. For him, the holiday punctuated his losses. He cast a sidelong glance at Allie. She'd lost her mother, too, yet she radiated joy in her bounding step and beaming expression. How did she do it?

Levi broke the silence. "How old were you when your mother died?" He offered Allie his arm.

Allie looped her arm in his, folding her hand around his elbow. She took a deep breath in through her nose and released it slowly. "Twenty. How old were you?"

"Fifteen."

"So young." Her breath caught. "How did your father handle it? I imagine a loss like that would bring a father and son closer together."

"We're not close. He walked out on us on Christmas Eve." His throat constricted. "Haven't seen him since."

The silence grew heavy between them. He couldn't bear to tell Allie that he was responsible for his mother's death and his father's leaving. What would she think of him if she knew his family's unraveling was his fault?

"What about your father? Was he there for you?"

Allie closed her eyes, drawing another deep breath. "For a time. He became more closed off as the year dragged on." She opened her eyes, brows knit together. "Eventually, he told me I reminded him too much of my mother. It was too painful to be with me. That's when he married Julianna and began a new adventure. That was Christmastime two years ago."

"He left you?"

"Not alone, but yes. He left me with his brother in St. Louis."

He stopped and turned to look her in the eyes. "How do you do it?"

"Do what?"

"Stay so open to everyone around you?" Levi swallowed hard. "How do you let them in?"

"I ask God for help and take a deep breath in." She breathed in through her nose. "And then I breathe out like this. One breath at a time." She exhaled a long stream of air, coughing at the tail end of it.

"Are you okay?"

She sputtered. "The air is chilly, that's all."

"I want you to see the doctor tomorrow."

"It's nothing."

"I mean it, Miss McLaughlin. You coughed up a lot of water when I tossed you on that barrel the other day. We need to ensure there's nothing more serious going on."

They walked a little farther before stopping in front of the mercantile. Levi shifted the cookie tins to one side. He rested his hand on hers, holding it in the crook of his elbow a moment longer. "Better get inside."

"Just a minute." She broke away, hurrying down the boardwalk. "I want to check the notice board."

"What are you looking for?"

"It occurred to me that if the nativity owners are looking to settle down here, they may have come straight away to place an advertisement if they have a service or product to offer."

"Smart thinking." Levi winked.

Allie perused the board. She shook her head. "No Zimmermanns. None of these names even sound German. I'll keep an eye on the board, though."

"Miss McLaughlin, thank you for inviting me along today." Levi handed her a cookie tin and took the nativity box before she entered the store. "Take care of that cough. I'll check on

51

you tomorrow, and if you're feeling better, maybe we'll visit Cobb."

9

Allie gazed at her reflection, pressing her fingers against the puffy orbits of her eyes. She should have listened to Uncle Shadow's suggestion to stay home and rest, but she had been anxious to meet the people he wrote of in his letters. Going to church seemed like the perfect opportunity to begin making acquaintances. Plus, she wanted to make inquiries about the nativity. It was only four days until Christmas, after all. There was no time to waste if she and Levi were going to find the owner.

Brushing her hair, she pulled it to one side, braided it, and secured it with a hair ribbon. She thumbed the corner of the rumpled envelope in her lap. Her uncle had given it to her the previous evening. He waited until she'd eaten supper and was warming herself by the fire.

Allie ran her thumb across the clean tear at the top edge of the letter. It was from her father. Through bleary eyes, she had read it ... how many times?

She set the letter to the side. Her chest tingled with a desire to cough, but she suppressed it long enough to gather a deep breath. She permitted herself one strong cough as quietly as possible so as not to alert her uncle. He wouldn't allow her to continue the search with Levi tomorrow if he suspected she was ailing.

She rearranged items, placing a wash bowl between herself and the mirror. Next to the bowl, she placed a pitcher of hot water, ground mustard, and a wide swatch of muslin. Dipping her fingers into the pitcher, she confirmed the water was a tolerable temperature and poured some into the bowl. She submerged the muslin in the water and wrung it out. Sprinkling the swatch with a generous amount of ground mustard, she stretched it across her chest. Then, adding half a dozen drops of peppermint extract to the hot water in the wash basin, she made a steam vapor. Finally, she pulled a towel over her head and leaned over the bowl to inhale the warm, thick air.

A knock sounded, and the door creaked open. Uncle Shadow poked his head in. His crooked smile didn't mask the deep concern in his gray eyes. "How are you?"

She lifted the towel, turning to face him. "I'm almost ready to be put in the oven."

He chuckled. "So, as I asked, you applied the mustard paste?"

She nodded.

"And you've added peppermint to the wash basin?"

Another nod. "Though I think all this fuss is completely unnecessary."

"Humor your old uncle." He eased into the room and edged up behind her. "I've got plenty of gray hairs."

"All your hair is gray, Uncle."

"Precisely. Next, my hair will turn loose, so let's not rush that process." He rubbed her back. "Here is that piece of bread you wanted. Put the towel back over your head and breathe."

Allie did as he instructed. She took a few deep breaths. The peppermint vapor warmed her inside and eased the stuffiness in her head and chest. Was the vapor helping? Perhaps. She took another deep breath, the essence of Christmas saturating her lungs.

"Well, what about your father's letter?" He tapped the envelope on the edge of the dressing table. The hesitance in his voice was unmistakable. "Did you read it?"

"I read it." She held up the envelope.

"Are you considering his request?"

"I don't know." She sat up, pulled the towel from her head, and turned to face him. "Julianna left him. It seems she couldn't handle the wilds of the West. He wants me to join him. Says we'll have a grand adventure."

"It might be a good opportunity to reconnect with your father."

"One thing troubles me." She turned to look in the mirror. "I still look like my mother."

"Yes, you do. I drew this picture of your mother the day she stood up to Martin Stafford." Uncle Shadow retrieved a framed picture from across the room. "As her big brother, I was ready to step in, but she didn't need me to. I couldn't have been prouder. You favor her in more ways than one."

"That's why father left me to begin with." She turned to face him, taking the frame in hand. "What if I go west, and he decides my presence is too painful once again?"

"I'll come for you." He kissed the top of her head. "You'll always have a home with me. Take your time and think it over. For now, get some rest." He slipped out as quietly as he'd entered.

Allie opened the top drawer of the dressing table, sliding the letter inside. Sighing, she shut the drawer. She pulled the towel over her head and drew a deep breath. The sensation of relief and comfort was gone. She dipped her fingers in the water. Too cold. Removing the swath of mustard-covered muslin revealed splotchy, red skin across her chest. She rinsed her hands and patted them on the towel.

The hint of peppermint took her back to that afternoon in the pastry shop. Levi's warm hand on her back, the inviting aroma of cinnamon and other spices, his easy conversation with Mr. Hildesheim. It lifted her spirits to witness his curiosity grow as they puzzled through the information Mr. Hildesheim provided. Could he learn to recognize the hope that Christmas had to offer?

She moved the wash bowl to the side and replaced it with a smaller bowl. She added some rosewater. Picking up the bread, she tore it in two, dipped the pieces in the soothing liquid, and squeezed the excess from them. Moving to the bed, she laid down and placed the slices of bread over her eyes.

How should she respond to her father's letter? Sighing, she pushed the thought away. Time to rest. She conjured images of the nativity, candles lit, figures revolving. She had a grand adventure of her own to pursue.

10

"I sure was surprised when Miss Allie mentioned your ma at the riverfront the other day." Justin worked at the anvil opposite Levi at the work table, tapping and turning, tapping and turning. "I think I'd known you over a year before you mentioned anything about your folks."

On the other anvil, Levi extended a piece of metal over the edge, tapping lightly to create a bend. Then, flipping the rod over, he tapped the tip a few times, rolling the metal over on itself.

"Just to be clear, is it your ma we're not talking about or Miss Allie?"

"Make sure you're following that pattern I gave you." Levi stepped back over to the forge to reheat the rod. He rolled his shoulders forward and back, trying to alleviate the tension.

"Both, then." Justin tapped the piece of metal around the horn of the anvil. "Not that it's any of my business."

Returning to the anvil, Levi struck the piece of metal several times, red-hot scale flying. He turned the rod and continued shaping it. "If you're having trouble focusing, you can start another box of nails."

"Doing great. Following the pattern." Justin dipped the piece in the water barrel, dabbed the excess water onto a rag, and then laid the work over the scale drawing. "I made a box of those star ornaments yesterday after I finished taking care of the horses. You stayed out a long time with Miss Allie following Sunday dinner. It went well, I suppose?"

Levi dropped his hammer on the table. "You want to talk about Miss McLaughlin? Let's talk about Miss McLaughlin. What do you want to know?"

"For starters, why are you so tense at the mention of her?" Justin set his hammer down. "You're usually more at ease when you're smithing."

Levi paced a few steps from the table and turned as though looking for something. He walked back and put his hands on his hips. "This is not working. I can't get out of my head."

"You can't get out of your head, or you can't get *her* out of your head." Justin's boyish grin didn't set well with Levi.

"You're not helping." Levi's chest tightened. "I start talking to her, and before I know what I'm doing, I'm opening up to her about things I don't talk about."

"What's wrong with that?"

"That's not me. I don't do that." Levi threw his hands up. "I don't even know her."

"You're getting to know her. That's a good thing, right?"

"Is it? I don't know how long she'll be here." Levi picked up the metal rod and shoved it back into the fire. "Sam never mentioned she was coming. Maybe she's not staying long."

"Who's not staying long?" A cheery voice interrupted.

Levi's heart stopped. He peered around the potbellied stove to see Allie coming in the door. He and Justin exchanged an uncomfortable glance.

"Mrs. Pratt's niece. She is expected for Christmas, but we don't think she'll stay long." Justin stammered in his rush to answer.

"Oh, and why are the two of you concerned about how long she stays?"

"Justin is sweet on her." Levi pulled the rod from the fire and brought it to the anvil.

Justin shot Levi a glare. Levi shrugged, and Justin returned his attention to Allie. "It's nothing serious. What brings you out to the forge?"

"Levi and I planned to talk to Captain Cobb and visit the courthouse today." She walked over and warmed her hands near the stove. "So, I chatted with Mrs. Hogue for a few minutes, and she directed me out here."

"I planned to pick you up at the store."

"I couldn't wait. Too excited." She bounced on her toes. "May I see it again?"

"The nativity?"

"What else, silly?" Allie shoved her hands in her pockets and pulled out four votive candles. "Can we light the candles?"

"Again?" Levi quenched the metal rod in the water barrel. "You're going to use up Sam's candle inventory."

"These are the same candles we used the other day." She retrieved the box from the sitting area and brought it to the work table. Lifting the lid, she grabbed a fistful of packing material.

"No, ma'am." Levi grasped the material from her hand. "We are not unboxing here."

"But it will look so enchanting in the forge's light."

Levi tipped his head at Justin. "Hand me one of those crates."

"Sure." Justin reached around Allie with the crate in hand. "Miss Allie, we can't have the packing material so close

to the forge or the anvils. We're back and forth with hot metal."

"And one of us needs to keep working. We have too much for both of us to stop." Levi removed the rest of the scrap material from the box. "Which means searing bits of scale flying through the air could catch all of this on fire."

"Oh, I didn't realize—"

"You can't come in and take over to suit your whims." He placed the crate and the nativity box on the waiting area table. "I'll let you have your enchanting moment, but you'll do it my way. Have some patience."

"One step too far?" She smiled weakly.

Levi nodded.

"Patience ... comes before lighting the lamp."

Levi gave her a questioning look.

"Hope is patience with the lamp lit. My mother's favorite quote. It's by Tertullian." She arranged the pieces and placed the candles. "I sometimes forget that patience must come before lighting the lamp."

Levi smiled, returning to her side. He took one of the votives. Picking up the fire shovel, he scooped some charcoal and fire from the forge and lit the candle. He emptied the shovel, returned it to its stand, and lit the remaining candles. "You enjoy the scene. I'll tidy my area and step next door to the bunkroom to change shirts."

"I'll tidy up for you." Justin pointed at him. "You don't forget to keep it capped."

"Keep what capped?"

"My head. Justin thinks he's being funny." Levi grimaced at Justin's playful attempt to remind him not to overshare. "He's reminding me to grab my winter hat."

"So all his grand metalwork ideas don't spill out the top of his head." Justin winked, laughing at his own joke.

"Funny. Very funny." Levi removed his leather apron and hung it on a nearby hook.

"Remember to open that gate so the gases don't build up in the bottom of the forge. Especially if you need to step out for a bit." Levi patted Allie's shoulder. "I'll be right back."

When Levi returned, he found Allie, elbows propped on the work table, her head resting on her hands, gazing at the nativity. He was drawn to her starry-eyed fascination. Joining her at the table, he assumed the same pose.

"Mr. Snow, are you making fun of me?" She cut her eyes toward him.

He quickly straightened. "Not in the least. I'm trying to see what you see. Trying to understand your sense of wonder."

Allie's cheeks pinked. Levi's heartbeat pounded like a hammer on an anvil. Hopefully, she couldn't hear it.

Across the table, Justin cleared his throat, jolting Levi from the moment. Levi crossed the room to the sitting area and picked up the nativity box.

"I guess we'd better pack it away again."

"Are you taking it with you?" Justin twisted the metal he was shaping.

"No, I don't think we need to bring it along today."

"Are you sure?" Allie stood. "It makes a strong impression. It might encourage people to help us."

"Cobb will help with anything I ask. Always has. And we don't want to take too much of the clerk's time setting it up."

"In that case, don't worry about boxing it up." Justin placed the metal rod back into the fire. "I enjoy seeing it. I'll put it up before I tend the horses later."

Levi returned the box to the table and rejoined Allie.

"Are you sure you want to go down to the wharf?" Levi offered her his arm, and she curled her hand around his elbow. "You ought to be warm and cozy by the fire at your uncle's. I could take you home and come by before heading to the courthouse."

"The whole journey." Allie stifled a cough. "I want to be here for the whole journey. I don't want to miss a single moment."

"Justin, don't forget—"

"To open the gate on the forge if I need to step away. I know. I know." Justin shooed them out the door with a wave.

11

"Have you made plans to see Doc Ewing?" Levi asked as they started down Cane Hill towards Main Street.

"I'll make time later today if I need to." The cold, dry air irritated Allie's throat, and she swallowed hard to smother the rising cough. He'd put a quick end to their day if he noticed so much as a sniffle from her.

"I don't think it's a good idea for you to be on the steamboat in this wind. Pull your bonnet down over your ears." He tugged at her hat. "Don't you have one made of fur?"

"It was so warm when we departed St. Louis that I forgot to bring it." Allie jogged a couple of steps to keep pace with him, and he slowed.

"Stop. Stop." Grabbing her arm, he turned her toward him. He unfastened her scarf and pulled it up over the bonnet, tying it under her chin and wrapping the tail ends around her neck. "Maybe that will hold."

"You're making such a fuss."

"You're right. I'm making a fuss. I didn't dive into that river to save you so you could miss Christmas with an illness." He tucked loose tendrils of hair into the edge of Allie's scarf, his fingers lightly brushing her cheek. Her breath swelled at his touch. "Allie, why won't you let me take you home? I could visit Cobb and the courthouse while you rest."

She smiled.

"What is it?"

"You just called me Allie."

"My apologies." His cheeks flushed.

"I liked it. Levi, I want to see this through. Let's go see the captain." Allie looped her arm in his, marveling at the change in him since she appeared in the forge Sunday. He'd been so adamant about keeping her at arm's length. So much so, it had taken her aback when he'd asked about her father during their walk from Conrad Hildesheim's shop.

They continued, turning onto Main Street. She pulled herself closer to him, savoring the warmth. "Do you have any family keepsakes? Something that connects you to family or inspires hope when times are hard?"

"No. I didn't have a strong relationship with my family." His jaw tightened. "I think I could have been close to my mother after my father left if she had lived."

"Levi, what happened to your mother?"

Levi tensed at the question. He looked away. Allie remained silent and relaxed. She wanted him to be comfortable sharing with her. She might not have fared so well if she hadn't been able to share her feelings in letters to Uncle Shadow. Levi hadn't had that. He took a deep breath.

"My father stumbled home Christmas Eve with a bottle of whisky. He was so angry. I never understood why." Levi's voice strained as he rubbed his wrists and adjusted his gloves.

Allie's heart ached at the sound of his thready voice. "He'd never done that before?"

64

"He did it often, but I never understood it. That was life with Pa." He rubbed the back of his neck. "He threw the bottle at Ma. Knocked the oil lamp over, setting the bed on fire in our one-room shanty. I was trying to put out the fire when he attacked Ma."

Allie slid her hand from his elbow to his palm, lacing her fingers with his. Levi looked away. She waited for him to continue.

"When I turned, her body lay crumpled on the floor. He'd thrown her against the wall. He was about to hit her again when I got between them. We had words, and he left. Never came back." His voice caught and moisture filled his eyes. "Ma died a few hours later. Christmas morning."

"You were fifteen." Allie's voice was barely a whisper. A heaviness spread through her chest. "And alone." She tightened her hold on his hand. Then she wiped a tear from her cheek. "When my father left, I felt like it was my fault. I felt like I had nothing. I needed something to cling to, and I had my mother's Bible. On a slip of paper inside the cover, I found that quote, 'Hope is patience with the lamp lit.' So, I read every verse I could find about hope. That's what keeps me going." She paused to look at Levi. "I don't know how you did it, Levi. Alone ... with nothing to hold on to. Most of us aren't as strong as you. Someone needs that nativity to keep going."

Levi blinked hard as they approached the gangplank to the *Resilient.* "Let's go see a man about a manifest. Coming aboard!"

Levi's shout shook her from her thoughts. Her gaze drifted up the gangplank, and her breath froze. She felt herself falling, the frigid water engulfing her.

"Allie?" Levi steadied her. "Are you coming?"

"I felt like I was falling." She sucked in a deep breath. "I got lightheaded."

"Allie," Levi turned her towards him. "You don't have to go aboard. Are you sure you want to do this?"

"Oh, yes." She took a tentative step onto the gangplank. Then, clearing her throat, she paused. "I didn't expect to feel this way returning to the boat."

"It was a harrowing ordeal, being run aground in one vessel and knocked into the river from the other." Levi pulled her close, and she found his warmth comforting. "I can walk you up the hill to the fuel depot. I'm sure they'll have a fire going. I'll talk to Cobb and come back for you."

"No, I'll be fine. I can do this." She closed her eyes, gripping his arm. Then, opening her eyes, she plunged forward with a determined stride. "Why aren't you nervous? You went into the river too."

"By choice." He chuckled. "I think that makes all the difference."

At the top of the gangway, they stopped for a moment so Allie could get her bearings. A young boy ran past, brushing against her. She tipped backward, the handrail pressing into her back. She clutched at Levi, and he drew her into his arms. He leaned close, his breath warm on her forehead. "I've got you. You're not going anywhere."

Gulping air, she began to cough. Her brows furrowed in defeat.

"You're still coughing." Levi pulled back to look her in the face. Flecks of gold popped in his warm brown eyes like the first embers of a fire lighting.

"Please don't take me home. We're already here."

He pulled her close again, rubbing his hands across her back to warm her. "Allie, have you got a fever? Your forehead is hot."

"Of course, it's hot. Look how you've bundled me up." She

wiped the back of her hand across her forehead. Determination sparked in her eyes. "I'm not leaving."

"We'll stay. But another fit like that, and it's straight home with you. And I'll be fetching the doctor for a house call."

The scrawny young deckhand returned. "Are you all right, miss? I'm real sorry."

Resting her head against Levi's chest, she smiled weakly. "I'm good."

"Perhaps you could offer us some help to make up for it. Point us in the direction of Captain Cobb?"

"I'll do better than that. I'll take you to him." The boy ushered them to the captain's quarters, leaving them at the door.

12

"I see you're sitting around, as usual, Cobb." Levi chuckled.

"Levi! Good to see you!" Captain Cobb stood and shook Levi's hand, pulling him in for a one-armed hug. "Who is this you have here?"

"This is Sam Mooney's niece, Allie McLaughlin. She had the great misfortune of traveling with you on your ill-fated journey." Levi wrapped an arm around her, moving her forward. "Allie, this is Captain Hale Cobb."

"Miss McLaughlin." Cobb tipped his chin to her. "My deepest apologies. However, I believe the whole ordeal could have been avoided if we had a better blacksmith looking after the maintenance of this vessel."

Levi slugged Cobb's arm. "No blacksmith's work will hold when you run your boat into the dirt."

They shared a hearty laugh, and Cobb returned to his chair. He motioned to a red velvet banquette. "Have a seat. I tell you, Levi. That sandbar came out of nowhere. If lightning hadn't flashed at the right moment, we'd have torn the entire bottom out of this boat. God was watching over us, that's for certain."

"Listen, I was at the riverfront that day—"

"That's right. I heard you organized the cleanup and saved some young soul from the river."

Allie blushed at Cobb's comment.

"Oh, dear. Miss McLaughlin, were you that young soul?"

She nodded.

"You ought to be home in bed resting after such a distressing event. What are you doing here?"

"She's being stubborn, that's what." Levi shot her a sidelong glance followed by a wink.

"We're hoping you can help us find someone." Allie smiled.

"Find someone here in town?" He frowned. "I'm afraid I don't know many people in town."

"We'd like to check the ship's manifest for a name, Cobb." Levi leaned forward, elbows on his knees. "A parcel was left on Water Street. It might have belonged to a passenger of yours. Can you check for German passengers, last name Zimmermann?"

"No, I can't." Cobb scratched his head. "Manifest is missing."

"How can the manifest be missing?" Levi propped his hand on his knee.

"One of the boys sent the manifest to the *Valiant* with the passengers. I talked to Sterling Reed. He's the captain of the *Valiant*." Cobb offered the aside to Allie. "Reed said he never saw the manifest. So no one knows where it is."

"I see." Levi took Allie's hand and lightly squeezed it. "If it turns up, could you send word to the mercantile or the boardinghouse?"

"Of course, but why don't you put it in the lost and found?"

"Oh, it's vital we find the owner, Captain." Allie stepped across to his desk and grasped his hand.

"What makes that more important than the other things in the lost and found?"

"It's a nativity."

Cobb patted her hand and exchanged a knowing look. "I agree. That is important, especially so close to Christmas. Finding that manifest is my highest priority. I'll check for the name Zimmermann. If it's on the manifest, I'll send word."

"We better get going if we want to stop by the courthouse." Levi scooted Allie toward the door.

"Levi, could I speak with you for a moment?" Cobb straightened his shirt as he stood. "In private?"

Levi glanced tentatively at Allie. "Do you mind waiting?"

"No, of course not."

"Much obliged, Miss McLaughlin. We'll be right out."

Captain Cobb closed the door gently behind Allie. He turned to Levi with a somber look on his face. He opened his mouth as if to speak but then sidestepped Levi. He stood near the banquette, staring out the window.

"What is it, Cap'n?"

"Levi, we lost a soul in the storm that night." Silence hung between them. He turned to face Levi. "He didn't stay with the rest of the passengers. He came topside to help. Muscular fellow, ruddy complexion, wild red hair ... foreign accent."

Levi blew out a breath as though he'd been punched in the gut.

"With the manifest lost and the passengers scattered throughout town, we cannot identify who he was. Crewmen thought they saw him traveling with a woman and two children, a boy and a girl. Someone may have lost a husband, a father, a brother." Cobb's blue eyes dimmed. "It was my responsibility to deliver these passengers safely to their destination, and now this season of celebration may be a season of despair for someone."

"Hale," Levi grasped Cobb by the shoulder, "this wasn't your fault. That storm came out of nowhere. You did all you could."

"That man saved lives. If he is connected to this nativity in some way, and if he traveled with family, you must find them." Cobb pulled his hand down his salt-and-pepper beard. "They're going to need that nativity. And they need to hear about the sacrifice he made."

"I understand."

The men emerged from the cabin, rejoining Allie. Captain Cobb accompanied them topside, seeing them off, waving from the top of the gangplank. Levi steadied Allie as they descended the ramp. Then, their feet again on solid ground, she waved back at Captain Cobb.

Across the wharf, a man stood on the hurricane deck of the next steamboat. His pointed stare caught Levi's attention. With a gnarled finger, the man pointed to his pocket watch.

"Levi, who is that?"

"That's Captain Horn of the *No. 7*."

"Isn't that the man I saw in the blacksmith shop yesterday? Do you need to go aboard and talk to him?"

"He's trying to send me a message." Levi directed Allie toward Water Street. "And it is one that I fully intend to ignore."

"You can go aboard if you need to. I don't mind waiting."

"What we're doing is more important."

13

"Let me do the talking at the courthouse." Levi directed her up Main Street toward Thompson Street. "We need to make it quick and get you home."

"Are you calling me longwinded?" Allie's eyes narrowed.

"I, uh—" Levi stammered. "I'm sorry, but you tend to go on about that nativity."

"I'm teasing you." Allie laughed. Her smile faded. "Do you think stopping by the courthouse will do any good? We're right back where we started, aren't we?" Allie suppressed another cough, hoping Levi wouldn't notice.

"Not exactly. We still have the name from the bottom of the nativity piece." Levi stopped, grasping her hands. "We'll proceed as planned, assuming that Zimmermann is the owner. Of course, we could be wrong about that, but better to have one lead than none, right?"

"I don't know." Allie hesitated.

"Allie, you were right." There it was again, a glimmer of gold, a flame coming to life in his eyes. "This is important. I see that now. We'll make this quick and get you home."

Since when did Levi consider the nativity such a priority? Was it something Cobb had said? Allie pursed her lips. She hated being left out of conversations. She slipped her hands from Levi's.

"What did Cobb say to you?"

Levi turned her up the path to the courthouse. "Look, a few more steps."

Levi and Allie stared blankly at the sign on the courthouse door.

CLOSED FOR THE AFTERNOON
OPEN 8 A.M. TO NOON THROUGH DECEMBER 23.

"There's got to be something else we can do." Allie turned to Levi. "Let's go talk to Captain Reed. Perhaps he'll let us search the *Valiant* for the manifest."

"You don't need to be out in the cold. Besides, the *Valiant* left to take the soldiers to Fort Smith as soon as its passengers and cargo were unloaded." Levi rubbed her shoulders and then turned her toward the street. "Let's get you home. If you're feeling better tomorrow, we'll try again."

Along the path from the courthouse to Main Street, they met a man in a buckskin coat wearing a fur cap. He pulled a cedar tree across the courthouse lawn with a rope. His eyes briefly met Levi's, and he gave a curt nod.

"Where are you going with that tree?"

"Taking it to Mr. Styles. Found it pulled up by the roots while I was hunting." The man shifted the rope to his other shoulder. "Figured he could make a chest or something, and I'll earn a little extra to get through the winter."

"If you see any oak or hickory downed, I can use it at the forge. You don't have to bring it to me. Send word." Levi hitched his thumb in the direction of Hogue House. "Justin and I can pick it up in the wagon. I'll pay you a finder's fee."

"I'll keep that in mind." The man parted with a wave while Levi and Allie continued down the path to Main Street.

"A big cedar like that would be stunning in front of the courthouse." She paused, inhaling deeply. "I love the smell of cedar."

"I reckon it would."

Shoving gloved hands into her coat pockets, Allie walked with her head hanging low.

"What's the matter?"

"There's nothing we can do now except wait." Allie coughed. Her shoulders slumped. The hope of finding the nativity's owner had helped her fight against her worsening symptoms. Her head ached.

"Levi!" Pastor Turner called from up the street. "Levi! A moment, please?"

Levi and Allie ambled up Main Street toward him as the pastor jogged to meet them.

"Pastor Turner, what can I do for you?"

"You're a hard man to find." Pastor Turner took a few haggard breaths. "I've been all over town."

"Yes, Allie dragged me all over town today on a mission. She's set on restoring the hope of Christmas to the world." Levi winked at her. "But you've found me now."

"Thank the Lord. I'll walk with you a moment." He fell in line with them as they continued up Main Street. "The quilting circle is meeting at the church tomorrow. Some of them have taken in passengers from the *Resilient* who hadn't planned to stay in Van Buren. Several passengers are stuck here because they don't have the means to move on or were separated from loved ones or belongings."

Allie tugged Levi's coat, signaling she was ready to be out

of the cold. She stretched her scarf toward her cheeks. He drew her close, resting his arm around her shoulders.

"The ladies plan to collect clothing and other items to help them through Christmas, so they will be at the church daily." The pastor blew warm air into his hands and rubbed them together. "There's a problem with the hinges on the iron stove, and the door doesn't hang right. They're worried that someone might bump into it and get injured. I've tried everything, and I can't secure it. Would you mind stopping by to look at it tomorrow?"

"I'd be happy to. What time should I come by?"

"Any time tomorrow. But the sooner, the better." He winked. He peeled off from them with a wave. "Thanks, Levi."

"Are you okay?"

"I need to rest a moment." Short breaths delivered sharp, cold bursts of air to Allie's lungs, but she didn't dare complain. She released a puff of air, a ribbon of steam floating between them. She tilted her head. "What's that delicious smell?"

"That's Gray's Café. You hungry?"

"Famished." She clutched her stomach. "A bite to eat, and I'll be good as new. Then, we can figure out what to do next."

"Allie, we're done for the day."

"But it's only three days until Christmas." She tugged at Levi's sleeve. "Time is running out."

"We'll get you fed, and we can try the courthouse again in the morning." Levi held the door open. A burst of warm air flooded over them as they entered. "Let's get that table near the kitchen. Should be nice and toasty."

Levi hurried to pull the chair out, then helped her with her coat, his warm fingers brushing her neck as he grasped the collar. Allie removed her scarf, hat, and gloves, placing them on the seat beside her. He put his hat and gloves in the pockets of his overcoat. Allie smiled when he moved her things to the chair at the end of the table and sat in the seat next to her. Then, raising his hand, he waved to an older lady in an apron.

"Levi, we don't see you in here much." Mrs. Gray placed napkins and utensils on the table.

"Mrs. Gray, I stopped by last week for a piece of your famous pecan pie." Levi smiled. Then he leaned across to Allie, whispering behind his hand. "She makes the best pecan pie on either side of the river. But don't tell her I said that. Compliments make her head swim."

"Compliments do no such thing, Levi Snow. Besides, it's not a compliment. It's the truth." Mrs. Gray laughed and swatted at Levi. "And I can handle the truth fine. What'll you have?"

"We'd like two bowls of oxtail soup with cornbread."

"No cornbread for me, please." Allie rubbed her throat.

"Bring the cornbread. I'll eat it. Also, we'd like some hot tea." Levi glanced around the café. Allie's eyes followed his gaze until he paused, pointing to the candy jars near the counter. "And a peppermint stick."

"As you please, sweetie. I'll be right back."

Mrs. Gray reappeared with a younger woman who held a tea kettle. She arranged two saucers and teacups, tucking a spoon next to each cup. Then she swept across the café as the younger woman filled their cups. She returned, waving a peppermint stick in the air.

"Here's that peppermint, dear."

With a nod of thanks, Levi took the candy stick and placed it in Allie's teacup. "Before you know it, we'll be toasty. Thank you, Mrs. Gray."

"The soup will be out soon. I'm finishing up a fresh batch of cornbread." She patted Levi's hand. "Such a dear. You should come to see me more often."

Allie's eyes followed Mrs. Gray as she bustled away in a

flurry. "Mr. Snow, I do believe she was flirting with you."

"Mrs. Gray? No." Levi's ears reddened, and he fidgeted with the spoon on his saucer. He glanced back. Mrs. Gray was looking in their direction. She smiled and waved. "She's like that with everyone."

"She hasn't waved at anyone else." Allie grinned. He seemed so in control, and she enjoyed seeing him slightly unsettled. "Is there a Mr. Gray?"

"Of course, there's a Mr. Gray." Levi fished tea leaves from Allie's cup. "Drink your tea."

She sipped slowly, eyes closed, lashes fluttering. The warm liquid soothed her throat.

"Feels good, doesn't it?"

"It's just what I needed. Thank you." She swirled the peppermint stick in her tea. Bringing the cup close to her face, she drew deep breaths. Then she took another sip. "*Mmm.* This reminds me of one year back home when we had a peppermint taffy pull close to Christmas."

"I guess you experienced quite a few traditions growing up."

"Not so many. We began hanging evergreen boughs on the mantle when I was thirteen. First, we'd string beads and tie ribbons on the branches. Then we would make ornaments to give each other as gifts." She smiled at the memory. "It was great fun trying to make them in secret and hiding them away when I heard someone coming. What about your family? Did you have holiday traditions?"

Levi stared into his cup. He fiddled with his spoon, turning it over and over, then tapped it lightly on the saucer. "No, no traditions to speak of. Do you think you'll share many more Christmases with your father now that he's moved west?"

Allie shrugged. She still hadn't decided how to respond to her father's letter. If she shared it with Levi, he would probably agree with Uncle Shadow that she should join her father. She wasn't sure she had any interest in heading west. She cherished the security she had living with Uncle Shadow. And, if she was frank with herself, she felt more drawn to Levi every moment.

"Here you go, my dear." Mrs. Gray's silvery voice announced the arrival of their meal. She placed a bowl in front of Allie and then Levi. Her assistant delivered a plate of cornbread. "Let me know if you need anything else."

A thin boy came through the front door carrying an armful of evergreen boughs. He picked his way through the tables, trying to avoid diners. Finally, he stopped at Levi and Allie's table. "Mrs. Gray, where would you like these?"

"Sarah, dear, would you show him what to do with those?"

The young woman beckoned the boy to follow.

"Why, Mrs. Gray, are you decorating for Christmas?" Levi arched an eyebrow.

"Sam Mooney stopped by earlier talking about his idea for living displays in the shop windows. We had an old pine blown down in that storm, so I sent Tommy to cut some pieces for the café." She clapped Levi on the back. "You know I'm not about to let Sam Mooney outdo me. I've got to think about what else I can do for Christmas."

"Allie was telling me—" Levi gestured to Allie, "Have you met Allie? She's Sam Mooney's niece. Allie was telling me how they had a peppermint taffy pull one year at Christmastime." He winked at Allie, and her heart fluttered.

"Peppermint taffy, is that so? I believe I have a vanilla taffy recipe. It might do nicely to add a touch of peppermint to it." Mrs. Gray patted Allie's hand. "Thank you, dearest. And tell that uncle of yours he'll have to work harder to outdo Annetta Gray." Mrs. Gray was off again with a wink and a flourish.

Allie dipped her spoon in the soup, took a bite, and nodded

her approval. Levi crumbled cornbread over his bowl, fisted his spoon, and ate a hearty mouthful. After his fourth spoonful, he swallowed and paused to glance at Allie.

"I hope you don't mind that I'm not talking. I thought maybe your throat could use a rest."

"I do appreciate that." She smiled as the broth eased the irritation in her throat.

Levi downed the soup in record time. His eyes followed as Sarah flitted from table to table, clearing dishes. He scooted his bowl to the edge of the table, and Sarah picked it up without a word at her next passing. Moments later, Mrs. Gray appeared again.

"Could I interest you in some pie, Levi?"

"Not today, ma'am, but thank you."

Mrs. Gray smiled as though she had a secret. She leaned close. "I have pecan pie again."

"Oh, dear woman," Levi flattened his hand to his chest, "you know I cannot resist your pecan pie. May I have some coffee to go with it?"

"Naturally. Back in a jiffy."

"My, you do have a hearty appetite today." Allie giggled. She neared the bottom of her bowl.

"I'm stuffed after all that cornbread, but she doesn't make pecan pie every day. I'm not about to miss it." He drummed his fingers on the table. "If you're ready to get home, I can have Mrs. Gray wrap up the pie."

"You go ahead. I believe I'll have some more hot tea."

They ate the rest of the meal in comfortable silence. When they were ready to leave, Levi helped Allie with her coat. Then he grabbed her hat and pulled it down around her ears. Releasing a puff of air from the corner of her mouth, Allie blew a strand of hair out of her face. "Levi, I can put my hat and scarf on myself. I don't need assistance."

"I want to make sure you're bundled up tight. I'll be in trouble with Sam when he finds out you're still coughing, and I didn't bring you home."

"It's only a cough." Allie's mind plodded along, her thoughts sluggish. "One last stop, and then home."

"What do you mean 'one last stop'?" Levi narrowly eyed her. "There is nothing more we can do today."

"I know, but I would feel ever so much better if I could see the nativity one more time. Please?"

"I am well-practiced at saying 'no,' but I have difficulty saying it to you." Levi sighed as he ushered her through the tables. "We'll go to the boardinghouse, but you're not going to sit there moon-eyed over that thing. We'll box it up, and you can take it to your uncle's, where you can gaze at it to your heart's content."

Allie's energy quickly faded as they walked up Cane Hill toward the boardinghouse. Breathing became more labored. Had she been foolish not to allow Levi to walk her straight home after their meal? Would he be put out with her if she asked him to take her home in the wagon after she retrieved the nativity?

She halted. Squinting, she peered up the hill. Two more streets and they would arrive at the boardinghouse. She could do this. She had to do this.

"Allie, are you all right?" Levi returned to her side.

"Remember when I told you that I tend to go one step too far? This may be one of those moments, but I'll manage." She trudged ahead with determined steps.

"Do you need me to carry you?" He half chuckled as he slid his arms under her elbows for support.

"Of course not. I just need—"

A sharp clap split the air, and they froze.

14

"The forge!" Levi exhaled the words. "Can you make it?"

"Yes."

Levi clutched Allie's elbow as they ran toward the forge. Pushing ahead, his arm drew back as she slowed. Falling back, he urged her on. When in sight of the yard, he scooped her up, carrying her the rest of the way. He deposited her on the porch as Mrs. Hogue and a host of others spilled out of the house. Levi raced around the side of the house.

Justin emerged from the blacksmith shop, coughing. "Fire's out. Need to ... open ... the windows. Clear ... the air."

Levi's heart pounded as he helped Justin to the ground. He ran to open the windows and returned to Justin's side. "Are you okay?"

"Doc Ewing ... inside ... with Rebecca."

"In the house?" Levi knelt and patted Justin's back.

Mrs. Hogue appeared at his elbow. "Doctor Ewing is tending to Allie."

"Can you walk?" Levi looped his arms under Justin's armpits.

He nodded. Hoisting Justin up, Levi wrapped the young man's arm around his shoulder. He grasped the back of Justin's belt in one hand and placed his other hand on the apprentice's middle to steady him. Mrs. Hogue ducked under her son's opposite arm for added support. Then together, they guided him to the front porch.

Allie was nowhere in sight, nor was Doc Ewing. Levi choked on the words. "Where is Allie? You said she was here with Doc."

"They must have gone inside."

They clattered into the house, Mrs. Hogue slipping sideways through the door, followed by Justin and Levi. Doc Ewing rushed to Justin's side, taking Mrs. Hogue's place. They helped him to the sofa, and Doc began to examine him.

Levi glanced around the room. The three oldest Hogue girls stood at the ready, eyes trained on Doc Ewing. He heard brother and sister, Simon and Martie, upstairs wrangling the youngest Hogues. But no sign of Allie.

"Allie?" Levi grabbed Rebecca by the elbow. "Where is Allie? Is she all right?"

"She's here, Levi." Rebecca scooted aside, revealing Allie sitting upright in a chair behind the three young women. "Doc Ewing was about to give us instructions when you came in with Justin."

Doc Ewing leaned around Mrs. Hogue, who hadn't left Justin's side. "Basin of hot water for the feet. Lay a cloth covered with mustard plaster on her chest. Pepper tea and onion syrup, if you have it. I don't carry onion syrup, but there's pepper tea in my bag if you need it."

The sisters launched into action, dispersing throughout the house to collect the needed items before converging in the kitchen. Levi knelt by Allie's chair. Her flushed appearance and rough cough caused a pang in his chest.

"I knew I should have taken you home." He patted her hand. "I'm sorry, Allie. I'll get you home and to bed as soon as Doc allows it. Do you want me to tell Sam what's happened? I should let him know where you are."

Allie shook her head. "Stay. Please."

"Doc, shouldn't she be lying down?"

"Sitting up for now, Levi."

"How is Justin?" Levi craned his head around, spying Justin reclining on the sofa with his eyes closed.

"I believe he's okay." Doc grasped Mrs. Hogue's hand. "Mrs. Hogue, could you tell the girls to bring a few rags?"

Mrs. Hogue darted out of the room, and Doc returned his attention to Levi.

"He'll be fine. We'll clean him up, give him a few moments to rest, and then I want him to step outside for a little fresh air."

"Is there anything I can do? For either of them?"

"When he's ready, you can accompany Justin on a short walk for some fresh air. I'll move Allie to the sofa then. I don't want her fully reclined, but she can rest upright on some pillows for the time being. I want to keep her here overnight to watch over them both."

"I'll get Simon. He can run down and let Sam know what's going on. He'll be expecting Allie home soon."

Allie groaned. "My throat hurts."

Levi resettled her closer to the edge of the chair and leaned her head on his shoulder. He patted her back. "I'm so sorry, Allie. We'll get you better soon. I promise."

"Excuse me, Levi." Rebecca waited patiently with a basin of hot water for Allie's feet. Ivajohn and Cordelia stood behind her with the other items Doc had requested. "We'll take good care of her."

Levi stood and brushed Rebecca's shoulder, mouthing 'thank you.' He stopped at the sofa and leaned over Justin. "Looks like you're in good hands here. I'll fetch Simon and then step outside. Back in a bit to get you for that walk."

Justin nodded. "There's something I have to tell you."

"Not now. Rest first."

Since there was nothing more he could do, Levi sent Simon to update Sam while he went out to inspect the forge. If the damage were too bad, their gift to Mrs. Grace and all the steamboat work would be delayed. He had stayed in Van Buren longer than anywhere else he'd lived since his mother's death. He owed these people for their graciousness. If it came down to it, he'd have to abandon the search for the nativity owner to repair the forge and take care of the town.

Levi pushed open the shop door and crossed the room to the work table. His heart sank. Muted light from the gray December sky fell softly through the window onto the charred remains of the nativity display. Levi picked up the platform, turning it slowly. The propeller was broken, and one side of the frame was blackened.

The figures. Where were the figures?

Levi grabbed the fire poker and poked at the debris around the work table. The heaviest items near the forge seemed unscathed for the most part. The work table was blackened on one side, but the damage was minimal. Stones from the forge lay in a heap at the base. Bits of clinker radiated out from the blast point. Unfortunately, because the nativity pieces were made of wood and some wood burned down to clinker, there was no way for Levi to determine with certainty if the fragments were the remains of the nativity set.

Levi slumped to the floor. How could he tell Allie it was

gone? What about the woman and children traveling with the passenger who had drowned? If the nativity did belong to them, what hope could he and Allie offer them now?

Levi raked the fire poker across the floor, hoping something would take shape, allowing him to identify the objects of his search. He placed the poker on its stand and rubbed his hands down his face. He looked questioningly toward the ceiling and spoke softly.

"I've never believed this God with us stuff, but if it's true—if you came down to dwell among us—I'd love to see it. I want to understand what Allie sees in you."

The cold air from the windows had pushed out the warmth of the forge. Levi stood and crossed the room to shutter the window by the door. As the day waned from the sky, the shop became darker. Levi stretched, grasping at the shutter. His toe bumped against something. Reaching down, his fingers hooked on a small piece of carved wood. Scooting the carving into his palm, he quickly grabbed the candleholder from the table. Throwing open the stove door, he lit the candlestick from the fire.

Levi raised the piece into the light. It was the man from the nativity that Allie always placed near the woman and child. He set the figure on the table and crouched down with the candle. Slowly, he scanned the floor, moving the candleholder from side to side. Finally, he spotted another chunk on the floor under the far corner of the table. Retrieving it, he held it up to the light.

The woman.

His heart flip-flopped. Could it be here? Could the babe in the manger have survived the explosion? He continued to scan, pushing back the darkness with his small candle. He searched high and low. Nothing.

Levi returned to the place near the window where he found

the man. He traced a path with his eyes from that spot to where he found the woman. He allowed his gaze to drift along that trajectory. Was there something under the stove?

Levi eased across the room as though whatever it was might escape if he moved too quickly. The radiating heat of the stove intensified as he leaned close. Sweeping his hand underneath, he caught something with his pinky. Then, drawing it into his hand, he wrapped his fingers around it.

He raised the candleholder and his fisted hand inches from his face. He uncurled his fingers. There in his palm was the babe, resting in a manger. An unexpected warmth flooded through him.

"Here you are, Immanuel. God with us." He ran his rough thumb over the sleeping baby. Then he lifted his gaze and whispered. "Thank you, Lord."

The door opened a crack, and Rebecca Hogue's honeyed head appeared. "Levi?"

"I'm here."

"Allie is asking for you, and Justin is ready for that walk." She pointed with a long slender finger. "What's that?"

Levi held up the carving. "This is the babe everyone is so fascinated with this time of year."

Rebecca entered, pulling the door closed behind her. She sat down at the table, and Levi joined her.

"The baby Jesus?"

"I thought he was lost." Levi handed her the piece. "The nativity was on the worktable when the forge blew."

Rebecca took the piece and looked it over. Then, she scooped Mary and Joseph from the table. "Is this all that's left?"

"I think so." He patted the table. "I don't know how I'm going to tell Allie. She is so set on finding the owner, and now most of the set is destroyed."

Rebecca returned Mary and Joseph to the table. She held the babe in her open palm between them. "This is the most important part. Allie knows that."

"She's going to be heartbroken."

"She'll be thankful these treasured pieces can still be returned. She knows it was an accident." She handed the infant to Levi. "Better put those back in the box. Allie and Justin are waiting."

"I guess I'll put the stand in there too. Unfortunately, the propellor is broken, and it's blackened on one side, but perhaps a carpenter could use it as a model to create a new one."

Levi retrieved the display from the worktable and nestled all the pieces in the box before following Rebecca to the house. Justin and Allie had traded places. Justin sat upright on the edge of the chair while Allie reclined on the sofa under a blanket. Her eyes appeared dull and tired. Levi pulled a footstool next to her and took her hand.

"How are you doing?"

Allie smiled weakly. "Exhausted."

"How is your throat?"

"It's a little better. The tea helped."

He brushed her hair away from her face. Should he tell her about the nativity? No. He'd wait. Perhaps after she'd had some rest.

"You take it easy. Do whatever Doc says." He tucked the blanket under her chin. "I'm going to take Justin for that walk. Won't be gone long."

Levi squeezed Allie's hand and kissed her forehead. She lay her head back and closed her eyes. He stood, clearing his throat and straightening his shirt. He turned to Justin.

"Let's get you ambling, mister." He followed Justin out the door.

"Levi, I have to tell you something."

87

"You didn't finish the order of nails for the steamboats."

"Well, no. But that's not what I wanted to tell you." Justin hung his head. "It's about the nativity—."

"I know. I inspected the forge when I went out earlier." Levi patted Justin's shoulder as they walked around the house. "It's not your fault. I should have put it away before Allie and I left this morning."

"No, I told you I'd do it." Justin folded his arms across his middle, avoiding eye contact. He'd never looked more like a little boy to Levi. "It's just that Doc has been in and out of town the last several days. He showed up this morning saying he's staying for Christmas. I only intended to be gone a few moments to stall his horse."

"You didn't open the gate."

"Doc followed me into the stable," Justin shrugged, "and I guess we talked longer than I realized. You're right. I didn't open the gate. Now, the nativity is damaged because of me, and the forge is in shambles."

"It's my responsibility. You're my apprentice." Levi stopped and turned to face Justin. "I released you to work by yourself too soon. Mr. O'Rourke, my mentor, never would have turned an apprentice loose that soon. I let you down."

"No, Levi, I let you down." Justin kicked the dirt back and forth between his feet. "I've been working with you for almost a year. You've told me a thousand times about that gate. Twice this morning."

"Don't beat yourself up over it. It's still my responsibility." Levi toed the dirt. "Now I have to find a way to tell Allie."

15

A gentle nudge coaxed Allie from her sleep. She drew a deep breath of air through her nose. Her eyes fluttered open. Uncle Shadow leaned close with Levi standing over his shoulder.

"*Hmm.*" She stretched, taking in the unfamiliar room. "Where am I? The boardinghouse?"

"Yes. This is the older girls' room." Uncle Shadow stroked her hair. "I hear you're not feeling so well."

"I wouldn't say that exactly." She grimaced. "I couldn't handle the run up the hill in the cold air. I feel much better now, though."

"Doc wants you to rest here a good twenty-four hours." Uncle Shadow gave her a hard stare. "No more gallivanting around town. Do I make myself clear?"

"But Uncle—"

"Don't 'but Uncle' me. You'll stay here, and Doc will look after you, or you'll miss Christmas."

"You need your rest, Allie." Levi echoed over his shoulder.

Allie closed her eyes. They had to continue the search for

the nativity owners. Her mother's Bible was all Allie had left after losing her mother. Her father had taken everything else west with him. She couldn't imagine what it might be like if someone lost their nativity forever.

She placed her hand on Uncle Shadow's knee. "I have to take care of the nativity."

Uncle Shadow exchanged a hesitant glance with Levi.

"What? What is it?"

Uncle Shadow patted her hand. "You'll be in good hands with Doc Ewing. Levi and the Hogue girls will take good care of you. I must get back to the store." He wagged his finger in her face with a playful smile. "You get some rest. I mean it. You don't want to miss the Main Street festivities on Christmas Eve."

"Festivities?"

"Businesses up and down Main Street are planning something special." His grin widened as his chest puffed out. "Festivities will last all day."

"Did you know about all this?" Allie eyed Levi narrowly.

Levi shook his head. "First I'm hearing of it."

"It's all inspired by the two of you—and that little nativity."

"It's a German Christmas pyramid." Allie smiled as she pictured the sweet scene revolving in the candlelight.

"Whatever it is, it spreads hope and joy throughout the town." Uncle Shadow cleared his throat and pulled an envelope from his coat pocket. His eyes sobered. He passed the envelope to Allie. "Allie, this letter came for you today. Perhaps you should read it."

"Do you know what it says?"

"No. I didn't open it." Uncle Shadow shook his head.

Allie glanced down, reading the scrawl across the front. It was from her father. She pushed it back into Uncle Shadow's hand. "Take it back to the store with you. I don't want to read it."

"Allie—"

"Take it back." She gritted her teeth. "Please."

"All right." Uncle Shadow leaned in to kiss her forehead. "If Doc gives his blessing, Levi will bring you home sometime tomorrow."

She nodded. Uncle Shadow got up and headed toward the door.

"I'll walk you downstairs." Levi followed behind.

Allie sank deep into the bed, pulling the covers over her head. It had been more than a year since her father had written her. Now, a letter had been waiting for her at the general store, followed by this second letter only days later. Would it be another letter begging her to join him out west? Or was he writing to tell her that he'd already changed his mind?

She pulled the quilt back down to her chin. Why hadn't Uncle Shadow brought her mother's Bible instead of her father's letter? What she wouldn't give to join Levi tomorrow at the clerk's office and the quilting circle. It would be the perfect distraction from her jumbled thoughts. Instead, she had at least a day to wrestle with them.

The door creaked open. Levi poked his head in. "Still awake?"

"*Mm-hmm.*" She lifted her gaze toward him. "What time is it?"

"Close to nine o'clock, I'd say."

"Oh my, you'd better get to bed."

"I wanted to let you know Doc Ewing will be up soon." He leaned in a little further. "I'll sit with you a while if you don't mind."

"Oh, no." She pulled the covers tight under her chin.

"You've got to get up early to work before you go by the clerk's office and the quilting circle."

Levi blinked hard. He sat down, rubbing his hands together. "Allie, I'm not going to the clerk's office tomorrow. Or the quilting circle."

"Why not?"

"Well, the forge is damaged. It'll take me a couple of days to repair it by myself." He shrugged. "I can't very well do anything to fix the stove at the church with a busted forge."

"You've got extra time to visit the clerk's office then."

"Allie, did you hear me? I'll be working on that forge for two days."

"I've been thinking." Allie sat up in bed, pulling her knees to her chest and wrapping her arms around them. "You should still visit the quilting circle. Some church families agreed to lodge the steamboat passengers with nowhere else to go. Perhaps one of the ladies in the quilting circle is hosting German passengers. Or they might know who is."

"Allie." Levi rubbed his forehead. "You're not listening to me. I've got a responsibility to the town. I can't continue this search for the owners. Besides—"

"What?" Allie gave him a hard stare. "What aren't you telling me, Levi Snow?"

"Allie, it appears some of your color is returning." Doctor Ewing entered with a large pitcher. He crossed to the dressing table. "I had Rebecca bring up a wash basin. I'm going to get things ready here, and we'll continue the treatments you were doing at your uncle's."

She nodded. Then, arching an eyebrow, she returned her attention to Levi. "What aren't you saying?"

"It's about the nativity."

"Go on."

"Remember we left it on the work table?"

"No." Her breath hitched. "It's gone? Destroyed?"

Levi leaned his elbows on his knees and studied his feet. "Not entirely."

"What do you mean?" She swallowed hard. "Levi, tell me what happened."

"Most of it was destroyed." He laced his fingers together, steepling his thumbs.

"Joseph and Mary? The baby?"

"I found them. They survived." He lifted his head, a bewildered look in his eyes. "I don't know how, Allie. The frame is blackened on one side, and the other pieces were nowhere to be found."

"How did you find them?"

His voice dropped to a whisper. "It was the strangest thing. I talked to God. I said I don't believe this God with us stuff, but I wanted to understand what you see in Him." He shut his eyes tight and his Adam's apple bobbed. He drew in a deep breath, then opened his eyes. "I went over to shutter the window in the sitting area, and I stubbed my toe on the Joseph figure. So, I started searching by candlelight."

She smiled. "Keeping the lamp lit."

"I found the woman, but I couldn't find the baby." He paused. "So, I scanned the path from the man to the woman and beyond."

"And you found the babe?"

Levi nodded. "Allie, I'm so sorry I didn't put it away before we left this morning. The entire set would be fine if it were in the sitting area."

She reached up to cradle his stubbled cheek in her hand. "Levi, you told me from the very beginning I shouldn't be taking it out of the box. If I had listened—"

"If you had listened, we never would have known what was in that box." Levi pulled her hand to his lips and kissed the inside of her palm, causing her heart to flutter. "I never would have prayed a prayer that God answered."

"Levi, that's one thing we haven't done."

"What?"

"Pray. We haven't prayed for God's help in finding the owner." She took hold of Levi's hands. "Will you pray with me?"

"I-I—" Levi stammered. "Sure."

They bowed their heads, and Allie prayed. "Lord, we've been trying to do this all on our own. You know exactly who this nativity belongs to and where they are." She opened one eye to peek at Levi. "And You know who needs the hope of Christmas the most. Please lead us to them."

They opened their eyes. Levi let out a sigh, looking relieved.

Doctor Ewing walked over and placed his hand on Levi's shoulder. "Five more minutes, Levi. She needs plenty of rest."

Levi nodded.

Doc Ewing nodded to Allie. "I forgot the mustard paste. I'll be right back, and we can start your treatment." Doctor Ewing left the door open on his way out.

"You know you still have to go to the courthouse and the quilting bee tomorrow." Allie beamed.

"You are an exasperating woman."

"Always one step too far." She nudged him out of the chair. "Better get a good night's sleep."

"I don't know what I'm going to do about the forge."

"It'll be okay. God's got a plan."

"Couldn't the same be said of the nativity?"

"Yes, but Justin told me he finished the grate for Mrs. Grace's window before the explosion. Is there any other work that can't wait until after Christmas?"

"Perhaps not. Though I'll still have Horn to contend with."

"That settles it. The nativity needs to take priority. Then the forge."

He took an envelope from his vest and laid it on the bedside table. "If I must continue this search tomorrow, you must read your father's letter."

Allie arched an eyebrow.

"I asked Sam who it was from." He tucked his hands into his pockets. "When he told me it was from your father, I asked him to leave it for you."

"I didn't take you for the kind to meddle." She half-joked.

Levi stood and kissed her forehead. Her skin warmed. "Rest well. G'night."

Allie reached for the letter, then pulled her hand back. It could wait until morning. Snuggling her head against the pillow, she brushed her fingers across her forehead, remembering the soft touch of Levi's lips on her skin.

16

On the way to the courthouse, Levi made a side trip to check the notice board at the mercantile. Nothing new had been posted by anyone with the name Zimmermann or other German-sounding names. Levi continued to the courthouse and arrived at the door as the clerk unlocked it.

"Excuse me, sir." Levi nestled the box under his arm. "Are you the clerk?"

The clerk held up his hand. "Not until I'm in the office."

"I only need a moment of your time." In Levi's experience, entering the courthouse could cause a man to be tied up for an unnecessary length of time. He preferred to ask his question and be on his way. If he wrapped this up quickly and ducked into the quilting circle, he might have time to begin repairs today.

The clerk held up a finger, opened the door, and continued down the hall. Levi sighed and followed. The clerk stopped to unlock another door. Levi stepped around him and grasped the man by the shoulder. "If I could just—"

"Unhand me, sir." The clerk squared with Levi. "You will wait until I come to the window, or I'll throw you out of this courthouse."

Levi pursed his lips and stepped aside. Then, sitting on a bench near the clerk's window, he waited. Finally, the shuttered window opened with a sharp thwack, and Levi approached.

"Good morning." Levi cleared his throat. "I'm trying to locate a passenger who transferred from the *Resilient* to the *Valiant* after it ran aground early Saturday morning in the storm."

"You'll need to speak to the steamboat captains." The clerk turned abruptly and began sorting through papers.

"Excuse me, sir." Levi tapped the counter. "We've already spoken to the captain of the *Resilient*. It seems the manifest has been lost."

The clerk peered around Levi to the right and left. "We?"

"Yes, a young lady has been helping me with the search, but she was unable to join me this morning."

"I'm sorry to hear that." The clerk didn't look up from his papers. "We don't keep records of steamboat manifests. Good day."

"I came to inquire whether anyone new to town may have come to ask about land or something. Perhaps someone with a German accent."

The clerk turned. "Why, might I ask, are you inquiring?"

Levi placed the box on the counter and patted the lid. "This parcel was left behind. I want to find the owner and return it. The owner's family name may be Zimmermann."

"Yesterday morning, there was a young woman here with an unusual accent. She and her husband had planned to purchase land." The clerk pulled a piece of paper and a pencil from the counter behind him. "However, he is gone now, and she is trying to decide what to do. You're welcome to leave a note on the board in case she happens back by."

"Did she happen to have two young children with her?"

"No, she was alone. I remember because she was the only one who came in all morning." The clerk scratched his head. "You know, you could take the package to Hogue's boardinghouse. They keep a lost and found for items left behind on the steamboats."

"The lost and found is overflowing with items now. Thought I'd save the Hogues some space and deliver the package myself."

The image of Allie adoring the nativity at the work table popped into his mind. She wouldn't leave without showing it to the clerk if she were here.

"May I?"

"I'm quite busy."

"It will only take a moment." Levi pulled the singed platform and the trio of figures from the box.

"It is inspiring." The clerk fingered the loops of wood that formed the Christmas tree at the center of the piece. "Such delicate work. Who would have thought to put a tree at the center of a nativity?"

"Conrad Hildesheim is one of the tenets at Hogue House. Mr. and Mrs. Hogue allow him to erect a tree in the parlor at Christmastime. It's an enjoyable tradition." Levi boxed up the nativity. "We saw a man dragging a great cedar across the courthouse lawn yesterday. I could imagine folks gathered 'round that tree. I hope I haven't taken up too much of your time."

"If you don't mind my asking, what happened to the frame?"

"There was an explosion at my forge, and the frame was damaged. The rest of the pieces were destroyed."

"That's a shame. Your intentions are admirable." The clerk shook Levi's hand. "If anyone comes in with an accent, I'll mention this. Where can they find you?"

"Hogue's boardinghouse. I'm the blacksmith, Levi Snow."

Levi left the courthouse and headed to Water Street with the nativity box. A firm grip caught his arm, nearly pulling him off his feet. Turning, he found himself face-to-face with Horn.

"Blacksmith, you don't seem to be spending much time at that forge of yours."

"Back off, Horn."

"This is the last time I'm telling you. Move my work to the front of the line, or I'll take my work to the blacksmith across the river."

"I accept."

"Accept what?"

"Your offer to leave town and take your work with you. Send a couple of men to gather your pieces from the shop." Levi turned on his heel.

"Blacksmith!" Horn snarled after him. "Snow!"

Without turning back, Levi threw a hand in the air, waving Horn off, and kept walking. Keeping his promise to Allie was all that mattered now. And since the court clerk's office proved a dead end, the quilting circle was his last hope for a good lead.

17

A bitter wind bit at his cheeks as he trudged to the church, nativity box in hand. There were already several wagons at the small building. Folks carried in armfuls of items and quickly reemerged empty-handed. Levi held the door open for Mr. Pratt and a family carrying wrapped packages tied with ribbons.

"Good morning, Levi." Mr. Pratt steadied two boxes with his chin. "You're out and about early. Don't you usually spend your mornings working at the forge before venturing through town?"

"Usually." Levi followed Martin Pratt inside, pulling the door closed behind them. "Work has come to a full stop now, though."

"Oh? Why is that?"

"There was an accident yesterday, and the forge is busted." Levi rubbed the back of his neck. "I should be there trying to repair it—lots of work to do for the town in the wake of that storm the other day. But Sam Mooney's niece and I have been trying to find the owner of this nativity. She was with me when

Pastor Turner asked me to look at the stove, and she insisted I bring the nativity along."

"I've heard about your search. Very intriguing."

"Ah, Mr. Snow, so good to see you." The sing-song voice of Olivia Pratt interrupted their conversation. "It would also be agreeable to see you Sunday mornings. But that's all right. You're here now, and you'll soon see we don't bite."

Levi pressed his lips into a flattened smile. "Good morning, Mrs. Pratt."

"Good morning, love." Mrs. Pratt stretched on her tippy toes, kissing Mr. Pratt's cheek. "You know where the boxes go."

"Yes, I do." Mr. Pratt returned her kiss. "Don't forget that I'm heading to help a neighbor after this. I'll be there the rest of the day."

"Of course." She waived him off and turned to Levi. "He's such a good-hearted man."

"He is of fine caliber."

"Ladies, ladies!" Mrs. Pratt led the way to the front corner, where the women were seated. "Make room. Make room. Mr. Snow is here."

The group shifted, and a few women rose, scattering in different directions. Someone took the nativity box from him. He was beckoned to sit and handed a plate holding a biscuit with a swath of apple butter. In short order, a cup of black coffee was presented. The ladies all began to greet him at once. Some uttered thanks for various moments of upheaval Levi had set to order. Some thanked him for blacksmith work. Still, others mentioned daughters or nieces they'd like him to meet.

Levi had quieted a few dozen men at the river only three days ago with a raised hand. He'd called to order more men than that once everyone was gathered from the boats. However, he felt powerless in this group of slightly more than a dozen women. He didn't dare raise a hand in the air for fear of offending them. What was it Allie had said? *Take a deep breath in like this.* He breathed in through his nose. *And breathe out like this.* He let it out.

"Ladies, let's not overwhelm the man." Mrs. Pratt settled the group. She scooted an extra chair next to Levi so he would have a place to set his plate and cup. The women eyed him with rapt attention.

Levi's mouth went dry. He cleared his throat. "Mrs. Pratt, all this isn't necessary. Pastor Turner asked me to look at the stove doors."

"Oh, we can manage it." Mrs. Pratt took a seat next to him and patted his knee.

"You can?"

She gave a curt nod.

"All right then." With a look of confusion, he stood. "That's good because there was an accident at the forge yesterday, so I need to get back to make repairs there before I can fix the stove. I'll be on my way."

"Not so fast, Mr. Snow. We wanted to see the nativity, but Pastor Turner was not inclined to take that request to you. There is a problem with the stove door, and we would like you to look at it before you go. But we've been managing that door for weeks, so a little longer won't hurt."

Levi took a bite of the biscuit. A dollop of apple butter squished out the side, and he licked it off. The women stared in wide-eyed anticipation. He rested the plate on the chair beside him. Then he took a sip of coffee. The room was still and silent. Swallowing, Levi finally spoke.

"Ah, yes, well." He turned this way and that in his seat, looking for the box. Finally, he leaned over to Mrs. Pratt and whispered, "I seem to have been separated from the nativity."

"Oh, my apologies." She giggled and sprang from her seat.

"Let me get that for you. We wanted to make sure you felt welcome."

Levi smiled uncertainly. "You are quite the hospitable group of ladies. Your efforts are very much appreciated."

Mrs. Pratt handed him the box. "If you please, you may unbox it on the table in front of the pulpit, and we can file by to look at it." She shot a warning glance to the rest of the group. "In an orderly fashion. We all know Mr. Snow is fond of order."

"Mrs. Pratt, might I inquire of the group first?"

"Certainly. What would you like to know?"

"Pastor Turner mentioned that several of your families took in passengers from the *Resilient* who were stranded here for various reasons. I'm curious, are any of those passengers German by chance?"

Looking around the circle, Levi glimpsed heads shaking. Not a single *yes* in the whole group. That was it, the end of the search. He couldn't bear to tell Allie. He felt Mrs. Pratt's hand on his shoulder.

"Mr. Snow, is it true that you believe the owner of the nativity to be of German descent? Is that why you're inquiring about German passengers?"

Levi nodded. "Yes, ma'am. However, we can't be certain. We know the carpenter who created it is German. We're working off the assumption that this is a prototype, the first of its kind. It's possible the carpenter might have kept it for himself."

"Don't lose heart, young man." Mrs. Pratt patted his hand. "There are a few other church families who have taken in passengers. So, the passengers housed in town are not all represented by those of us in attendance today. I'll ask around and see what I can find out for you."

"I greatly appreciate that, Mrs. Pratt. Sadly, you will not find the nativity exactly as Allie described it." Levi unboxed the scene. He set the pieces in place, taking special care with the mother and child. "It suffered some damage in the accident at the forge yesterday. Some pieces were destroyed, and the frame was blackened."

He stepped back from the table. Even in its ruinous condition, Allie would say it looked perfect. He was anxious to return and see how she was doing. He fulfilled his commitment to visit the courthouse and the quilting circle. Had she satisfied her side of the bargain and read her father's letter?

Mrs. Pratt appeared at Levi's side. She touched his arm lightly, holding out four votive candles. "May I?"

"By all means." Levi smiled. He turned the damaged propeller. "If the propeller weren't broken, the platform would rotate as the candles heated the air around it. I regret that you won't get the full effect."

Mrs. Pratt smiled. "We can imagine it."

The quilting circle filed past the nativity, each woman admiring it in turn. Levi's heart warmed at the 'oohs' and 'aahs' that filled the church. After they passed by, several women came to him and grasped or patted his hand or hugged him to express their gratitude. He didn't understand what he'd done that was so special. He hadn't created the nativity. It was his fault it was nearly destroyed. He wasn't personally connected to it. Yet showing it around town made him feel more and more connected to folks. He was getting to know people beyond the occasional calamities they experienced together and the work he was doing for them.

"Mrs. Pratt, I'd like to look at that stove now."

"Mr. Snow, don't you worry yourself about it." Mrs. Pratt snuffed out the candles around the nativity. "You've given us such a treat today."

"I want to see what I can do." Levi carefully placed the

wooden pieces back in the box. "I appreciate the quilting circle going to such lengths to welcome me and allow me to share the nativity."

Mrs. Pratt showed Levi to the stove. He inspected the hinge and reported back to her. "As I've said, I won't be able to fix it before Christmas. I have a couple of fireplace screens back at the forge, though. I can bring one by to create a barrier, so people don't get too close. Then I'll get to that hinge as soon as I can."

"That sounds like an acceptable plan, Levi."

"I'll go get that straight away."

"Oh, nonsense. Come visit with us a spell." She motioned to his seat. "We have something we'd like to share with you."

Levi took his seat among the women in the quilting circle. The ladies all retrieved items from baskets beside their chairs. Each one held colorful quilt blocks in her lap.

"We enjoyed having Allie at church Sunday." Mrs. Pratt began with a beaming smile. "She described the nativity in such detail. It was delightful to hear her talk about it. We're so grateful you brought it so we could see for ourselves."

"It's been an honor to spend the morning with the quilting circle." Levi was surprised by the sincerity of his sentiment. He surveyed the room. These women had received him with generosity and graciousness, unlike anything he expected.

"When the circle met later Sunday afternoon, we decided that the theme of our Christmas quilting project would be the Light of Christmas. It was inspired by Allie's description of the candles bringing the nativity to life. What a treat to see it today."

"Allie would be delighted to hear about the project. I'm sorry she couldn't be here."

"Mr. Snow, we'd like you to be part of the project."

"I don't understand."

"We want you to make a square for the quilt."

Levi's eyes widened under arched eyebrows. "Mrs. Pratt, I have no idea how to sew. I don't even darn socks. I pay a little extra to have Mrs. Hogue do it for me."

"I will help you while the others assemble their pieces." She clapped her hands. "All right, girls, you know what to do!"

A few hours later, Levi sat back to admire his work—two neatly stitched quilt squares. He sucked his finger. He was bleary-eyed and had lost track of how often he'd poked himself with the needle.

Mrs. Pratt presented her uplifted palm. Placing the quilt blocks in her hand for inspection, Levi held his breath. Her shrewd expression gave nothing away. Finally, she handed the blocks back to Levi.

"It's lovely. Just lovely." Her face broke into an approving smile. "If you ever decide to give up blacksmithing—"

"I appreciate the offer, but blacksmithing is much easier." He laughed. "I better get back, but I'll drop off the fireplace screen a little later."

Mrs. Pratt walked with Levi to the door. "Dear boy, you must come to the candlelight service tomorrow evening. We'll finish the final touches, and you can see this wall quilt completed."

"Mrs. Pratt, could you do something for me?"

"Of course, dear. What is it?"

Levi leaned close to whisper in her ear. Her head bobbed, her smile widening.

"Happy to do it, dear boy." She squeezed him around his middle. "And I want to see you at church Sunday. You'll be my guest for dinner after."

"Thank you, Mrs. Pratt." Levi leaned in and kissed her cheek. "For everything. And remember, that last bit is a surprise."

18

s Levi returned to the boardinghouse, none of the Main Street businesses were open. Each one prominently displayed a "closed" sign in the window. Odd. He pulled his coat collar around his neck and shoved his hands into his pockets. Perhaps they were all preparing for the special festivities Sam mentioned. But there was no sign of movement inside any of the shops. Main Street looked like a ghost town. He shrugged.

Walking up Cane Hill, Levi saw several wagons along the side of the road as he approached the boardinghouse. Drawing nearer, he heard numerous voices and loud noises. His heart skipped a beat. Was something wrong?

He jogged the rest of the way. Then, rounding the corner of the house, he ran into Mahala Hogue. He gripped her shoulders to steady her. "Mrs. Hogue, my apologies. I saw the wagons and heard the ruckus. Is something wrong?"

"Everything is fine, Levi." Mrs. Hogue picked up the empty basket she'd dropped and smoothed her skirt.

"What's going on?"

"Folks are being neighborly. They heard you needed some help."

"Me? What kind of help do I need?"

"Rebuilding the forge, silly." Mrs. Hogue laughed. "Levi Snow, you beat all I've ever seen. First, you go out of your way to help folks and think we don't notice. Then, you try to convince us all that you do it to find work. But we know better."

"Who's in there?" Levi pointed to the smithy.

"Most of the business owners. They closed shop to help you."

"They can't do that. They'll lose a day's earnings."

"You lose a day's work every time you help the town. So let us help you as you've always helped us." Mrs. Hogue pecked him on the cheek. "You're a dear boy. I've got to get back in the house to check on Allie."

As she turned to go, Levi caught her arm. "How is Allie?"

"Oh, she's much better. She's got that spark in her eyes again." Mrs. Hogue patted Levi's hand. "Doc is examining her now, so we'll know more soon. Come see her when you're ready."

Levi thanked her and headed into the forge. His workspace had never been so crowded. Justin, Sam, Conrad Hildesheim, and Mr. Pratt were hard at work. He could hear noises coming from behind the shop as well. Justin spotted him first and elbowed Sam, who grasped Conrad and Mr. Pratt by the shoulders.

"Mr. Pratt?" Levi's eyebrows furrowed. "Weren't you going to help a neighbor today?"

They all laughed. Levi tried to sort through his muddled thoughts. He struggled to make sense of it all. Mr. Pratt crossed the room to the old potbellied stove. He poured Levi a cup of coffee and handed it to him.

"Son, you are my neighbor." He winked and went back to work.

"Sam?" Levi shot him a quizzical glance.

"I told you he'd be dumbfounded." Justin chuckled.

Sam joined Levi in the sitting area as the others continued to work. Sam motioned to a stool. "Sit down, Levi."

Levi joined Sam at the table. "What's going on here?"

"We're going to work until we have the forge back up and running again. We'll be here all night if that's what it takes."

"Have you all been here all day?"

"Pretty near." Sam smiled his cockeyed smile and wiped his forehead with a handkerchief. "Listen, if Doc says it's all right, I'm going up to see Allie in a bit. Want to tag along?"

"Have you talked to her today? Did she read that letter from her father?"

"She was asleep when I peeked in earlier. I didn't want to wake her. Mahala brought these out since you don't keep extras." Sam pulled a tin mug close and thumped the outside. "I sure hope Allie's Pa hasn't changed his mind about her coming west with him."

"Coming west?"

"It seems his new bride skedaddled, and now he's invited Allie to join him." Sam took a long sip from the tin cup. "She's worried he'll change his mind after she gets out there. But I promised I'd come to get her if that happens."

"She's planning on joining him then?"

"Oh, I don't know. But it makes sense she'd want to reconnect." Sam took another draw from his mug. "Go see her. She ought to be awake."

"Maybe I will." Levi took his coffee and went to the house. Doc came down the stairs as he entered.

"Levi, what are you up to?"

"I thought I'd visit Allie a spell."

"I'd rather you didn't see her until morning. She's doing much better and eager to hear your news." Doc Ewing grabbed Levi by the arm, turning him toward the kitchen. "However, I'm afraid it will stir her up, and she won't go back to sleep. I'll pop in and check on her tomorrow morning. With another good night's rest, I expect she'll be able to participate in the festivities. You can tell her about your day at breakfast. The bunkroom is apt to be rather noisy with all the work, so you'll share a room with me tonight."

"I can't see Allie until morning?" Levi's heart sank, but at least he could put off telling her the search had reached a dead end. He wished he could talk to her about her father's letter. Was this new letter another plea for her to join him? Was she truly considering leaving?

19

As Allie buttoned her collar, a gentle knock sounded at the door.

"Come in."

Uncle Shadow's bright smile warmed her heart. "It was nice of the Hogue girls to double up and let you have this room to yourself."

"It was." She sat on the edge of the bed to lace her boots.

"Did you read your father's letter? What did it say?"

Allie swallowed hard. "He's coming to get me."

"You don't seem happy."

"I didn't realize until I read this letter that's why you asked me to come." She didn't look up as she laced the other boot. "You've been planning this all along. Coming to Van Buren means he doesn't have to travel as far to get me."

"No, honey." Uncle Shadow grasped her shoulders, pulling her up from the bed. He folded her in his arms. "I didn't know he'd come. You don't have to go with him. I meant it when I said you could stay with me." He pushed her back, gazing into her eyes, that old familiar shadow who followed her in her toddling days. "What do you want?"

"I don't know. He's my father, and I love him. I do." A lone tear streaked down her cheek. "But I can't see myself going west with him. I can't see us having a home together—without Ma."

"I guess that's the question. Where do you see yourself at home?"

"Here in Van Buren with you. And the Hogues."

"And Levi?"

She ducked her head. "If he can open his heart to me."

Uncle Shadow pulled her close and laughed. "Oh, sweet Allie, he already has. There's been such a change in him since you arrived."

"You think so?" Hope flickered in her heart.

"I know so." He gently patted her head. "He's waiting downstairs in the wagon. He lined it with hay and put bedwarmers in the blankets. Allie, he wants to celebrate Christmas Eve with you."

After bundling herself up, Allie followed Uncle Shadow to the wagon. Levi placed a step stool at the back and offered her his hand. She climbed in, and he mounted the steps behind her.

"What are you doing? Who's going to drive?"

"I drew the short stick." Justin emerged from the stable. "Long stick sits in the back with the pretty girl. Short stick gets a view of the horses' backsides."

Allie laughed. She scooted over, making room for Levi to nestle in beside her.

"Listen. Doc said you're not to be outside long, so we've planned to get you warm in some shops." Levi tucked blankets around her before taking his place.

"Uncle Shadow, where will you be?"

"I've got to ride ahead and get to the shop." He kissed her forehead. "Mind you do what Levi says. We don't want you taking a bad turn."

"Mind you do what I say," Levi whispered in her ear with a sheepish grin. His warm breath made her skin tingle. She elbowed him playfully.

"Oh, Levi, what about the nativity? Did you find the owner yesterday?"

"No, nothing panned out." Levi's eyes dulled. "I'm sorry, Allie. I let you down."

"You went out of your way to help me. You stayed with me." Allie leaned her head against his shoulder. "I pushed my way into your life, always going one step too far, and you stayed. What more could I ask for?"

"Peppermint?" Levi smiled and held out a brown paper package. "To soothe your throat."

"You've thought of everything." Allie opened one end of the package and snapped off a bit of mint. "Let's enjoy the day."

When the wagon turned onto Main Street, a band of musicians fell in behind them. Allie's heart sparked with delight. The music struck up, and other merry-makers flooded into the street. Allie's eyes widened.

They paused in front of shop windows to watch scenes acted out like charades. Levi pointed out folks they knew. At the mercantile, Uncle Shadow, dressed as Scrooge, mimicked opening a door.

Allie jumped at the booming voice, "Come in! Come in and know me better, man!"

Justin leaned over his shoulder. "They told Captain Cobb a million times it's a silent scene, but he's determined to say that line."

Allie and Levi folded over with laughter. A few stops later, they ventured into Hildesheim's Pastry shop to make gingerbread houses. A young lady with blonde ringlets brought out a tray of gingerbread pieces.

"Levi, Allie, velcome." Conrad brought bowls of colored icing. "I beliefe you know Clara. She is joining me today."

"Did you see the lovely nativity scene Mr. Hildesheim made from gingerbread?" Clara pointed to the counter. "He's been teaching me the meaning behind the menorah. It's fascinating."

When Allie and Levi finished their creation, Conrad boxed it up for them. "I'll take it to the boardinghouse this evening when I return."

Nestled in the wagon again, they viewed a few more shop windows. A steamboat whistle sounded in the distance. Levi put his arms around her, rubbing her shoulders to warm her. She could have stayed there in his arms forever. Did he want things to stay this way as much as she did?

"I imagine you've read your father's letter by now. What did he have to say?"

She didn't want to think about her father now. "Nothing much. He's writing to ask how I'm settling in with Uncle Shadow."

"Sounds short and sweet."

"It was." The wagon pulled to a stop in front of Gray's Café. "Oh, don't tell me ... is it?"

"I think so." Levi nodded and helped her down from the wagon. "A peppermint taffy pull."

A short time later, the pair reemerged from the café with a package of taffy.

"My hands are all sticky." Allie giggled. "How am I ever going to get my gloves on?"

Levi grasped her hand. "Let me help."

He brought Allie's finger to his lips, his eyes locked with

hers. Heat rose in her cheeks. She glanced away and cleared her throat.

"I love peppermint taffy." Her voice was a hoarse whisper.

"Me too." Levi pulled a handkerchief from his pocket and wiped her hands. "Better?"

"Much." She leaned closer.

Justin burst through the door of the café, followed by a boisterous round of laughter from inside. "Mrs. Gray sure can tell a story. Where to next?"

Allie distanced herself. "You know what I'm thinking?"

Levi grinned. "Back to your uncle's store? To check the notice board one last time?"

"Precisely. I want to walk if that's all right."

Levi turned to Justin. "I think we'll be all right from here. Meet us at the church later?"

"Sure thing."

Allie looped her arm in the crook of Levi's elbow as they turned toward the mercantile. Her heart was soaring, and she half-hopped up the steps. Cheerful music drifted through the street, and Levi did a little crossover step. They laughed and turned their attention to the board.

There it was:

> Wanted: Help with passage to St. Louis
> See M. Zimmermann at Br

They stared at the board. Allie let out a puff of air, deflated. The bottom corner of the note was torn. She ripped the notice off the board.

"This is it. The last clue." She clutched it to her chest. "What are we going to do?"

"There you are, puddin." A deep voice resonated behind her. "I've been looking all over for you. We need to talk."

20

"Father, what are you doing here?"

"I told you I was coming. I arrived on the *Valiant*."

"Levi, is that you, dear?" Levi turned to see Mrs. Pratt waving a white lace kerchief across the street. He'd never been so thankful to see her.

"Excuse me." He slid past Allie toward the stairs. "I've got to go."

Sam's news of a westward-bound Allie was accurate. Yet she hadn't mentioned it. Why was she holding back? Levi jogged across the street. He screwed a smile on. "Mrs. Pratt, it's good to see you."

"Oh, I didn't mean to take you away from Allie." She tucked the fabric square into her reticule. "Who is that man?"

"That's Allie's father. She'll be traveling west with him soon." Levi caught Mrs. Pratt's elbow. "Walk with me a moment?"

"Of course."

Levi explained about the notice they'd found. "The notice

said 'M. Zimmermann,' not 'J. Zimmermann.' Do you have any idea who 'Br' might be? Whose residence is Zimmermann lodging at?"

"You believe you're looking for a woman with two young children?"

"With the information I have, yes, I believe so."

"It's got to be Bradley House. Paulette Bradley opens her house to women and children, just as Hogue House boards men." Mrs. Pratt indicated a storefront a few steps away. "Paulette stepped inside the tailor's shop to speak to the milliner."

Levi kissed Mrs. Pratt's cheek. "Mrs. Pratt, you are a peach."

"Oh!" Her face reddened.

Levi burst through the door of the tailor shop. "Mrs. Bradley!"

Everyone started and stared.

"My apologies." Levi's heart pounded. He crossed the shop in long strides. "Mrs. Bradley, it's urgent that I speak to you." He quickly unfolded the story to her. "Do you know who M. Zimmermann is? But, more importantly, do you know *where* M. Zimmermann is?"

"Marta Zimmermann, yes. She and her two children stayed with me after the steamboat accident. She's been trying to locate her husband. They were separated during the voyage." Mrs. Bradley gripped his arm. "But Mr. Snow, they are boarding the *Valiant* soon, headed back to St. Louis. She has no more money. So, they will return to their family in St. Louis, hoping Mr. Zimmermann will join them there."

"Mr. Zimmermann. Did Marta mention his name?"

"It's Josef. Why?"

"Thank you. You'll never know what you've done!"

Levi raced out the door, pausing briefly to talk to Mrs. Pratt. "I've got to catch Justin before he heads to the church with the wagon. Can you find Captain Cobb and tell him to meet me aboard the *Valiant*?"

"Of course. What about Allie? Do you want me to have her join you?"

Levi glanced across the street. Allie and her father were gone. His stomach tightened. Had her father loaded her onto the *Coffee No. 7* so soon? Captain Horn planned to depart this afternoon for Fort Coffee. Was she leaving without saying goodbye?

"No, that won't be necessary." Levi's voice dropped. "Tell Cobb to hurry."

Spying the wagon still in front of Gray's Café, Levi dashed down the street and collected the familiar box. Pushing past clusters of people, he cut through the courthouse lawn, narrowly missing a surprisingly large cedar. Then, heart pounding, he sucked in his middle and raised the box as children darted past, going in the opposite direction.

"Levi, wait!"

He whirled as his head spun around. Allie ran to catch up to him.

"Levi, stop!"

"Not now, Allie." He kept moving. He didn't want to hear her say she was leaving.

"Where are you going with that?" Allie caught his coattail and yanked. "You know. You know what 'Br" is, don't you?"

"Bradley House."

A steamboat whistle blew. Levi stopped to listen. He clutched Allie's arm.

"One long, two shorts. One long, two shorts." Levi turned Allie toward the mercantile. "Go back to the store and stay warm. I've got twenty minutes to talk my way onto the *Valiant* and find the owner."

"*We've* got twenty minutes. You're not doing this without me, Levi Snow."

"Didn't Sam tell you to mind what I say?"

"Every step of the journey." Allie propped her hands on her hip. "I'll go every step of the journey, even if it is one step too far."

"Stubborn woman." Levi shook his head. "C'mon then."

The pair sprinted to the gangplank of the *Valiant*, where Allie stopped short.

"We don't have time for this. I'll go." Levi scooted Allie aside and continued up the gangplank. Halfway up, he heard a plodding sound at his back. Glancing over his shoulder, he saw Allie charging up the footway. He reached the top and turned, extending a hand to her.

"Thank you." Allie grinned, blue eyes shining. "Who are we looking for?"

"Marta. Marta Zimmermann and her two young children."

"And her husband, the carpenter? What is his name?"

"He didn't make it." Levi shook his head. "He went overboard in the storm. And Marta doesn't know."

Allie's face blanched. She turned Levi toward a woman holding a carpetbag. A young boy clutched her hand and a little girl hung on her skirt. Levi's gut twisted.

"My Josef? He's gone?" Her voice trembled.

"Are you Marta Zimmermann?" Levi reached out to her. She nodded. "Do you recognize this box?"

"It is zee Christmas pyramid." Marta set her bag down. "Holt your sister's hand, Josef."

"Mrs. Zimmermann, I'm sorry, but it has been damaged." Levi handed her the box. "Some of the pieces are missing."

She opened the lid. The little family lay nestled in the packing material. A tear dropped from her chin onto the baby. She pulled the box tight to her chest. "Josef carved zis as anniversary gift. Ve married on Christmas Eve. Zank you for returning it."

Captain Cobb appeared at Levi's shoulder.

"Mrs. Zimmermann, this is Captain Cobb of the *Resilient*." Levi patted Cobb's shoulder.

As Levi turned to disembark, he heard Cobb say, "Mrs. Zimmermann, I'd like to tell you about the sacrifice your husband made. Because of his efforts, many lives were saved."

21

L evi slipped in the door of the church and sat at the back. While Pastor Turner announced Sunday services, Mrs. Pratt left her seat to join Levi. She handed him a small box tied with a red ribbon.

"As you requested, dear boy." She patted his hand. "I shared your prayer request with the circle. Now, don't waiver. Stick to your plan."

Levi responded with a tight smile, and Mrs. Pratt returned to her seat. His gaze wandered toward the front. Allie sat on the second row between her uncle and father. What was she doing here? Hadn't they departed with Horn?

Pastor Turner spoke of the light of the world, the hope for all mankind. Levi couldn't keep the lamp lit any longer. Not on his own. Perhaps he never had. He surveyed the room. Sam drummed up work for him whenever business was slow. Mr. Pratt brought Levi projects he knew the man could do without his help. How often had he found a basket of Conrad's pastries near the stove in the forge? And the Hogues provided a space for his shop. They didn't even charge him extra. It was included with the usual boarding fees.

What had Allie said? *Most of us are not as strong as you.* Perhaps he wasn't as strong as she thought. He had worked hard to keep his home from falling apart as a child and failed. He had done nothing to build a home in Van Buren, but hadn't one grown up around him while he wasn't looking? Had God been with him all this time? His heartbeat quickened.

Simon Hogue approached with a basket of candles. Levi nodded and took one.

"If you'll all stand in a circle, we'll have the candle lighting while we sing 'Silent Night.'"

People shuffled from their seats. Folks scooted by Levi to find others they wanted to stand beside. It wasn't long before Levi found himself standing next to Sam. Sam traded places with him.

"I'd like to stand by Mrs. Grace if you don't mind."

Levi caught Allie's eye. "I don't mind if you don't mind."

"I've been looking for you." She smiled. "You disappeared after we returned the nativity."

Pastor Turner began to sing. Light spread around the circle as the wick of one candle touched another. Levi basked in the moment, allowing the harmony to resonate through him. Sam's deep bass, Allie's honeyed alto, Mrs. Pratt's lilting soprano. Allie touched the tip of her candle to his, completing the circle. The light washed over him, and peace settled in his soul.

The song ended, and Levi and Allie blew out their candles and returned them to the basket. Mrs. Pratt joined them, pointing at the wall behind them.

"Did you see the wall hanging? It was inspired by your description of the nativity, Allie."

The small quilt displayed a star encircled by several

candles. Mrs. Pratt pointed to a block of three blue candlesticks. "Mr. Levi Snow handcrafted this one."

Allie's jaw dropped. "Levi?"

"Don't look so surprised." The heat of embarrassment crept up his neck. "I take instruction well."

"See you at church Sunday." Mrs. Pratt squeezed his hand before filing out after the others.

Levi and Allie stood alone in the little church. *Don't waiver. Stick to the plan.* Levi moved back to his seat and picked up the ribbon-tied box. He returned to Allie's side. Clearing his throat, he started to speak but stopped again. He took a deep breath and released it slowly.

"I had planned to make a gift for you at the forge, but then the accident." He fidgeted with the ribbon. Then he shoved the box toward her. "I wanted to give it to you before you left. Well, here."

Allie opened it, revealing a single quilted square. She fingered its neat edges. Fabric scraps formed the image of a candle holder and candle with the flame lit.

"It's ... uh—" Levi cleared his throat again. "Hope is patience with the lamp lit. The Tertullian quote. Your mother's favorite."

Tears formed in Allie's eyes, threatening to break free. Levi took her hands in his, and his skin tingled at her touch. "Allie, you've been patient with me. For some strange reason, you believe me to be a better man than I am. You've taught me the importance of keeping the lamp lit. But more than that, you've taught me how to open my heart again. I couldn't let you leave without telling you."

A tear rolled down her cheek, and she wiped it away. "Leave? Where am I going?"

"Sam told me your father plans to take you west with him."

"Oh, Levi, I'm not going west." She half-laughed as another

123

tear sprang loose. "Yes, my father wrote asking me to come west. I'll admit that's what I thought he had in mind when he showed up today. But between the time he wrote those letters and when he arrived in Van Buren, he met Camila. Did you see the woman sitting next to him?"

Levi shook his head. He had seen only Allie. How could he have noticed anyone else?

"He is so lost without my mother. I've tried to help him, but I can't. I need a place to call home, but he's trying to escape from home. I won't go west with him. He and Camila are staying through Christmas, and they'll leave the day after."

"Really?"

"Really." She took his hand and led him to a bench. "Since my mother's passing, I haven't felt at home anywhere. Until now."

"With Sam."

Allie took Levi's face in her hands. "With *you*. I want to sit at the table in the forge, watching you work. I want to take care of the town with you. I want you to tell me *'whoa'* when I go one step too far. Because I'm at home—with you."

"Allie, I can't promise I'll always be the man you deserve." Levi caressed her cheek. Her lips met his, and his breath stalled. Finally, he wrapped her in his arms, whispering into her ear, "But I promise there will always be a warm fire waiting."

THE END

Author's Note

Though set in the real-world city of Van Buren, Arkansas, this story is fictional. Some historical information, such as the date of incorporation and street names when they could be found, has been used to ground this story in time and place. However, people, places, businesses, groups, and other things are not intended to depict any real-life figures, organizations, etc. Any resemblance is unintentional.

Thirty years ago, I planned a long weekend trip to Eureka Springs, another delightful Arkansas town. Along the way, I wandered off the interstate and into Historic Van Buren. I instantly fell in love with its historic buildings, riverside location, and welcoming people. This charming city sparked my creativity.

Years later, I returned with a friend and inspired both our imaginations. Before we knew it, there we were. Two grown women standing inside a bank vault pretending we were in a time machine being transported back to the 1800s. I've visited Van Buren several times since then. There are three things I know I'll leave with every time—new ideas, a perfect latte, and a good book. (Thank you, Chapters on Main!)

About the Author

Tonya B. Ashley is an award-winning writer who loves a thread of adventure, whether in story or in life. Along with her publication credits as a devotional writer, she received first place in an ACFW First Impressions contest for mystery and suspense.

She and her firefighter/paramedic husband are the parents of an adult son, also a firefighter, and a school-aged son. With experience as a 911 dispatcher and volunteer firefighter, she enjoys all sorts of adventures, including hiking trips well off the beaten path.

CARVING out LOVE

Ellen E. Withers

Carve out Love for
yourself —
Ellen

For Jenny Carlisle and Tonya B. Ashley. These ladies are fabulous writers and the best collaborators anyone could wish for while creating a novella collection. Their kindness, support, encouragement, and faith in me and our project never flagged.

1

July, 1861
Mexico, Missouri

A warm, humid breeze buffeted George Hunter as he bounced on the family buckboard into town. Beads of sweat covered his neck as the temperature rose. Since dawn, he'd spent hours doing chores for Papa on the farm, then loaded lumber into the wagon. This drive into town should have been easier. Instead, guiding the draft horse around the more prominent furrows was challenging as the wagon pounded through a sea of ruts along the dusty road.

The town's recent occupation by the Union Army left the main thoroughfare damaged from their constant vigil against secessionist raids. New posts dotted the road—likely poles for telegraph lines—an additional gift from the Union troops upon the landscape.

Once in town, George guided his horse into the alley behind Dawson's Mercantile, where the owners accepted deliveries to their storage barn. He slid off the wagon seat and limped to the back to unload the lumber.

Moments later, Johnny Dawson flung open the back door of the mercantile. "Morning, George."

George nodded at the young man as he approached. "Thank you kindly for your help."

Johnny was a gangly lad with a perpetual smile on his freckled face. "Are these dried or fresh cut?" He leaped on the wagon as easily as a cat claims a windowsill, then grabbed the opposite end of the board George struggled to unload.

Observing Johnny's dexterity, George experienced a pang of jealousy. Even though he was a few years older, he should have the same nimbleness. "They've had some time to dry. More air could get to them if they're stacked for a while."

"With the call for building materials now, we'll be lucky if this lasts more than a few days."

They stacked the lumber in the barn, allowing space for air to reach most of the boards. When they'd finished, George followed Johnny into the mercantile.

The aroma of spices, coffee, and stale air greeted them. Although it was technically still morning, the air hung thick in the room as if it were late afternoon. George limped his way to the cash register manned by the elder Dawson.

"Morning, George. Did you bring the usual white oak?"

"Yes, sir, Mr. Dawson. I wish I had more mature red oak or black walnut to cut, but those trees are too small to fell this year. Maybe next year. This lumber's had some time to dry, but needs more. Young Johnny says you have a high demand and no drying time is available."

"I will take all you can cut and bring to me. Fresh cut or dry. You can even throw in some short boards. With such high demand, length doesn't seem to matter. Either the Army or our local people will take all we've got." He gestured to the brass register. "Are you looking for payment in trade or coin?"

"Papa said to trade." George pulled a list from his pocket. He handed the paper to Dawson. "Between everyone in my family, we're always hankering for something."

Dawson glanced around the store. "Can we go to the barn for a moment? I have some business I'd like to discuss."

George hesitated. He couldn't imagine what Dawson could want with him. Since he'd returned from the war, they'd conducted business in the store, in public. A talk in private usually meant something illegal.

"I see your concern, George. I promise this is a legitimate business deal. Just hear me out."

George noted the strain in Dawson's voice and nodded his assent. He'd never seen the man rattled before. That was saying a lot. He'd been coming to this store since before he could see over the counter.

Dawson turned and looked around. "Johnny, come here."

Johnny appeared by the register, broom in hand. "I was going to sweep while George was here."

"Hold off on that for a bit. I need you to gather things up for him." Dawson handed him the list. "He and I are stepping away, but we'll be back."

Johnny eyed the list. "I think I can find everything."

Dawson patted Johnny's shoulder. "Much obliged." Then he nodded at George, and together they made their way to the barn.

ONCE INSIDE, George stood silently as Dawson shifted his weight from one foot to the other. He had no idea how to relieve the man's anxiety. George resigned himself to waiting for Dawson to find the right words to explain.

After some time shuffling, Dawson spoke.

"I have a job I'd like to offer you." Dawson held up his hand to stop George from interrupting. "Please, let me finish. You don't want another obligation besides everything you do on the farm. I understand. I'm in a bad way. A real bad way."

"What is it?"

"Two days ago, the new colonel ordered me to do something."

George sucked in air. "The federal colonel? Grant?"

"Yes, I believe that's who he said he was. It surprised me to have any officer appear in my store. Before this, they'd always sent some foot soldier. The whole time he talked, I stared at him, stunned that he'd come in person instead of sending one of his men. When he told me what he wanted, I was speechless."

"What did he want?"

"He demanded a weekly delivery of supplies to their encampment in the area called 'the commons,' about a half mile from John Clark's house."

George nodded. He knew the location.

"A runner will drop off the order at the beginning of the week. I'm to fill requests and deliver them by the end of the week. Weekly! They will pay me if a man sympathetic to the Union delivers it."

Dawson paused and fiddled with the top board of the lumber he and Johnny had just stacked. "Since John Muldrow gathered the 'Audrain Rangers'—foolish secessionists—the Union forces find it hard to trust anyone local. Even after Muldrow surrendered himself to Grant and took an oath of loyalty at Clark's house. They don't want a spy anywhere near their camp, yet they want the supplies brought in. I tried to talk him into sending their wagon to pick them up, but he refused to consider any other way I suggested."

"Why can't you do it yourself?"

"I'm unacceptable because I sell to both sides of this conflict. Puts me under suspicion." Dawson paced. "I've hardly slept since he's been here, trying to think of a solution. I thought about sending young Johnny but wondered if the Audrain Rangers might shoot someone delivering to the camp, even if he wasn't a soldier. I already have his father, Big Johnny, at risk in the war. I'll not have my grandson in danger."

"No. Don't put young Johnny in harm's way. He'd be subject to a random attack, with no experience in such situations. Besides, since he's your grandson, the Army would think he's as objectionable as you. So, why don't you tell Grant you won't do it?"

"He threatened to cut off my railroad shipments if I didn't take on the responsibility. That would put me out of business in a matter of weeks."

"Why are they approaching you now for these supplies? They've been here for nearly a month."

"He wasn't specific, but I got the feeling a lot more troops are coming in. Speculating about that could get me in trouble. It's just a guess." Dawson threw his hands up. "Bah! This is a fine mess!"

Dawson stopped pacing and walked to George. He was so close that a drop of sweat slid from Dawson's nose onto George's arm that was crossed in front of him. "See my dilemma? I don't know what to do. When you entered the store, it gave me an idea. You were a soldier for them. What if you did it?"

"I was a soldier for the militia, which was under federal rule. But when they thought I would die, they discharged me and loaded me onto a train."

"Did they give you discharge papers?"

"Sure. I'd have been mistaken for a deserter without them."
Dawson pulled out a handkerchief and wiped his sweaty
brow. "Those papers would be proof of your service and proper
discharge."

George's face twisted into a wry grin. "You mean my limp
isn't enough?"

"Oh, George, it's your saving grace."

"How's that?"

"Your injury got you out of the fighting before you got
yourself killed. Everyone in the county respects your service. So
much so, I don't believe any of the rogue secessionists would
try to kill you for delivering supplies there. They might jump
you, but I don't think they'd kill you."

"No, Dawson. My limp isn't my saving grace. God is. He
allowed me to survive when men to my right and left fell in
that battle. I'm left to walk with a limp. My brothers in arms
don't walk this Earth anymore, with or without a limp."

Dawson stared at him for a moment, twisting his
handkerchief. After several moments, he asked, "Know of
anyone else I could hire? Someone who'd be trustworthy to
Grant and his troops?"

George pondered the question. "I'm the only one from my
militia discharged and sent back home. The ones I enlisted
with have either committed to a three-year enlistment as full
federal troops—or they're dead."

"This terrible war. Here we are, caught in the middle
between both sides."

"I'm not caught in the middle. I know what side I'm on.
Almost gave my life for the cause."

"Will you do it? I'll pay you all the profits from their
purchases to do it. Or, give you an equivalent in trade for
goods. Whatever you want."

"I'll have to think about it. We sure could use the money or trade, but it's a dangerous job. I'll need to pray about it."

"Pray. Think. Just make a quick decision. I don't want to be forced out of business. I take care of young Johnny, his mother, and his siblings while Big Johnny is off to the fighting. I'd let them shut me down if it were only me."

"I'll let you know. In a day or two." George reached out and squeezed Dawson's shoulder. "You have my word."

Both men stepped away from each other at the sound of an approaching cart. "Not a word to anyone about this." Dawson started toward the barn door. "Not until you decide."

George nodded. Then he led the way out of the barn.

OUTSIDE, a female easily halted a horse-drawn buggy. Sitting beside her was a young boy, who sprang into motion when they stopped. He hopped onto the ground and ran to the back of the cart.

Only a bit of the girl's face was visible, hidden as it was behind the sides of her straw bonnet. Yet, George caught a flash of blue eyes and long lashes. What he spotted piqued his interest.

Dawson greeted the new arrivals. "Ah, Miss Zimmer, isn't it?"

"It's Zimmerman, Mr. Dawson." The young lady smiled down at him. Then she motioned toward the rear of the buggy. "That rude young man is my brother, Albert."

George hitched over to assist her out of the buggy. She took his hand without hesitation. Then, when she stepped to the ground without incident, she flashed him a slight smile for his courtesy.

"Morning, ma'am. I'm George Hunter." He tipped his hat.

"Pleased to meet you, Mr. Hunter." She gave a slight curtsey. "Alice Zimmerman." Her blue-eyed gaze was steady on his face. She didn't search his lower extremities for the reason he limped, as some people did, nor comment on his awkward gait.

Dawson joined Albert at the back of her buggy and surveyed the contents of the wooden crate. "How many eggs do you have for me here?"

"Six dozen." The boy beamed.

Alice turned from George and walked behind the buggy. "Albert, you say 'six dozen, Mr. Dawson' or 'six dozen, sir.' You've forgotten all your manners. Aunt Berta has been spoiling you."

George moved to help unload the crate. "You must be the relatives Mrs. Schumacher's been expecting."

Her face showed surprise at his remark.

"It's a small community and word gets around." George shrugged. "My family has a farm next to your aunt's land. She mentioned that family was coming when I returned one of her goats. He thought our pasture was tastier than hers."

Albert ran to spread the doors wide as they entered the barn. The men carried the crate while Alice followed.

"My father is Aunt Berta's brother. When Uncle Otto went to be with the Lord, she offered Papa the management of her farm. We took over many of the chores around the property. My aunt suffers from a weak constitution." She opened her reticule, removed a handkerchief, and dabbed her upper lip. "My apologies, gentlemen. Growing up in Boston, I haven't developed a tolerance for the heat here."

After placing the crate, George and Dawson looked at each other with amusement. Dawson pulled his handkerchief and wiped his face while George fought to keep his laughter from erupting.

Dawson returned the handkerchief to his pocket. "None of us have developed a tolerance for this heat, Miss Zimmerman." He gestured toward the mercantile. "Come inside, and we'll conduct business while George picks up his order."

George helped Albert latch the barn doors, then shadowed the three of them into the mercantile. While he followed, he admired the back of Miss Zimmerman's bonnet and gingham dress.

Today had been interesting. It offered a life-threatening duty to consider and the discovery of a pretty maid who now lived a short walk down the road. He might take the wagon delivery job for no other reason than to have an excuse to pass her aunt's house once a week.

This new job would be dangerous. Possibly deadly. Was this job his fresh path in life? Did God spare him to keep the peace in his hometown inhabited by two warring nations?

2

Alice and Albert made their way to their aunt's farm, melting in the hot afternoon sun.

"Missouri sure differs from Massachusetts." Albert removed a handkerchief from his pocket and wiped his brow. "How do you stand it in all those layers?"

"I grit my teeth and push through it. Ladies have no other choice but to cover up everything. My bonnet keeps the sun off my face, but otherwise, I'm so hot I'm soaked to the skin."

"So am I."

"This dress is the lightest material I own. You're lucky you get to wear short pants. No complaining out of you."

"We need to make these deliveries early in the mornings. When it's cooler. I'll have Papa wake me earlier to do the morning chores." He shot her a glance. "Are you willing to get breakfast on the table earlier?"

She nodded. "You've got a good plan there. I might have to bake at night. Things like bread, pies, and biscuits require time near the fire. I can tolerate the fire much better when the sun's down."

They bounced along the rutted dirt road for several minutes before Alice could no longer contain her curiosity. "Papa is nowhere around, and neither is Aunt Berta. I want your honest thoughts about our move down here. I promise I won't tell anyone what you think."

He squinted up at her, then shaded his eyes with his hand to study her. "Promise?"

"I vowed to promise, and you know my promise is an oath."

His hands fiddled with the edge of the buggy seat. "I can see the good and bad of it. It's so hot here. I had to leave my friends. I work on the farm and everything is new to me. I'm not very good help for Papa." He sighed. "I miss our mother, but I'd miss her no matter where we live."

Alice teased him. "I'm guessing that's a list of the bad things? What do you enjoy about living here?"

Albert fiddled some more, then answered. "After losing Mama, I enjoy living with Aunt Berta. Even though her health keeps her mostly sitting or lying down, she's happy. She doesn't let anyone know how much it bothers her to be nearly an invalid."

Alice nodded.

"Even with all that, she hugs me and sneaks me a sweet when I fetch her something. The farm animals are also something I like. I suppose I'll get better at wrangling them in time. I would love to find a friend." He glanced at her. "No offense, but you're my sister. I want a friend who's my age. One who'll go fishing, hunting, and stuff."

She grinned. "I understand. We used to enjoy fishing together, but now that I'm older, I have things to do. Cooking, cleaning, sewing, and running a household." She guided the horse around a significant dip in the road. "It was good that Mama taught me how to do all those things. She never figured

I'd run the household, much less Aunt Berta's, but God had a different plan."

"I wish I knew His plan for me."

"It's not our place to know God's plan until He's ready to reveal it." She sighed. "I miss Mama every day. Every night I pray she's happy and knows we're doing the best we can without her. You can always talk to me about her. Whenever we mention her around Papa, he gets that sad look in his eyes and excuses himself."

"He does. He disappears. I wonder if he needs a friend too." Albert hesitated a moment, then smiled. "Speaking of friends, you made a new friend back there. That George guy."

She smiled. "You're right. And he's a neighbor, so we'll see more of him. We should have asked if he has family your age. A brother or a cousin. Did you think Johnny was too old to be friends?"

"No, we could be friends. I just figured he has a lot of chores. He looked busy working at that store today. I guess he works most days."

"When you hopped out of this buggy and were rude to Mr. Dawson, your lack of manners embarrassed me. You've been raised better than that."

He frowned. "I wondered when you would lay into me about that."

"You deserve to be 'laid into,' young man. Johnny Dawson and any young boys in George's family won't be allowed to visit you if you don't remember to be a young gentleman."

"I've spent too much time taking care of the chickens. They don't care if I use my manners on them."

Alice laughed. "Blame it on the chickens. Well, I admit, I'd love to make friends with some younger people, especially girls. Now that we're settled in, we must attend church on Sunday. I don't know if Aunt Berta can tolerate a ride in the buggy. It may have to be the three of us. If we are three or four, we need to go to church. We'll meet most of the town and get some scripture to guide our way."

"How do you feel about the move? Are you sad you turned down the offer from Mr. Talley?"

Alice adjusted her bonnet and chuckled. "I never gave one serious notion to Mr. Talley's offer. He is a wealthy man. But being offered a comfortable home by a man I didn't love, much less like, was a straightforward decision. I didn't feel the calling to marry him despite him being a widower with children. Some older woman would find his offer most attractive."

"He had hair growing out of his nose, and his eyebrows were like caterpillars."

"What a wicked thing to say, Albert. We all have our faults. It's our character that's important."

"You called him old."

"That's not wicked. It's the truth. He was much older than me. But it wasn't just our age difference that caused me concern. It was his business practices. He valued coins more than people. I'd never marry someone like that."

"I don't know how you'll marry, considering you now care for Aunt Berta, Papa, and me."

She momentarily pondered Albert's declaration. "You're right. I have obligations that'll keep me from making other choices. But I'll accept them. I love all of you, and this path appears to be God's plan for me."

Albert shuffled in the seat. "Is it God's plan that you always drive the buggy? With all of your chores, why don't you teach me how to handle this? I'm old enough to learn. Besides, you won't have to do it when I know how."

Alice chuckled. "Good idea." She handed over the reins. "Let's start now."

~

WHEN GEORGE RETURNED HOME, he unhitched the wagon in the barn and brushed down Clyde in their small corral. Before he'd finished with the horse, his sister Mary appeared with a pitchfork of fresh hay.

"I'm proud to say this is my last outside chore today." She pushed away a stray lock of dark hair that stuck to her face. "I'm sure Clyde would like his supper after taking you to town. And Mama says to wash for your own supper."

"Be right there."

"Have you seen Frankie?"

He shook his head. "Not recently. I suspect he thought I'd put him to work. Might try looking near the creek."

Grumbling about chasing down a spoiled little boy, Mary left him the pitchfork to return to the barn and went off in search of Frank.

At the dinner table, after Papa said grace, George grinned before delivering his news sure to please his Mama and sisters. "I met two of Mrs. Schumacher's relatives today. One of them seems to be about your age, Mary."

Mary's head whipped in his direction. "Who'd you meet? Girl or boy? Were they nice?"

"The niece near your age is Alice Zimmerman. I figured she's about twenty years old. She has a younger brother, older than Frankie, but not by much."

Frankie smiled at this news. "I'm happy to have a boy move within walking distance. When can we go see them?"

Once he described the new arrivals, Mary and Frankie left him at peace. His thoughts returned to his decision, and Mama's beans and cornbread seemed to stick in his throat. He glanced around the table to see if anyone noticed his problem. Mary and Mama were deep in conversation about their new neighbors. Papa took a sip of his coffee and turned his knowing gaze to him.

"Something the matter, son?"

George pushed beans around his plate briefly, then cleared his throat. "I'd like your permission to ride Clyde into town tomorrow. I won't need the wagon."

"Why do you need to go again?"

George put down his fork and turned to Papa. "I've been offered a business arrangement by Mr. Dawson. I promised him he'd know my answer tomorrow or Thursday. It is the best day to be gone since enough storm clouds are building up outside to deliver rain by morning."

Papa fingered his coffee cup. "Want to tell me what this is about?"

"Nothing underhanded, Papa. I've promised not to say anything to anyone else until I've brought my answer to Mr. Dawson."

After another glance, Papa picked up a wedge of cornbread. "Good of you to keep your promise. Clyde is yours for the day, son. I'm sure whatever you tell Dawson will be the right decision." Then he returned to his meal.

Mary picked up on their conversation and launched an idea with enthusiasm. "George. If you're going back into town tomorrow, why don't you hitch the wagon again and take Mama and me to visit with Mrs. Schumacher's relatives? I'm dying to meet the girl. Alice, you said?"

"Yes, Alice."

"When you finish your business in town, you can stop and pick us up."

"You'll get wet, if you go with me. It's going to rain."

"I'd swim there if it means I'd meet Alice." Mary turned to Mama. "Isn't that a lovely idea? We'd get to meet them and start a friendship. I long for the friendship of a girl my age and now one's moved nearby."

"I want to go." Frank's loud voice earned him a scathing glance from their Mama.

Mama turned back to Mary. "I suspect you need a friend, Mary. We must bake some things to take as welcoming gifts once we finish supper." Then she flashed her brown eyes at Frank. "You're not going with us unless you get up from this table and do all of your chores tonight and in the morning. You've been slacking."

Frank dipped his head. "Sorry, Mama. I'll get them done. Promise."

George listened as Mary and Frank chattered with excitement about the new neighbors. He'd welcome another opportunity to lay eyes on the pretty Alice tomorrow. Too bad tonight's pending decision was not allowing him to enjoy her newfound proximity. He eyed his papa after he grew tired of pushing the beans around his plate. He prayed he would make the right decision. Especially since he didn't know what to do.

AFTER SUPPER, George excused himself from the table and went to one of the rocking chairs on the front porch. Whenever he needed to decide or work his mind through a problem, he picked a new piece of wood to whittle.

Papa joined him about an hour later. Mama allowed no smoking in the house, and Papa enjoyed a pipe every evening. He claimed it settled his nerves. George had tried it during his time in the Army, but whittling was much more relaxing than sucking foul-tasting smoke through a pipe.

After several minutes of silently watching the storm clouds gather, George spoke to Papa. "This decision I have to make, it's between the Lord and me. Whatever way is right, God will lead me."

Papa rocked for a moment. "God has strange ways sometimes of leading us down the path He's chosen for us. So go with what your heart is telling you. God talks to you through your heart, not your head."

"Whittling is the only activity that turns off the voice in my head. It allows me to hear my heart."

Papa pointed his pipe at George's hands. A barn owl with a heart-shaped face appeared in the wood. "The only way I can explain how you find those animals inside the wood is to credit our Creator for the talent He's given you, son. Try not to worry. He'll lead you to make the right decision."

3

The following day after they completed chores, including the ones assigned to a surprisingly eager Frank, George hitched Clyde to the wagon. He drove Mama, Mary, and Frank to Mrs. Schumacher's farm. Although the air was muggy and rain threatened, the clouds held their moisture during their journey.

Alice burst out of Mrs. Schumacher's house when they arrived, her younger brother Albert close on her heels. Her hands fluttered to her hair, which was the color of ripe wheat.

George tipped his hat to her. His heavy heart lightened simply by seeing her smiling face. George realized he'd been staring too long when Mama, suppressing a grin, elbowed him. He averted his gaze and climbed down to assist his mother and sister from the wagon.

Mrs. Schumacher made it out the door in time to offer introductions. Alice curtseyed when introduced to George's mother and sister, while Albert and Frank disappeared into the barn, probably to find mischief.

Mrs. Schumacher gestured to George. "Won't you partake of some tea and cake with us?"

"Thank you, Mrs. Schumacher, for the kind offer of refreshments." George dipped his head. "I'm afraid I must decline, as I have business in town. But I'm sure you ladies won't miss me. It shouldn't take too long to handle, so I hope to get everyone home again before the rains come."

As the ladies turned toward the house, George removed his hat and called to Alice. She'd been talking with his sister. "Miss Zimmerman, may I speak to you for a moment?"

Alice turned to him, appearing surprised by his request. "Of course, Mr. Hunter." She schooled her expression before she spun toward Mary. "Excuse me for a moment, please."

George waited for her on the steps of the porch. His face heated with embarrassment, but he remained committed to his purpose. He reached into his pocket and pulled out a lumpy handkerchief. Inside the bundle was a small carving of a horse and a large, more delicately carved, barn owl. George's worry gave him time to finish the bird. The small project helped to soothe him to sleep.

Alice gasped in amazement. "Oh, they're beautiful. The owl looks like he is going to fly away."

"He's my attempt at presenting you with a welcome gift. It's a barn owl."

She pulled her gaze from the owl and met his eyes. "You did this?"

"Yes, ma'am." He placed the owl in her hand. Then he pressed the horse into her other palm. "Albert will like this horse, I imagine."

Alice chuckled. "He will be delighted, as I am. I'm much obliged by such a gift." She ran her fingers along the owl carving. "The eyes and beak are exceptional. It's so realistic. I'm amazed at your talent. But I have nothing for you."

"Your delight is all the gift I need, Miss Zimmerman." George bowed and limped over to the wagon. "I'll be back soon."

ALTHOUGH THE WEIGHT of his decision gnawed at him on the way to Dawson's Mercantile, the image of Alice's smiling face cheered him. He prayed he was making the right decision.

When he arrived at the store, Johnny was helping with a delivery. George entered through the back door. The place was empty of customers.

"George. Good to see you."

George walked over to the register and shook Mr. Dawson's offered hand. "I've made my decision about your proposal."

Dawson eyed him with concern. "What did you decide?"

"I'll do it on one condition that's in addition to what you've already offered."

"What would that be, son?"

"I can't ask my Papa to give up one of his horses for a day every week. Our horses are a team. He needs them to help with the plowing, heavy work around the farm, and the harvest. I'm already leaving him a man short one day a week by doing this." George fingered the nearby scale for a moment. "You understand. I can't walk to town because of this leg. If you can help me find a way to get here. Perhaps loan me a horse or send young Johnny to bring me to town and take me home when needed, then I'll do it."

Dawson pondered this for a moment. "You on horseback today, or did you bring a wagon?"

"I brought a wagon."

"Good. I've got a Morgan at my place. He's the only bay in

my corral. Buster is a gentle fellow, but a bit long in the tooth for a real workhorse. When Big Johnny went to serve, he didn't take him."

"That sounds fine."

"You can take his saddle, blanket, and bridle too. I'll send Johnny to help you get him and his tack. Whenever this is all finished, you can return him."

"You've got a deal, Mr. Dawson."

They shook hands.

"I'm mighty relieved. I didn't know who else could do this." He patted George on the shoulder. "I'm proud of you for taking this on. It won't be easy and it might be dangerous, but you've got a level head and some military experience."

"I'd like you to tell everyone I'll be making the deliveries. They know I'm a former soldier. Might keep some of the riffraff away."

"I'll do that."

"If you get any complaints, send them to me, and I'll try to talk some sense into them. I want to make deliveries during the greatest light of day, but I plan to stagger the times so my deliveries won't be predictable to those looking for trouble."

"You've given this a great deal of thought."

"Yes, sir. I plan to be armed with a rifle. Using it could be a mistake that could rile up both sides of this war. I'll only use it if forced."

Dawson shook his head. "I pray the fiery tempers will die down after some time. With the demands of an occupying Army, what choice do we have?"

"Sir, I'm not trying to pick at you, but it's not an 'occupying Army,' because Missouri is still in the Union. Use of terms like that can cause tempers to flair."

"Sorry. I'll do better at watching everything I say."

"I'm telling you, so you'll be extra careful about what you say. You've got young Johnny and his mother to protect."

"What else do you need from me?"

"Since they've asked for Friday deliveries, I'll come every Friday, but at different times, as I mentioned. If you'll load your wagon and keep it in the barn, I'll ride Buster inside and hitch him up there."

"You want the wagon in the barn?"

"I'd like to keep the wagon out of sight. It'll keep my departure time more secret. A loaded wagon sitting in front of your store is likely to catch the attention of anyone inclined to raid deliveries to the Union encampment. We might consider some deliveries on Thursday afternoon or early evening. That would keep people guessing when it will happen."

"Good thinking, George. Let me know after each delivery when the next one will be. I'll try to keep you informed if what they've ordered will be delayed beyond a Thursday delivery."

"There is a war going on. Deliveries are going to be delayed. They'll have to understand you can't deliver everything they want, all the time."

Dawson rubbed the back of his neck. "I doubt any military leadership is inclined to understand much of anything these days. Seems everyone yells or shoots first and then figures out the problem when it's too late."

ALICE'S HEART fluttered with delight as she stole away to prepare a tea tray for their unexpected guests. She was happy she had something tasty to serve them that went well with the strawberry scones Mary brought. Yesterday, after her trip to the mercantile with Albert, she'd made good on her pledge to bake at night and made bread, two pies, and a sponge cake.

To serve the delectables and tea, she scooted into the kitchen. It was a small brick structure, built about ten feet from the main house as a fire preventative. There was an enormous oven for cooking, with several iron hooks used to cook meat on a rotisserie and for hanging stew pots. Along the middle of the chimney, Uncle Otto had built areas for bread baking and slow smoking meats. Shelves and tables used for utensil storage and food preparation lined the three remaining walls.

She gathered Aunt Berta's tea service and placed it on a tray with the sponge cake and scones. Within moments, she had warm water for the teapot, put the tea leaves in it, and added strainers for the cups. After the addition of napkins and forks, she gathered the tray to head into the parlor.

The ladies sat on various pieces of furniture. The room had a fireplace, but the house was cool on this stifling summer day because the cooking was done in the separate kitchen.

Mrs. Hunter arranged her skirts. "I must convince Mr. Hunter that we need a separate cooking shed. Your ability to keep the main house cool in the summer is enviable."

Mrs. Schumacher looked pleased. "It is a wonderful thing to have. When my husband was a boy, he lost his home to a cooking fire. He was always afraid such a thing would happen again, so he built our kitchen separately."

Alice interrupted. "Inform them about all the ironwork."

"Yes, Alice. He was handy with a forge, so he made hooks and iron tools to make the cooking easier. He was so thoughtful about my poor health. He was always trying to make my chores easier."

Alice served tea to the ladies and George's sister, Mary. "Now, I've taken over all the cooking and baking." She shot a smile at her aunt. "I'm enjoying that kitchen, and the family seems to like what I make."

"That is wonderful." Mrs. Hunter took a sip of tea. "You're doing a fine job."

"I'm happy to help Aunt Berta, and baking is my favorite pastime. I've figured out how to use the places Uncle Otto made. He designed them for bread baking. I've found they also work as a place for baking pies and cakes."

There were questions about "the places Uncle Otto made for baking." Aunt Berta explained where they were and how it allowed for heat without direct heat or flames.

Alice then sliced pieces of the sponge cake for everyone. "I'd like to hear your opinion about this cake. I think I've figured out the proper cooking time."

The guests had murmurs of appreciation.

Mary took one bite and sighed happily. "Alice, I beg you to teach me how to bake like this."

Alice laughed. "I'm sure your efforts are equal to mine."

Mrs. Hunter grinned at Mary, then turned to Alice. "I can attest that her efforts are nowhere close to this exquisite cake. If you would teach Mary, I'd pay you for your time. We made the scones together, and Mary was uncomfortable helping with them. I'd like her to gain confidence in her cooking abilities."

"Thank you for the offer of payment, Mrs. Hunter, but I would delight in teaching Mary a bit about baking. Just yesterday, Albert and I were discussing our need for friends here. Today, God seems to have delivered one for each of us. Right to our door."

GEORGE PULLED up to the Zimmerman farm. His wagon held Buster's saddle and blanket. Buster trailed behind the wagon. George hopped down and walked to the porch. He moved to knock on the door, but his hand hung in the air for a moment as the laughter from inside washed over him.

He grinned as he listened to them, surprised their happiness filled his soul with warmth. If Mary and Alice formed a friendship, he'd likely see more of Alice. And that was a splendid thing indeed.

4

It was hot and muggy the morning George set off to make his first delivery to the Union Army camp. Good to his word, Mr. Dawson sent Johnny to him the night before with a message that the order was ready and waiting in the barn. George dispatched the boy home with one of his mother's sweet cakes to enjoy.

When George neared Dawson's Mercantile, Buster recognized his territory and quickened his steps to the barn. Even though he was an older horse, Buster's good nature and steady gait suited George. His injured hip felt better at a slow pace on horseback. Buster, so far as he could tell, only had two speeds. Slow and "not quite so slow," when near his home.

Mr. Dawson's head appeared at the back door of the Mercantile, soon followed by the rest of him. He scurried down the back steps, stumbled, and flung out his arms for balance. The actions kept him from rolling to the ground.

"Whoa, there, Mr. Dawson. Take care."

"I must build a handhold for those stairs." Dawson reached him, his face red from the heat, embarrassment, or both. "I can't imagine how you're so calm, George. This entire business is an abomination. I'm worried sick."

George slid off Buster, unbuckled the leather scabbard holding his rifle, and slid it under the wagon seat. Then he unhitched his saddle. "I'm sure it will turn out fine."

"I'm glad you brought that rifle."

"I hope I don't have to use it on anyone, Mr. Dawson. I'm on the same side as this Army. They're not the enemy to me."

"Me, either. But you will be the target of all the secessionist riff-raff. And they'll make trouble as soon as they figure out what we've been forced to do."

"I'm friends with most of them, even if we don't see eye to eye about this country's future. I don't want to hurt them, either."

"You've got to protect yourself, son."

"Ah, give it time. Maybe the hot heads will cool down." George led Buster to the water trough. "Did they tell you where I was supposed to deliver the load? Say who was going to unload the wagon? I need to know these things."

"The corporal who brought the list said they'd expect you on Friday. Nothing else. Don't you unload the wagon or let anyone touch the goods in this wagon until you've seen federal coins or dollars to pay for it." Dawson dug into his pocket and pulled out a crumpled list. "This is the inventory and the amount they owe."

George pocketed the list and led Buster to the wagon tongue. Buster stood steadily while they hitched him in. "Mr. Dawson, this whole thing is in God's hands. No amount of your worrying, or my worrying, will change anything."

Mr. Dawson checked the reins and then patted Buster. "Buster doing okay for you?"

George patted him. "He's perfect."

"Then Godspeed, George. I'll say a prayer for you."

With some tugs on the items loaded in the wagon, George assured himself they'd make a safe trip. "Thank you, Mr. Dawson. Be back as soon as I can."

Missouri in July was always muggy, but lately, the threat of rain made all the state's inhabitants miserable from the uncommon heaviness of the air. George's time in service had been during the spring, and he'd been blessed to avoid these conditions. The men could suffer from lice and fleas on them, their clothing, and bedding. When ants, crickets, chiggers, grasshoppers, cicadas, and other insects that roam the rolling hills during the heat of summer were added in, the soldiers had to be extra miserable.

He topped the hill that led to the headquarters area of the camp and, with a glance, knew he'd reached the leaders. These were men who planned and thought and studied maps. In the distance, they'd arranged two groups of larger tents in a semi-circle, with a cooking fire in the middle of each.

A young sentry strode to him, a rifle held across his chest.

"State your business."

"George Hunter. Delivering goods ordered from Dawson Mercantile."

Another soldier arrived. After exchanging words with him, the sentry turned toward George.

"Wait here."

The newly arrived soldier strode toward one tent while the sentry stared at him and spat tobacco. George looked away. He had no desire to engage in conversation with this armed sentry.

Soon an older, beefy sergeant arrived, followed by a group of young privates. The sergeant, at least ten years older than his charges, didn't waste time proving who was in charge.

"You there," he pointed at George. "Are you armed?"

"I have a rifle by my feet, under the seat of this wagon. Nothing else."

"Show me your papers."

George slowly reached his right hand into his pocket and pulled out some papers. He handed one sheet to the sergeant. "This is the itemized list and payment tally owed to Dawson Mercantile." After the sergeant had reviewed that, George unfolded a second paper and handed it to him. "This is my final muster record from the 16th Illinois Infantry. They put this in my pocket when I was sent home."

The sergeant studied the muster record. "Aren't you local?"

"Yes, sir. My family has a farm north of town."

"Why'd you join the 16th Illinois?"

"When the war broke out, Governor Claiborne Jackson refused to raise troops here to serve in the Federal Army. So I went to Illinois to enlist."

"Feel that strongly about preserving the Union?"

"Yes, sir."

The sergeant strode over to him and stuck out his hand. "Sergeant Samuels, here. Pleasure to meet you, Private Hunter."

George shook his hand. "Since my injury, it's just George now. My wounds were such that they sent me home to die. But the joke was on them. God allowed me to stay on this side of the dirt."

"I'm sure you're aware General Pope is the commander of this." The sergeant gestured toward the tents. "We're the Army's Department of Northern Missouri. I serve Pope and his officers. What I say is what Pope wants."

"Yes, sir."

"Drive that wagon over near that farthest tent on the left, and we'll unload the headquarter supplies. Then I'll ride with you down to deliver to the men."

George nodded. "When I get this wagon over there, nothing gets unloaded until I'm paid. Orders of Mr. Dawson."

Sergeant Samuels nodded. "I'll respect the wishes of the man you serve, if you'll respect the man I serve."

"You have my word."

They shared a quick grin before the sergeant started spouting orders. Within moments, they'd moved the wagon, the appropriate amount of money was provided to George, and the supplies for headquarters were unloaded.

The sergeant hopped onto the wagon, forcing George to make room for his ample girth. George kept a poker face—seemed those who served at headquarters didn't miss any meals.

After a short drive past the command area, they rolled into a valley surrounded by small hills. A grin tugged at the corners of George's mouth when he spotted the acres of white tents spread out across the valley about a quarter mile in front of him. The regular Army was here. Men like he'd been. These men did the fishing, hunting, sweating, and cooking when in camp. They did the shooting and dying when fighting.

Sergeant Samuels must have noticed George's reaction, because he sat up straighter in the wagon and bragged about the discipline the men were developing.

George listened with half an ear as his thoughts carried him away. He loved the regimental unevenness of the tents. The unit marching on the parade ground to the taps of the drummer boys warmed his heart. He'd only been a part of the Army for a few months, yet the pride he felt for those still serving surprised him. He yearned to be back among them.

When they drew closer to the tents, Samuels had George stop so he could round up some men to unload. The sergeant approached the lieutenant taking the men through their drills.

After a brief discussion, the lieutenant dismissed the unit and ordered them to unload the wagon.

The sweaty men teased each other as they unloaded the remaining supplies. While the men worked to move and stack everything from eggs to lumber, a drummer boy caught George's eye. The boy did not return to his tent but stayed off the side. When he looked at George, his sad countenance made George's stomach twist. Why was he unhappy? Was this lad trying to get a message to him through his proximity to the wagon? If so, what was his message?

George slid along the wagon bench to speak to the boy, but the youngster ran away, the sound of his drum slapping against his body fading away within a moment. George looked to see if anyone else had observed the exchange but it appeared no one noticed. The melancholy of the boy's sadness accompanied George back to the Mercantile and beyond.

TWO DAYS LATER, because one cow roamed her way into the cornfield, George sent the family to church without him. After successfully shooing the cow back to the proper pasture, he completed a quick fence repair and wasn't far behind them. Even with his usual slow pace, Buster had come in handy today. He'd have had to miss services altogether if not for having the extra horse.

He opened the church doors as quietly as he could. He didn't enjoy calling attention to himself or his limp. Now, thanks to the squeaky hinges on the door, he faced a building full of turned heads and the steely gaze of Pastor Collins, who was already leading the worshipers in the scripture lesson.

George cringed as his boots thudded on the wood floors, ringing out his uneven gait to all in attendance. Eyes focused on the shiny boards, he tried to step lightly. He gritted his teeth when he spotted his family seated near the front, leaving him no choice but to stride almost the entire length of the aisle.

The cooing of a baby caused him to glance to his right, where just past the infant, he spotted the bonnet of Alice Zimmerman. She sat by her brother, father, and aunt. His heart lifted. Perhaps he'd have an opportunity to talk with her after services.

He slid into the open space next to his brother, Frank. Too young to get much out of the service, Frank played with some wooden animals George had made. After watching him for a moment, George realized he needed to make Frank some biblical figures. That way he'd be entertained with appropriate items during church services.

When worship ended, George looked around for Alice. She was surrounded by family while they introduced her to other church families, including the Smiths. His heart sank when Jedidiah Smith smiled and tipped his hat to her. The family owned a tannery, with Jedidiah in line to inherit it. This alone made him a man of interest to mothers with marrying-age daughters. Jedidiah had his pick of all the eligible girls, and Alice was the prettiest.

George sighed and queued in the line to talk to Pastor Collins. He owed him an apology for his earlier disruptive entrance, so he waited patiently for his turn. He hid a grin while he watched Pastor trying unsuccessfully to remove himself from the never-ending fountain of words spouted by the widow Harney. The widow's granddaughter finally pulled the old lady away, which allowed Pastor to turn to George with a relieved sigh.

Pastor Collins was about a foot shorter than George but made up for his lack of height by allowing his thick, gray hair to add inches. With a glance to ensure he was free to speak,

Pastor Collins motioned for George to lean over toward him. "Sometimes I wish all of God's children were as quiet as you, George."

This made George smile. "I came to apologize for my interruption when I arrived late. Unfortunately, one of our cows got into temptation."

Pastor Collins nodded. "Cows are no more resistant to temptation than people. Your folks told me you would be late before services started. It is my call to apologize. I thought you were the Lackey family. They always arrive late, and I've lost my patience with them. I cut you that mean look before I realized it was you."

"No harm done. I did more than give a mean look to our wandering cow."

This brought a smile to the Pastor, but it faded quickly. "Your folks also mentioned you were delivering goods to the Army for Mr. Dawson. This makes me worry about you, son. You're putting yourself in danger by doing that. I know you're likely getting paid for it, but your life might be the price paid. I value your life more than whatever money you'd earn."

George kicked his boot in the dirt before replying. "I am being compensated, but I feel I've been called to make these deliveries. The Army needs supplies delivered by someone they trust. I'm loyal to their cause, even if I can't fight for it anymore."

"But the bushwhackers aren't going to like you helping the Army. I've heard some Union soldiers were killed a week ago near Martinsburg for no good reason. That's violence in our own county. It's too risky."

George set his jaw. "The majority of the bushwhackers are local men. Men I've either known all my life or met one way or another. They believe strongly in their cause, but I believe strongly in mine. I've already put my life on the line for my country, and God spared me. Maybe He spared me because of this. I can't fight anymore, but maybe I can help keep the peace between the two sides right here. In the town I love."

"You are but one man."

"Esther was but one woman, and she helped save the Jews from annihilation. I appreciate your concern, but all I ask is that you pray for me, Pastor. I believe this is something I've been called to do."

Pastor Collins gave George's shoulder a squeeze. "I must accept this as God's will and will say prayers for you."

George nodded. "I'd appreciate you praying for me to make a good impression with Alice Zimmerman too."

Pastor Collins smiled. "Can't fault your taste in women, son."

5

For several weeks, the deliveries were uneventful. George altered his delivery times and avoided any trouble. Nevertheless, he remained cautious about his journeys. Each trip included his rifle, stowed in the wagon, with a prayer that it not be needed to harm a human being.

With the eager whispers of county citizens, he felt sure everyone knew what he was doing. Those sympathetic to the Union Army wouldn't object, but those with Southern leanings would consider his deliveries as aid to the enemy. Dangerous business, but necessary. George hoped the deliveries would help keep the peace between the two factions.

With the arrival of August, the encampment saw one of their most popular leaders reassigned. Colonel Grant, one of the regimental commanders, received orders to transfer to Ironton, Missouri. Weeks after his departure, news returned to camp that Grant was promoted to brigadier general.

Most citizens in and around Mexico appreciated Grant during his time in town. When he'd arrived, he put a halt to the act of forcing locals at gunpoint to swear their loyalty to the Union. He also stopped the military from seizing local property and supplies. Thus, he'd been the one responsible for George's mercantile deliveries.

As the weeks passed, his mercantile assignment gave George the opportunity to pass by Alice's house eight round trips. He'd only been able to speak to her five times, yet each encounter had lifted his spirits. His admiration for Alice increased every time she smiled at him. Whenever possible, he tried to show her his appreciation of having her acquaintance. These visits made him hopeful for more time together in the future. Could she possibly feel the same?

It was a warm September day as Sergeant Samuels and George made their way from headquarters. Their mission was to drop off the men's supplies at the main area of the camp. George called it the "valley of tents."

As they rode, Sergeant Samuels lamented the lack of good chewing tobacco. "The Army deserves more than a few twisted leaves. Why, that's poor man's chaw, it is. Don't you agree?"

George grinned at him. "I must be a really poor man because I've never justified the price of 'poor man's chaw,' as you call it, much less that expensive store-bought flat black plug. I suspect the Confederates have all the good tobacco."

"True. I hope they choke on it." Samuels spit to emphasize his point. "Too bad there's nothing grown local."

"There's never been a good tobacco crop here. They raise cotton in Cape Girardeau, so they might raise tobacco there." He shrugged. "I don't know for sure. Despite what this summer has led you to believe, winters are too cold up here, and the crop depletes the soil."

The sergeant eyeballed him with disgust. "You are a farmer, that's for sure."

"Yes, sir."

"Tobacco relaxes me. What do you do to relax if you don't chew?"

"I whittle. Started as a pastime when I was younger. Then I found it allows me to think, without the worry behind it. If such a claim makes any sense to you."

He shook his head. "It don't. Some fellas in this camp are continually honing their whittling skills. You want me to introduce you to them? They could teach you something, and you could teach them. I'm sure you know things they don't."

George nodded. "I'd like that."

When they arrived, Samuels rounded up a unit to unload the wagon and disappeared. Within minutes, he returned, as good as his word, bringing two men with him.

"George, this here's Private Martin and Corporal Danny."

George stepped down from the wagon. He offered his hand to Martin. He was a thin, lanky man about ten years older than George. Martin's long, slender fingers were harbingers of artistry with wood. A glance at the smiling Danny had George returning a smile as he shook hands. Danny, who was younger, had a freckled face and hair the color of fire. "I'm pleased to meet you both."

Martin studied George a moment. "Sarge says you's a whittler."

"I do my best. I'd like to see your work if you have time to show me."

Martin and Danny exchanged a glance.

Danny's smile didn't fade. "I'll get a few things and grab a few of yours, Martin. I'm faster at retrieving than you, old man."

George and Martin watched Danny hustle off. Martin shrugged. "I can't even argue with what he said. I am an old man. He's faster than me, and he outranks me."

Within a moment, Danny brought back some amazing

carvings. The men discussed techniques and materials until the sergeant returned. Samuels's eyes held a spark of impatience as he approached them.

George took Samuel's hint. "I best be heading back. I'll bring some of my work on my next visit."

Samuels shooed the men away and turned to George, who climbed onto the wagon. "While you were jawing, I had some fellas load a few empty barrels and a handful of baskets that belong to the mercantile. We don't need 'em here, and I'm sure Mr. Dawson can reuse them."

George nodded. "Mighty thoughtful of you to give them back. Dawson will be obliged. See you next week."

Samuels pointed at him. "Mind you, tell him to put some good plug in the next load."

George chuckled as he turned the wagon. Of course, a higher authority than the sergeant would have to order that plug. He called over his shoulder, "Talk to your officer, the one who makes the orders. I deliver what they ask for, if we can get it."

BACK ON THE ROAD, the afternoon's heat drained George's energy and Buster's too. The horse's naturally slow gait became a snail's pace. Dust from the road stayed stirred up due to so many wagons and riders passing.

The Army's presence on the outskirts was a good thing for the growth of the town. Now, if they could eliminate the threat of skirmishes and potential battles fought here, growth would be assured. They didn't need conflicts related to this War Between the States to harm the citizens or burn down the town.

When the wagon neared the mercantile, Buster was so

weary, he failed to increase the speed of his steps near his old home. George hopped down, led Buster near the water trough, and then worked to unhitch him. He could tie the horse up in the shade and give him a break.

While George unloaded the empty barrels and baskets, he spotted a buggy hitched behind the store but didn't recognize it. Times had changed. He used to know every cart and buggy in the county.

Albert Zimmerman burst out of the store. "George!" Albert rushed to him, a smile lighting his boyish face.

Did that mean Alice was inside? He'd welcome another chance to talk to her.

"I should have thanked you personally for the fine horse you carved for me. It's a wonderful gift."

George reached out and ruffled Albert's blond hair. "Your sister told me how much you liked it, but I appreciate you telling me yourself, Albert. Even if it took you some time to say it."

"I'm sorry about that, George. My sister adored that owl you gave her too. She's put it up on a shelf in her bedroom and told me she'd give me a hiding if I even thought about touching it."

George grinned. Although he knew Alice was fond of the owl, it was nice to hear she'd placed it in a protected location. He knew first-hand how damaging younger brothers can be.

Albert took the baskets from George's arm and headed toward the barn. "Would you show me how to whittle like that?"

"If you'll hop in this wagon and grab the rest of those baskets, I'll consider it."

Albert ran the original load of baskets into the barn and then reappeared to shimmy into the wagon. Once he'd gathered the remaining baskets, he asked, "What kind of knife will I be needing? I may have to earn more egg money if'n I need a special knife."

"You can learn the basics with any small, sharp knife or a folding knife."

Albert's mouth dropped open. "You mean a regular knife?"

"As long as it's sharp. You have to know how to use it without cutting yourself. Once you master that, almost any knife will do."

George pulled himself into the wagon bed to reach the final barrel. He pulled on it, but it didn't budge. The barrels were supposed to be empty, so the weight of this barrel made no sense. Surprised by the resistance, he pulled up the lid to see what they'd left inside.

"Oh, my!" He pushed the barrel over and rushed to pull out the person inside. As he did, he shouted at Albert. "Go get help. Somebody's in here. Passed out. Probably because of the heat."

Albert scrambled away.

George tugged on the arms of the victim and extracted him from the barrel. It was a young boy, the drummer he'd seen a few weeks ago. Dark hair. Near the age of Albert and Frankie.

George laid the boy on his back while he climbed down from the wagon, groaning when his feet hit hard, radiating pain through his bad hip. He searched for a bucket and found one inside the barn. Then, as quickly as he could move, he filled the pail in the horse trough and went to the wagon to pour it over the boy.

The flood of water caused the boy to flutter his eyes. George moved to refill the bucket as Alice, Albert, and Old Mr. Dawson came running.

Mr. Dawson yelled, "What's happened?"

"I had a stowaway. I think the heat's gotten to him. He's just a boy."

Alice, skirt in her hands, ran faster than Mr. Dawson and peered into the wagon. "Is he alive?"

"Yes. The water revived him." George returned with another full bucket. "He must have climbed in there when my attention was elsewhere."

George gave Alice a hand as she scrambled into the wagon. She sat down near the boy's head and loosened his shirt. "He's nothing but bones. Didn't they feed him?"

"He might have been sick. The sergeant said there's been some dysentery making its way through the encampment."

Alice frowned as she inspected the boy. "I still question whether they've been feeding him properly. Poor thing."

Mr. Dawson stared into the wagon, his face revealing the horror of the situation. "The Army will be furious with us for helping him escape, stowaway or not, when they find out we have him!"

George bowed up. "I wasn't an active party in his escape. I simply found him. He's lucky to be alive."

Mr. Dawson turned to him. "What are we going to do, George?"

Alice called out to George. "Do you have a canteen of water? I believe he's coming around. He'll need to drink."

"I do." George limped to the wagon seat, pulled out his canteen, and handed it to Alice.

She turned to her brother. "Albert, go find a rag and dip it in the water. I want to keep cooling his face and neck."

Albert ran off to do Alice's bidding.

George studied the boy for a moment. His color seemed better. His eyes were darting around as if trying to place where he was. "Son, are you feeling better?"

The boy glanced over at him but remained silent.

Mr. Dawson approached the wagon. "What are we going to do with him? We've got to get him back to the encampment."

Alice whipped around to Mr. Dawson. "For Heaven's sake, Mr. Dawson. Take pity on this boy! He nearly died in this unfortunate escape. He needs to be in better condition before you return him to the camp. He might even need a doctor."

Mr. Dawson shot a look at George.

George shrugged. "She's right."

Albert came running back with the wet rag and hopped onto the wagon. He approached the boy with it, but the boy leaned away.

Undeterred, Albert asked him, "What's your name?"

The boy furrowed his brow and tried to slide away from Albert.

George studied the boy for a minute. "Odd. He seems to be afraid of Albert. Any idea what that could be about?'

Alice frowned. "Get back from him, Albert. For whatever reason, you scare him." She smiled at the boy and asked in a soft voice, "Are you feeling better?"

The boy frowned at her statement but didn't seem afraid of her.

George watched him for another minute. "He isn't trying to answer you at all."

Mr. Dawson said, "Maybe he's deaf."

George pulled a face and turned to Mr. Dawson. "He's a drummer boy. Of course he can hear. He couldn't drum without being able to hear."

Alice offered more drinking water to the boy, and he drank his fill. She watched him for a moment. "Maybe it's not a matter of whether he can hear. Perhaps it's a matter of understanding."

"Like he's touched or addled?" Mr. Dawson asked.

"No, Mr. Dawson. I was wondering if he doesn't speak English."

As if to prove her point, Alice started speaking in a foreign language. This caused the boy to smile and then respond with enthusiasm in similar gibberish.

George stared at them, surprised by the exchange, but relieved that the boy could communicate. "What language is that?"

Alice smiled up at him. "With a name like Zimmerman, I'd think you could guess."

"German?" He was amazed by this. "How'd you learn that?"

"My grandmother. Papa and Aunt Berta's mother. She was born in Bavaria, a part of the German Confederation. She lived with us. From the time I was a baby until God took her a few years ago. She told us she came to America when she was old and could only speak one language. But she insisted that Albert and I were young and smart enough to learn two."

George smiled at her. This girl was smart as well as pretty. "Looks like your grandmother was right."

Albert shifted close to the boy and also began speaking German. Within a second, both boys smiled.

Alice looked at George. "Isn't that sweet?"

Before George could reply, Mr. Dawson strode close. "They'll be looking for him."

Alice stood. "Well, you can't take him back yet. He's too weak."

Mr. Dawson paced. "What if he tries to run away from you? He's proved he can be a runaway. The Union Army will be mad we have him, but madder still if we let him escape from us."

George held up his hands. "Hold on, both of you. Why don't we have Albert run and get the sheriff? Sheriff Carter won't send him back to the Army without making sure he feels better."

Mr. Dawson nodded. "That takes the matter out of our

hands. It puts it into the hands of the law. Good idea, George. That's the right thing to do."

Alice pondered the idea for a moment. "I suppose that's a good plan. I have no other to offer."

Mr. Dawson appeared relieved at her acceptance.

George leaned into the wagon. "Sorry to interrupt you, Albert, but we need you to get the sheriff."

Albert rose to do George's bidding, but gave Alice a questioning look.

She reassured Albert. "I'll explain to the boy that we must involve the sheriff. It'll be fine. Run on, now."

6

Within minutes, Albert was running back to them. "The sheriff," he gulped air, "says he's coming." He hopped into the wagon and resumed his conversation with the stowaway.

Alice watched them briefly, then leaned down to whisper in Albert's ear. Albert nodded. A few minutes later, she motioned George over to her. "We have to get this child out of the sun."

"Of course." George turned to Mr. Dawson. "Will you help me get the boy out of the wagon?"

Mr. Dawson nodded. "I'll pick him up. Why don't you figure out somewhere for me to put him?" He gestured toward the barn. "In the barn, not the store. Other customers may see him. We need to keep this mess a secret. At least until we figure out what to do."

Alice stood. "Shame on you, Mr. Dawson. This boy is not 'a mess' to be hidden." She pierced him with her meanest glare, but he didn't seem fazed in the least. Alice leaned down and explained to the boy in German that they were moving him.

George shot her a sympathetic look and helped her from the wagon. Then, they moved out of the way to make room for Mr. Dawson to pick up the boy.

Alice plucked on George's upper shirt sleeve, drawing him close. In a low whisper, she stated, "I refuse to leave this boy with Mr. Dawson or Sheriff Carter. When the sheriff arrives, I'd appreciate your help to convince them I should take him home. He needs nursing back to health. Plus, all of us there can communicate with him. I'm sure the sheriff and his deputies don't speak German. Getting him healthy is imperative. Especially if he's going back to that camp."

George whispered, "I agree with you. I'll do my best to get them to allow it." In a louder voice, he asked, "Where might be a place for the boy?"

After a glance around the barn, they arranged a horse blanket on a bale of hay. George gestured for Mr. Dawson where to set the boy. When he did, George said, "Mr. Dawson, you'd better get back into the mercantile. If customers get past young Johnny and come looking for you, they might spot this boy."

"Oh, dear me." Mr. Dawson turned and left the barn.

Once Mr. Dawson was gone, George winked at Alice. "You feel more relaxed with him out of the way, don't you?"

Alice laughed. "You sent him off on purpose."

"Maybe."

"Thank you. I'm glad he's gone. You can handle the sheriff. It's your story to tell. We don't need Mr. Dawson hovering around, making us all nervous." George sure was smart for his realization of the problem and then offering a solution to solve it.

George grinned. "Thanks for your confidence in my abilities. Do you need anything else to help this boy? If the sheriff said he's on his way, then he'll soon arrive."

"I'm sure he's hungry. Maybe we could get him some crackers out of the cracker barrel?"

"Good thinking." George called Albert over and dropped a few pennies in his hand. "Run into the store. Get all the crackers this money will buy for you and the boy."

Albert's face glowed with a big smile as eager feet set him on a mission to fulfill George's request.

Alice approached the boy, spoke to him in German, and then turned to George. "I told him Albert was coming back with some crackers. Then I explained what a cracker is. This boy must be new to America."

"You're right. He gives little signs that he's familiar with the language. Now, we've established he's unfamiliar with common food too. I wish we knew his background and how he ended up here."

Alice studied George's concern for this boy. It was a sign of his character. Sympathetic, yet helpful.

Albert returned to the barn, the front of his shirt pulled out and filled with crackers. Both boys laughed in delight when Albert dumped the crackers onto the makeshift hay bale couch. In seconds, they made them disappear.

Alice and George stood nearby, watching the boys. After a moment, Alice tugged on George's shirt again but didn't say a word nor take her eyes off the boys.

"So what good thing just happened?"

"We have a name. A name for our mystery boy. I asked Albert if he could get him to tell."

George bent near Alice's ear and lowered his voice to a whisper. "What's his name?"

His breath on her cheek caused a flutter in her midsection. "I think he told Albert it's 'Hans.' I'll make sure when I can get Albert away from him. It's obvious the boy seems comfortable with Albert now."

George shrugged. "Seems he likes you too. You figured out what language he speaks. That's quite an accomplishment."

She ducked her head as she basked in his compliment. George always treated her with respect and kindness, qualities she yearned for when she allowed herself to consider a potential mate. "I can't imagine how lonely he's been in that camp. Do you think anyone could talk to him?"

"I doubt it."

"How did he get there?"

"I'll find out. I'll go back to the camp tomorrow. Try not to worry in the meantime."

"Thank you for offering to find out more about him. It will help us take care of him, in addition to tending to his basic needs of rest and good food. At my aunt's farm, all of us speak German. He'd be able to communicate. Hopefully, he could regain his health and perhaps a bit of happiness too. He seemed so sad initially."

George gestured toward the boys with his head. "Maybe his lack of English causes him to be afraid. Because he doesn't speak the language, he doesn't know what's happening around him. That can be frightening. Look at what a few minutes of water, food, and talking with a boy his age has done. He already looks better."

She smiled. George was right. The boy looked better.

THE SOUND of a horse approaching spurred George to leave the barn. He pulled down the brim of his hat and squinted in the sun until he spotted the sheriff making his way to the front of the mercantile.

"Back here, Sheriff."

Sheriff Carter turned and made his way to him.

"Thanks for coming."

The sheriff led his horse to the nearby hitching post and doubled the reins over it. Then he walked over to shake hands with George. Carter was thin and lanky, but strong from years of farm labor. Besides his sheriff duties, he also owned a working farm in the northern part of the county. His horse was a good-looking crossbreed that was part of his farming operation.

Amazing that Sheriff Carter could keep such a good horse for his own use. Both sides of the conflict were buying good horseflesh, and Carter had excellent stock.

"So what's happened? That boy you sent said, 'come quick' and mumbled something about a boy from the 'old country'?" The sheriff, originally from Kentucky, still carried a slight drawl in his speech.

George launched into the circumstances of the stowaway and his discovery. He ensured the sheriff understood how close the boy had come to dying in his escape attempt.

"So you don't know where this boy comes from originally?"

"Not yet."

"No knowledge how he came to the Union camp?"

"No. He hasn't spoken any English in front of us. Mrs. Schumacher's niece, Alice Zimmerman," George gestured toward the barn, "she and her brother are inside with him right now. Alice tried speaking German to him, which appears to be his language. He could have come here by foot, train, riverboat, or wagon."

"Could he be Amish?"

"They don't believe in war or fighting. I can't imagine an Amish child being comfortable associating with an Army. One on either side of this conflict."

"What about Mennonite?"

"They're like the Amish. If I were to guess, I'd say the Army took him in. I saw him wearing a uniform, and he had a drum. They may have a claim on him."

The sheriff entered the barn, tipped his hat to Alice, and watched the boys converse for a moment. "He speaks no English?"

"Hasn't yet."

While the sheriff pondered this, Alice approached.

"Sheriff," George said with a note of pride in his voice, "I'd like to introduce you to Alice Zimmerman. She's the niece of Mrs. Schumacher. She and her father and brother have moved here to help Mrs. Schumacher run her farm."

Carter tipped his hat again at Alice. "Nice to meet you, ma'am. I've had the pleasure of meeting your father. Klaus, isn't it?"

Alice nodded.

"He mentioned he'd brought a daughter and young son with him."

George gestured toward the boys. "Her younger brother, Albert, was the one we sent to get you. He's doing his best to make the stowaway feel comfortable."

Alice smiled at the sheriff. "I'm happy to report we have a name for him. Albert was able to get him to reveal his name, Hans. I told him to keep pursuing more information."

The sheriff put his hands in his pockets and blew out air. "Last thing I want is to have anything to do with that invading Army."

Sheriff Carter's comment did not surprise George. The sheriff made no secret of his opposition to the Union cause and their Army encampment within the county.

"You're aware I've been making a weekly delivery to the camp?"

Sheriff Carter frowned. "Heard about it. Can't say I think it's a good thing."

"Yes, sir. But I hope to deliver their supplies and keep the peace between them and the town. Otherwise, they might go back to stealing from the locals if they don't get their deliveries."

The sheriff nodded. "Mighty dangerous situation. Dawson told me he had to find someone with Union leanings to deliver the orders. You watch your back, son. I know you fought for the Union but were out of it. Now you've jumped right back in."

George resisted the urge to argue any further. "As far as the boy, tomorrow I'll return to the camp and explain what's happened. I won't take the boy with me. He needs to regain his strength. It appears he's been sick or near starved. Not sure which. Miss Zimmerman has volunteered to take him to Mrs. Schumacher's place with her and nurse him back to health. Since they can talk to him, I think that's a good idea."

"You going to that camp alone?" The sheriff eyed George for a moment. "Or you want me to go with you?"

"I'd rather go alone, sir. They know me now. They haven't given me a bit of trouble. One sergeant has been my initial contact and unofficial escort while I make deliveries. I suspect I could explain the situation to him without incident."

The sheriff nodded. "If you're believing that's the way to do it, then that's the way we'll handle this. You've always been sensible, except for this delivery idea." Carter shifted his weight. "To be honest, I figure my appearance out there might rile them up. They know which way I lean, if you know what I mean."

"I do."

The sheriff turned to Alice. "Let's clarify that I've assessed the situation and I'm allowing you to take the boy home to nurse back to health. I'll write a report saying just that."

"Thank you, sheriff. I think we'll be able to help him."

"Does he need a doctor?"

Alice didn't hesitate to answer. "I don't believe so, sir. He was overheated. Combined with the fact that he's just skin and bones, the heat harmed him more than it would a healthy boy. I think some nourishing food and rest will cure him."

George puffed with pride at Alice's confident manner. He liked the determination she had when she felt she was doing the right thing.

Carter nodded at Alice and turned to George. "Report to the sergeant that I asked you to approach them on my behalf. I want them to understand I've taken control of the lad. You're my appointed messenger to explain what happened."

"I understand."

"Come to the jail when you get back in town tomorrow. I want to know what happens. They may fight me and say this is a military matter. They might even insist we return the boy. If they do, I'll look into how to prevent them from taking control."

"Thank you."

After the Sheriff watched the boys for another moment, he added, "Take him now. Don't say anything about this. The fewer wagging tongues we have regarding this matter, the better."

"I'll follow her home and make sure all goes well." George glanced at Alice and she seemed pleased with that idea.

"Can the boy walk?"

Alice turned toward the boys. "We haven't asked him to yet. We carried him here from the wagon."

George turned to the sheriff. "I'll bring Alice's buggy close to the barn doors and we'll get him out of here."

The sheriff nodded. "Get the buggy, and I'll carry him."

As George limped off to do the sheriff's bidding, he noticed Alice radiated happiness about the sheriff's agreement to allow Hans to recuperate at her family farm. Even if it was only temporary, George hoped she would remember he helped make it happen.

W hen George arrived at the Union camp, unexpected and with no supplies, his reception differed significantly from his previous experiences.

A young soldier with a rifle nearly as long as he was stepped forward and pointed the weapon straight at George. "Halt. State your business."

George pulled Buster to a stop. "I'm George Hunter. I'm unarmed. I need to talk to Sergeant Samuels."

"Why?"

"I had a stowaway from your camp in my wagon yesterday."

The soldier stepped closer. "Get off your horse. Hitch him up over there." He gestured toward a shady area with a water trough. "Follow me."

In silence, the men walked toward the headquarters area of the camp. As they grew near, a middle-aged lieutenant appeared and approached them. The young soldier explained why George was there, then returned to his watch assignment area.

The lieutenant appraised George for a moment, then spoke. "Seen you here before, I believe."

"Yes, sir. I deliver supplies to the camp every week."

The man frowned. "You were here yesterday. What could you possibly need from Sergeant Samuels today?"

"Sir, I had a stowaway from camp yesterday. He hid in a barrel in my wagon. It was a young boy. Didn't know he was hiding there until I got back into town. He nearly died from the heat. I need to know his association to this camp. Then we'll figure out what to do about him, sir."

The lieutenant nodded. "I think I know that boy." He sighed. "It's a sad situation. I believe Sarge is the best one to handle this. I'll send a runner to get him." He turned and strode into a nearby tent. Within a moment, a young soldier popped through the tent flaps and raced down the hill toward "tent city."

The middle-aged lieutenant didn't return, leaving George standing in the morning sun, dripping with sweat. With his detached reception from the camp guards, George decided against aggravating anyone by relocating into the shade. At least Buster had a decent place to wait.

Several minutes later, Sergeant Samuels approached the hill toward headquarters, red-faced and stomping with anger. When Samuels reached the top, he was wheezing from the effort. His face was so red it looked like it might burst into flames. He stormed into the headquarters tent without a glance toward George, reappearing a few minutes later. The sergeant's eyes scanned the field until they settled on him.

George approached the livid man as quickly as he could. "I'm sorry you had to come up here, Sergeant. I wasn't given the choice to come to you."

Samuels narrowed his eyes. "Whatever made you come here better be important. I have a job to do."

"Yes, sir. I needed to report I had a stowaway in my wagon yesterday. A young boy."

Samuels jerked in surprise. "A boy? One of ours?"

"Appears he was, but we're not for certain. He doesn't seem to speak English. Thin lad. About eight to ten years old. Looks sickly or starved, or both. I might have seen him here before. Maybe a drummer boy? Do you know him?"

Samuels nodded as he looked down. "I think I know exactly who it is. We call him 'Lost' but that's not his real name, of course. Someone joked we should call him 'Hungry,' because we can't feed him enough. He has never spoken here. At least, not as far as I know."

"He's not an official drummer boy?"

"No. One of our boys spotted him wandering along the banks of a stream in northern Missouri, trying to catch a fish with his hands. Our drummer boy thought he was starving and snuck him into his tent to feed him and gave him some clothes. No one ever came looking for him. We inquired about him at a local community, but they didn't know him. When we moved out to come here, we brought him with us."

"He didn't communicate with anyone while here?"

Samuels shook his head. "Nope. I thought he was deaf until the boys taught him to play the drums. Figured you can't play when you're deaf. I guessed he must be a mute."

"Was the boy ever sick since he's been here?"

"Never. Just so thin. It's been a struggle to put some flesh on his bones."

George explained how the heat had hurt the boy when he was discovered inside the barrel. He also told Samuels about Alice finding out what appeared to be the boy's native language.

The sergeant removed his cap and wiped his handkerchief over his sweating brow. "I'm ashamed of myself. We should have figured out he was a foreigner and spoke an unfamiliar language. I thought he was touched or simple."

"I assume no one in camp speaks German?"

"Not that I know of. Most of the guys here are Irish, from Illinois and other parts north. Some speak Gaelic. I think that's the only language besides English."

"So you have no hold on him?"

"None that's legal. A few of the boys are right fond of him, silent though he was. They'll want him back."

"He's being cared for by a local farm family. They all speak German. They're willing to nurse him back to health, and the sheriff agreed to let them take him home."

"The sheriff?" Samuels's face clouded. "We know all about the sheriff. Why is that Southern sympathizer involved?"

George spoke cautiously. "Sergeant Samuels, when I discovered the boy, and it became obvious he would recover from his ordeal, we called in the law. Regardless of his leanings, Sheriff Carter is still our sheriff. I had to report what happened."

Samuels spat in the dirt. "He sent you here to be his messenger? Too afraid to show his face?"

"Nothing like that, Sergeant. He offered to come with me, but I wanted to come alone. You and I have developed a sense of trust between each other from my deliveries."

The sergeant grunted.

"I'm walking a thin line trying to keep the peace between this Army and my town. You must be aware this town is split nearly down the middle between Union and Confederate. Many dislike me making the deliveries."

"I'm aware."

"I don't want a young boy to suffer because of a wrong step

I've made. Do you object to the boy recovering with the local family?"

Samuels hesitated, then seemed to decide. "Let them nurse the boy back to health. Maybe they'll find out where he belongs. How he got here."

"Any idea why he picked yesterday to stowaway on my wagon? Was he having problems with someone?"

Samuels shrugged. "Nope. I'll ask around about that. His friends need to know this escape nearly killed the boy. And I'll let them know what's happened to him. We all want the best for him. Just keep your sheriff out of dealings with us. Do we have a deal?"

"Yes, sir." George stuck out his hand and Samuels shook it. "If you'll accompany me to my saddlebag over there in the shade, I have something I'd like to give you."

Samuels's eyes twinkled. "Does it have anything to do with a finer cut of chewing tobacco?"

"Let's just say that the mercantile owner, Mr. Dawson, understood that keeping you happy was key. Especially since it was his wagon that rolled away with a stowaway."

Samuels clapped George on his shoulder. "Good man, that Dawson. Thank him for me."

As GEORGE RETURNED TO TOWN, his thoughts were on Hans. Called 'Lost' by those who found him, unable to speak to his rescuers, he had squeaked out a lonely, silent existence in a camp bursting with men and boys.

Dear God, I ask you to show me how to help Hans. To give him what he needs. To guide him to You and his family on earth, so...

George's prayer was interrupted by sounds of breaking limbs

in the nearby woods. Here in the wilderness, the dirt road was empty of travelers. The sounds he heard could be a dog, a wild animal, or something more nefarious. A scan of the trees to his right revealed nothing. As he swung his head toward the left, a figure atop a horse stepped out from behind a clump of bushes. He spurred Buster to move faster out of instinct, then sighed in relief when he spotted who it was. He pulled Buster to a stop.

"Will. You surprised me. What are you doing?"

The unexpected visitor guided his horse around a tree and up to the road. "Better question is, what are you doing? Today isn't Friday."

George frowned. "No, it's Saturday. I had business at the camp."

Will brought his horse to George, where they faced down on horseback, nearly eye to eye. "What kind of business do you have with those Yankees outside of your deliveries? You know I don't approve. Now you're running there every chance you get?"

"Let me explain, Will. Yesterday, I had a stowaway on board my wagon. I had to go to the camp and set things right. I did it for everyone, Union or Southern."

Will shook his head from frustration. "I can't protect you if you go above and beyond your original agreement."

"Protect me? I appreciate your protection, but I've volunteered for this. I don't want you to get hurt trying to help me."

"You can't do this alone. There are men out there who want your hide. Right now. Simply because you're aiding the invading Army."

"Those men who want my hide are fellows I called friends before this conflict became a war." George sighed in exasperation. "And you're wrong about an 'invading Army' because Missouri's still part of the Union, Will. The Army isn't invading. It's OUR Army."

"It may be your Army, but it ain't mine." Will pointed a finger at him. "You keep doing this, and I can't stop them from hurting you. They want to put an end to your deliveries. When they figure out how, you'll be their target."

"I'm willing to take that risk. Don't they realize if I don't deliver these supplies, the Army'll return to stealing from local folks? Then the local people will retaliate by shooting the soldiers. Then the soldiers will shoot back. There is no reason people on both sides of this conflict should end up dead. I'm trying to keep the peace. For my town. Regardless of anybody's politics."

Will stiffened. "George, you and I have been friends for years. I'm not willing to stand by and let you get hurt. You almost didn't survive your short term as a Union soldier. I saw your suffering when you were healing. Don't let all your pain be for nothing. I don't want you killed for something here in town."

George's fury faded. "Of course. You're a good friend. The best. I'm sorry I was angry. You were there when I woke up at home. You helped Papa run our place when I was gone. There's no better friend than you."

"So, figure out a way to stop the deliveries."

"And how do I stop them from taking—no, outright stealing—their supplies from the locals again if I do? Then my neighbors and friends are going to die. To make these deliveries, I'm putting God and my neighbors above my personal safety."

"People understand you're trying to help, but you can't be perceived as being more sympathetic to the Union."

"But I am more sympathetic to the Union. I volunteered to

serve. I was willing to give my life for it. I still will, if that's what happens with these deliveries."

"The Union loaded you onto a board and put you on a train bound for home, thinking you were as good as dead from your wounds. The rest of us figured that might have hardened your heart a bit."

"Maybe. But not enough to change my feelings. Do you need to tell your friends we've severed our friendship? If you do, I would understand."

Will grinned. "They would never believe such a thing if I said it. Which I won't."

"I thank you for trying to warn me. If you hear of anything specific, I'd appreciate you telling me. I know this puts you in danger."

"Enough of this." Will spun his horse toward town. "When this war is over, one of us will be right and the other wrong. Will it make any difference to us?"

"I doubt it."

"I agree. We'll still be friends. You got yourself into this mess, but I'll help you get out of it, if I can. When you figure it out, let me know." He spurred his mount.

George smiled as Will rode away.

God, thank you for giving me my best friend, Will. Please keep him from harm as he tries to keep me from harm. I would also appreciate any solutions to supply the Union without upsetting the locals.

8

When George arrived at the Schumacher farm, Mrs. Schumacher insisted upon escorting him into the parlor. "So good to see you. Please take a seat." She gestured to a sofa and took his hat, hanging it on a stand near the front door.

He remained standing. "I'm quite dusty, Mrs. Schumacher. I don't think it's wise for me to occupy a chair in your best receiving room."

"It will be fine for you to sit, George."

"I stopped by because I know Miss Zimmerman has been waiting for news about my activities related to Hans. In addition, I wanted to see how he's feeling today."

The sound of the boys calling out to each other reached them.

Mrs. Schumacher smiled. "You can hear that Hans and Albert are getting along very well. They've been playing all day. Quietly, at least until now. It's been a blessing having him here. Albert loves having a friend. We've also refreshed our German by speaking it with Hans."

George nodded. "That is good news. Is he looking better? Getting stronger?"

Alice entered the parlor wearing an apron over a pale blue dress. "Mr. Hunter. I've been on pins and needles, wondering how things were going today. So good of you to come." She turned her back to her aunt. "Will you help me get this apron off? I knotted it, trying to remove it when I heard it was Mr. Hunter, and ..." Her face turned red.

The blue of her dress matched those eyes he'd already admired many times. He didn't realize he was staring until Mrs. Schumacher cleared her throat. He stammered, then changed the subject. "I was telling your aunt that I'm too dusty to sit, but I have some information to relay that should make all of you happy."

Freed of the apron, Alice smoothed her skirt. "Please, sit down."

George looked around the room. He resolved not to ruin the good furniture.

"Over there. On that wooden chair, if you're worried about dirt," Mrs. Schumacher said. "Tell us everything."

George sat in the chair suggested once Mrs. Schumacher and Alice sat on the divan. "The Army said they know nothing about this boy's background. They never figured out he couldn't speak English."

Alice asked, "Are they claiming any hold on him?"

"No, not now. Likely no time in the future, either."

She breathed a sigh of relief. "I'm delighted to hear that. But what about Hans? Did they say where he came from?"

"The sergeant said one of their drummer boys spotted him trying to catch a fish with his bare hands in northern Missouri. They checked with a community in the area, but no one recognized him. When the Army moved, they brought him with them."

"Poor lad."

"They called him by the nickname 'Lost' at the camp. The sergeant joked that they later realized they should have named him 'Hungry' because he's always hungry. The sergeant seemed glad you discovered the boy's language and will provide a place for him. I got the impression they want what's best for him."

Mrs. Schumacher asked, "What about the sheriff? Did you go see him too?"

"I did. He seemed relieved the Army had no hold on the boy. There is no reason for him to deal with the Army. He sends his regards to you, Mrs. Schumacher, and said he'll stop by in a few days to check on Hans."

Alice looked as if she was going to ask him another question, but her attention was diverted to Mrs. Schumacher as she rubbed her swollen fingers. "Are your hands hurting again?"

Mrs. Schumacher stilled her hands and a flush crept across her cheeks. "I was reading. I must have done it too long. The weight of books makes my fingers hurt when I hold them too long. It's not an easy burden to have these weaknesses."

Alice's expression took on a look of sadness. "I'm so sorry you have that complaint. Reading is one of your great joys."

"I will persevere." Her aunt smiled. "God never gives us more than we can handle."

Alice gently patted her aunt's swollen hands, then turned to George. "This is all such good news. Hans seems to feel better, and we've even found a hint about where he might be from."

Mrs. Schumacher said to Alice, "Go get the *weihnachtspyamide*."

George pulled a face. "The what?"

Alice stood, and George jumped to his feet, as a gentleman should.

She smiled. "That word roughly translates to what Germans call a Christmas pyramid. Aunt Berta has part of the original piece. Be right back. I think you'll love it."

While Alice was gone, Mrs. Schumacher explained. "Because of some words he uses, we wondered if Hans is from the area of Bavaria where our family originated. Then I thought of some of our family Christmas ornaments my mother gave me when I moved here. Alice showed them to him and he called them by their names. He's familiar with craft items found in the Erzgebirge Mountain region."

Alice returned with a box. She removed miniature carvings of Mary, Joseph, and baby Jesus in the manger. Her face was radiant as she handled each item with care and placed them on the table. All the pieces of the set were wooden and unpainted.

Mrs. Schumacher explained, "My father brought my mother, brother, and me to America in 1845. We took a steamboat, the *Resilient*, I believe, down the Arkansas River, which ran aground in a storm. There was such confusion, but my father got us to safety before volunteering to help the steamboat crew. We never saw him again after that. Later we discovered he died in the accident somehow. Whether he drowned or got hurt by something remains a mystery."

"That is so sad," George said.

Mrs. Schumacher nodded. "My mother, now left a widow, eventually took us back to her relatives in Massachusetts. This nativity set was part of the cherished items my mother brought from the Old Country, most lost in the steamboat's wreck. My father made it for my mother as an anniversary gift before we sailed here. We understand that when the set was found in Arkansas, a woman worked hard, with the help of the local blacksmith, to discover who owned it and returned it to our family."

George picked up the tiny Joseph figurine. "Did the steamboat catch on fire? This appears to have suffered some scorching damage."

"I don't believe so. My mother said they were damaged in an explosion in a blacksmith forge. I was a girl at the time. I didn't get many details about how it happened."

"I understand, Aunt Berta," Alice said. Then she turned to George. "The traditional piece would have been a much larger tiered carving with spinning paddles at the top. The paddles would revolve, powered by heat from small candles. The nativity scene would be at the base of the structure."

"Really? I've seen nothing like that before," George said.

"Traditionally, it would have shepherds, sheep, a donkey, the three wise men, and the angel. Unfortunately, we lost all those pieces in the explosion or the riverboat's wreck."

George studied the remaining pieces as Alice talked. Could he improve his skills enough to match the expertise shown in these figurines and replace the missing items? They were so tiny, smaller than any he'd attempted before. Though unpainted, they were polished to a sheen through the hard work of oil and smoothing cloths. He knew better than to try to replace the whole tiered, spinning design. Perhaps he had the skills to carve the figurines.

George noticed his interest in the carvings pleased Alice. He studied the carving of baby Jesus. He'd wanted appropriate wooden pieces for his brother, Frankie, to play with in church. He could practice replacing these pieces by carving a miniature nativity set for Frankie.

Alice treated each item with reverence. She loved this set. It showed on her face and the protective way she handled each piece.

That settled it. He could practice by working on a set for Frankie. Then he could do a collection for Hans and Albert too. When he'd improved his skills, he'd attempt to replace the missing nativity pieces from this set for Mrs. Schumacher. Then, he'd carve an entirely new set for Alice, one that belonged only to her. She would have a complete copy of her aunt's set. Perhaps showing her how much time and effort he put in to make things she cherished would catch her attention.

"I see you like them too," Alice said. "As a wood carver, you can appreciate them, can't you?"

"I surely do." George smiled. "I'm of German descent. Sadly, I don't know of any heirlooms like these in my family. We've been in America too long, I suppose. I appreciate you teaching me things I should already know."

She smiled at his compliment.

He also wondered if there was something he could make that might help Mrs. Schumacher enjoy reading again. Some sort of stand to hold the weight of the book for her. With the weight of the book off her hands, she should enjoy reading again. He would have to think about it.

After Alice repacked the set, the three walked to the kitchen. They'd made a pallet for Hans by the fire.

The reaction Hans had to his entering the kitchen pleased George. The boy seemed happy to see him, and George was glad to spot some color in his cheeks.

Alice translated for Hans what George had determined today. When she finished, Hans was beaming.

George asked, "What did you tell him? Just now, that made him so happy?"

"He was told that he would stay here. The Army wished him well, and the sheriff would visit in a few days. I don't know a word for sheriff in German, so I substituted a phrase that means roughly 'the man in charge.'"

"Thank you for keeping him." He looked at both Alice and Mrs. Schumacher as he spoke. "For giving him a home and speaking the language he speaks. Please keep working on what he can tell you about himself. Such as where he comes from or how he ended up alone. If you get enough information to search for relatives, I'd like to help."

"Thank you, George, for all you've done for him," Mrs. Schumacher said. "He can stay here as long as he likes. If we can't find any family for him, he can become part of ours."

Alice beamed. "Oh, Aunt Berta. Thank you. I've been worrying about what he's been through and what might happen to him. Now we don't have to worry about his future."

George nodded. "Mighty nice thing to offer, Mrs. Schumacher."

Mrs. Schumacher blushed. "No need for us to get soft about it. When Otto died and left me alone, I was sad and lonely. With the house filled with family, God's given me a purpose again." She gestured at the boy. "I feel he's part of God's purpose too. If we can't return him to his family, we can see if he enjoys farming."

Alice nodded. "Town offers work opportunities too. He'll have several paths to choose from when he gets older."

"Speaking of paths, it's time for me to go. I need to take the path to my farm and get to work." George moved toward the front of the house. "Let me know if you need anything. For him or the farm."

He rode home, pondering how to create those tiny carved figurines. At least with his idea of making three sets, he should improve his skills with each group of figures. He might have to get pointers from Private Martin and Corporal Danny to improve his technique. It would take a lot of work. But Alice was worth it.

9

December arrived, reminding Audrain County citizens of the harsh reality of winter. The afternoon before, the sky produced freezing rain. That, along with frigid temperatures, continued through the night.

George, his father, and Frankie were up long before dawn. They had much to do to care for their animals in miserable weather. His mother and Mary rose early to cook for everyone. They also threw more wood on the fire to fight the cold and dampness inside.

Frankie's chores included going to the henhouse with fresh water and coarse-ground corn. With weather this cold, the chickens needed sustenance while they remained shut in the coop for the storm's duration. He hurried back to the house with the few eggs he'd gathered, slipping and sliding to the kitchen.

George and his father cleaned stalls in the barn, then returned the horses and mules with the addition of water and fresh hay. It was a day when the livestock would best dwell inside.

"We're going to have to check that water throughout the day," Pa said. "We must make sure it isn't freezing. Frankie will have to check on the chickens too."

"I'll take care of the barn animals, sir. But today's Friday and I have another delivery to make. I'll check them before I leave and when I return."

"Are the roads too icy to get a wagon to the camp?"

"Let me look." George went to the barn doors and pushed one open wider to study the results of the freezing rain. When he returned, he said, "It appears it's not freezing on the ground. Just on the tree limbs."

"You need to watch the temperature. If the day doesn't warm, ice accumulation on tree limbs covering the roads could fall and hurt you or Buster."

"I'll do that. Thanks."

They worked in silence for a few minutes before George paused again and returned to his father. "I know you don't like these deliveries. I appreciate you not trying to convince me to stop them. You know they're dangerous, even without freezing rain, and yet, you support me."

Pa pushed his pitchfork into the soft dirt and leaned against it. "You, George, are a grown man, able to make your own decisions."

George nodded.

"If you believe these deliveries will help keep the peace in town, then I support you in wanting to do them. What I can't do is stop the worrying I have about your safety. Every day, I pray to God to keep you safe. So far, He's done a good job. Back when you came home wounded and near death, your recovery was nothing less than a miracle. I put it down to prayer. I've always believed in the power of prayer, but God seems to use you to prove it beyond any doubt."

"Perhaps you better pray for God to ease your worry."

His father smiled. "I suggest you're the one who should ask God to ease my worry. If I didn't care about you, I wouldn't worry. Now, get back to your chores. You need to make that delivery."

BECAUSE OF AN IMPROVEMENT in the weather, George made it to Dawson's safely and relatively dry, thanks to his heavy overcoat. Johnny ran out of the mercantile as George rode Buster into the barn.

"We weren't sure you'd show up," Johnny said. "Save a spot for the perishables. Grandpa didn't want them loaded until he knew you were taking the delivery today."

George dried off Buster as best he could and gave him some water. Then he and Johnny went to get the rest of the supplies.

Mr. Dawson approached and shook George's hand. "Wasn't sure you were going to make it today, George. I should have known I could always count on you."

After they loaded the perishables, George and Johnny covered the wagon bed with several horse blankets to keep the items dry. They secured the blankets with rope because of the windy conditions. Then George hitched Buster to the wagon and led the horse back into the rain.

"Take care, George. It's a horrible day."

"Every day God gives me is a good day. Thanks for your help, Johnny." The rain had George hunkering down in his damp overcoat. He grimaced. His hands would take the worst of the trip—even covered in gloves—continuously exposed to the rain and near freezing temperatures. No help for that.

On this gloomy morning, the thought of visiting Alice on his way home was a bright one. Lately, he'd been stopping by to see her every time he returned from his army camp deliveries. She seemed to appreciate his attentions, and his fondness for her increased with every encounter. As someone who'd previously admired women from afar, she'd captivated his interest immediately. He couldn't keep his distance from her and didn't want to try.

She was polite and kind to him, but he didn't know if her feelings went further. What could he offer her? Part interest in a farm? Scraping out a living for a family, raising a small crop and some animals. All that was available to him was a tough life for a woman.

ALICE SCANNED the landscape from the window again. It was near dusk, but there was no older horse making its way down the lane.

Aunt Berta called out to her. "Maybe he canceled because of the weather? It's a right terrible day to be out. Perhaps he's going to make the delivery tomorrow."

"I don't believe he'd let some rain stop him. Even freezing rain. Something's wrong."

"Did you see him go by this morning?"

Alice shook her head. "No. But I was working in the kitchen. I can't see the road from there." Then, after a pause, she added, "Maybe the wagon broke down or his horse went lame."

Aunt Berta nodded. "Those things are possible. You've been pacing for an hour. Can't you settle somewhere for a moment? If I was speculating, I'd say you're quite fond of that young man."

"I'm worried about him. I guess that means I *am* fond of him. If I've judged his character correctly, he would not be late except for some mishap."

"You won't let the worry go?"

"No, ma'am."

"Well then. You must act. Run and call your father in from the barn. Maybe he'll go to the Hunter place. If George took the delivery today, they'd know when to expect him back. If he's past due, your father can help with the search for him."

Alice brightened. "Thank you. I know in my heart something's wrong. I feel it." Then she scurried to find her pa.

GEORGE WOKE WITH A START. His head pounded. Was he having a nightmare?

He tried to piece together images and memories he'd had right before he woke up. What brought him to this place?

It took a moment or two to realize his hands were numb. He looked down. In the dim light of the space, he could see well enough to tell his hands were tied together with rope.

He remembered pulling up to Dawson's barn, loading the wagon, and heading out to the encampment. Did he make the delivery? After thinking a moment, he realized he didn't know.

Where was he? His mind was murky. He wasn't sure about anything.

His stomach growled. Add in his powerful thirst, and he knew he had to take action somehow. His tongue felt sandy. Lips were dry. How long had he gone without water?

He might be thirsty, but his britches were wet. That must be from the rain today. Surely it was still today. He wouldn't have slept so long that the whole day had passed. At least he hoped that hadn't happened.

He squinted to make out shapes in the dimness. A shed or barn gave him a bit of shelter. Light filtered through the cracks in the boards that ran along the sides and roof. He was seated in straw in a dry area. The gable above him was the only area that seemed solid. Water dripped nearby, and it made him all the thirstier.

His legs were also tied together at the ankles. With a shift of his weight, he could roll onto his side. He rolled onto his stronger side and rose to his knees. Hobbling over to an area with a leak, he turned his mouth up to the raindrops. The moisture eased a tiny bit of his discomfort.

Someone kidnapped him. The Audrain Rangers? Another group of Southern-leaning men? Either way, they wanted his deliveries to stop, and now they'd crossed the line into action. He tried, but couldn't remember how they got him or where it happened. He remembered nothing beyond leaving Dawson's and going toward the encampment.

Why had they hauled him into this desolate shack? They could have shot him along the road and left him. Why put him in hiding?

He worked to make sense of it all. Were they trying to negotiate a payment for his release? Who had the money for such a thing? George's stomach dropped. His parents didn't have much, but they'd use everything they had as a bargaining chip for his safe return. Including their farm. They loved him that much.

Dear Lord, I've been selfish to think I could handle these deliveries. Now my folks may pay the price for my decision. Please keep them from suffering because of me.

If his parents paid for his release, his kidnappers would use the ransom against the military, creating even more animosity and hostility toward the citizens on both sides of the war.

Maybe they wanted to kill him, just had to wait for a better time. After dark rather than in daylight. If they wanted to halt deliveries to the Army, killing him or ransoming him would ensure no one else would consider delivering the supplies.

The light outside grew dimmer. His thoughts turned to Alice. She would have been expecting him to visit. She would know something was wrong by now. How much time had passed? No way to know in here. Would she worry? How long it would take her to switch from expecting him to worrying about him, to getting a search party sent? Too long to save him.

To live another day, he must figure out a way to escape.

God, please hear my prayer ...

10

Once Papa left for the Hunter farm, Alice resumed pacing. Her instincts communicated something was terribly wrong. Her father had refused to let her be a part of the search. He told her it was "man's work." That she had no business being involved. His bold statements made her resent being a woman, perceived as incapable of a search to find George.

"Alice," her aunt called. "Please come here. We need to pray together."

While her aunt remained seated, Alice fell to her knees beside her. They prayed silently together for several minutes. Then Aunt Berta prayed aloud, requesting God's holy support.

When Aunt Berta finished, Alice stood and hugged her aunt. "Thank you for knowing exactly what I could do for George. It's terrible to feel powerless when your heart hurts."

"Asking for God's help is always the right thing to do. Then, accepting the path He's chosen for us is usually the next step. Sometimes that can be hard."

"How did you know marrying Uncle Otto was the right

path for you? Choosing to accept him took you away from all you knew."

"Yes, it did."

"He brought you to Missouri, where you had no friends or family. That must have been a hard decision for you."

"Yet, it was where God led me, and I'm so happy He did. Sit down, dear, and I'll tell you about it." Aunt Berta patted the space beside her.

Alice took a seat and tried to relax.

"You were wrong to say I had no friends or family here."

"Really? Who was here?"

"I had two members of my family with me. My husband and God. That was all the family I needed. I yearned for more, but God and Otto helped me through the hard times. I relied on both of them when I developed rheumatic fever and it weakened my heart. But I recovered, even if I some weaknesses linger. When I recovered enough to get out and about, I made friends. Many are still nearby. These ladies taught me so many things, and each one brought me joy. They taught me how to accept my condition and not try to do too much, how to be a better cook, how to make rag rugs, and how to laugh."

"But didn't you feel separated from the rest of your family?"

"Christmas would have been the hardest for me, but Mama prepared me for that. I believe it's the reason she sent me here with what was left of the family's nativity set."

"How clever of her."

Aunt Berta nodded. "She knew it meant so much to me, even as a child. Before it was damaged. My father made it for her, but she let me take it. As our time in Missouri passed, I understood she gave it to me so I'd have a piece of my family's legacy. A reminder of my family to help me celebrate the birth of Christ with a full and happy heart. I wasn't discouraged by longing for what I couldn't have."

"Christmas is almost here. We need to display your nativity," Alice said. "Somewhere high enough so Albert and Hans can't get to it."

Aunt Berta grinned. "Perhaps on the mantel above the fireplace?"

Alice eyed the spot and nodded. "That should work." Then she turned to her aunt. "Do you have a solution for my feelings for George?"

"I don't understand."

"Is he the right man for me? How do I know?"

"Does he cherish you?"

"I believe he's quite fond of me."

"A man who will cherish you is rare, but I found one in your Uncle Otto. Building a life with a man who loves you like that," she paused. "It's a gift from God. May I say, a rare gift from God."

"How did you and Uncle Otto stay happy all the time?"

"We didn't. There were many hard times. Also, there were many sad times when we were forced to be apart. Marriage is not about happiness as much as it's about love. We loved each other through the good and the difficult times."

"It sounds challenging."

"It's work. It's a choice you make to strengthen the bond between you. Our biggest disappointment was that we were not blessed with children. Now, because of your mother's and my Otto's early loss, I think God's plan was for me to be alone when your mother was taken."

"Why would he do that? It sounds cruel."

"Through my need for someone to run the farm, God provided a place for my brother to come and overcome his grief. For him to have a purpose in life. For his children to have another woman to love them. God provided children to me in the form of a beautiful niece and a handsome nephew."

"I've never thought about our circumstances that way."

"You've been such a blessing to take over the household chores. My health no longer allows me to do much. And now God's added another boy. He needs a home and a family who will love him."

"And I'm essential to keep this household running. God's chosen path for me is to take care of my family. I can't possibly add a husband to that."

Aunt Berta frowned. "I don't see why not. God placed a respectable man at the adjoining farm. A man who appears to have captured your heart. If George cares for you as much as you care for him, he'll work it out."

"How?"

"George, his father, and brother can work with your father and brother and handle both farms. None of us will starve between his mother, sister, and you. My job will be to love all of you."

They shared a smile.

"Thank you, Aunt Berta. I feel better. But I'm still worried about George and where he must be."

"The rain has stopped, so the weather is improving. You must trust God's plan. Have faith in God's love for you and that special man named George."

GEORGE'S FATHER, Ernst, was in the barn saddling one of his horses when he heard an approaching rider. Was it George? Had he returned? He ran out of the barn only to see Klaus Zimmerman riding down the lane.

It was an odd time for Zimmerman to pay a call. Ernst's

211

stomach lurched. Did he have news of George? He stood firm, though his worry washed over him like an ocean wave. Something terrible must have happened to George. Otherwise, he'd be home by now.

As Klaus drew near, he stopped. "Alice was worried, so she asked me to come here." From atop his horse, he stated the obvious, "George is not here."

Ernst shook his head and turned back toward the barn.

Klaus dismounted, leading the horse into the barn behind him. "Tell me how I can help."

Ernst continued saddling his horse. "I'm going to report him missing to the sheriff. I hope he'll put a search party together."

"Fine. I'll be part of that search party. Want me to pick up Dawson on our way to the sheriff?"

Ernst nodded. "I'll take anyone willing to help."

"At least we have several hours before dark, and the rain has stopped."

Ernst mounted his horse. "Thank the Lord for small favors. Now let's see if He'll grant me a huge one. One that lets me bring George home safely."

SHERIFF CARTER KNEW George was not the type to make his family worry. After being briefed about the situation with George, Carter issued orders to his deputy on duty.

"Go round up the other deputies. Then gather some more men. We need anyone willing to help search for George. Have them meet here. Once you've done that, I want some of you to ride to the Union encampment. Look for signs of a broken wagon or an altercation between George and some ruffians."

He looked at Dawson. "He was out in your wagon?"

"Yes, sir."

"No sign of the wagon or the horse since George left?"

"No, sir."

"When did he leave your place?"

"I'd guess about ten or so this morning."

The sheriff turned to Ernst and Klaus. "I'll be right back. Don't leave without me. When I return, we'll divide up North, South, East, and West. I'm going to gather some extra men. One man in particular."

Sheriff Clark walked at a fast clip to the local men's boarding house. A certain young man named Will Winston was boarding there while he worked at the tannery in town.

At the boarding house, Carter didn't bother to knock. He pushed open the front door and strode into the dining area. He found Mrs. Abercrombie standing with a platter of biscuits in her hand near a table covered with food and surrounded by hungry men.

Carter tipped his hat. "Sorry to barge in, ma'am. I'm on business of the law."

He spotted Will at the far end of the table. "Will. Your friend George left for the encampment at ten o'clock this morning and hasn't come home."

The blood drained from Will's face. Visual proof that George's best friend wasn't involved in his disappearance.

Will stood up. "What's happened?"

"We don't know. But we're going to find out. Go get your horse."

"He's at the livery. Wait for me while I saddle him."

"Come to my office when you're ready. While saddling him, think about where your friends might have taken him. Places you know beyond the town. Where no one could hear what's going on. Assuming they haven't already killed him and left him on the side of the road."

Will groaned and ran from the table.

The other men mumbled to themselves. Many stood and offered to ride along.

"We'll take all we can get. Bring your weapons."

As word spread through the town that George was missing, possibly in trouble, more men arrived at the Sheriff's office to join the search party. Carter expected men would help because that's what folks do, but he was taken aback at the number of volunteers. Old, young, all shapes and sizes, whether their politics were Union or Southern supporters. They came with their horses and guns. With one unifying purpose. To find George and help get him home.

When Will arrived, he gave Sheriff Carter several options for places George might have been taken.

"Which one is the most secluded?"

"There's a crumbling shack west of Davis Creek on the Campbell property. It's several miles out of town."

Carter nodded. "You and I will go there, along with a few others."

Once Carter had the men divided into groups and appointed a deputy as the leader for each group, he said, "Let's ride. If any group finds George, send a runner to alert the rest of us."

Twenty minutes of hard riding brought the party near the shack Will felt was the most likely location.

Carter stopped the group. "Everyone dismount and tie up your mounts here. Will and I will scout the area to see if they're here. One of us will come back for you if we find them. Keep those horses quiet."

"Right, boss."

Will and Sheriff Carter approached the shack with caution. Will spotted a horse he recognized and told Carter who owned it. The sounds of men inside stopped them when they were about a hundred yards away. Angry voices, yelling at each other. As they stepped closer, sounds of a fistfight broke out.

Although unsure if George was there, Carter sent Will back for the rest of their group. "Have them approach the shack on all sides so it will be surrounded."

Within a few moments, the group was stationed around the shack, with every man pointing a loaded gun toward the angry voices erupting from inside. Deputy Benskin joined Sheriff Carter for the potentially dangerous entry.

The sheriff and deputy approached the shed with caution. A few feet away, they sprinted and broke through the shed door.

11

The fight among the angry men stopped when Sheriff Carter and Deputy Benskin burst into the shed. All five young men stared open-mouthed down the rifle barrel Deputy Benskin pointed in their direction. None of them moved.

Sheriff Carter grinned at them as they remained motionless, rendering the Kerr revolver in his hand unnecessary. "Put your hands up! Slowly!"

They complied.

At the sound of someone approaching, the sheriff turned toward the entryway. More of the search party entered, each carrying a drawn weapon. He waved them to various points around the shed.

"You've got nowhere to go. You're all under arrest."

One of the captured men crept his hand toward a pistol strapped to his leg.

Carter pointed his revolver directly at him. "Don't even think about it, Robert. You might be an excellent shot, son, but you're not fast enough for me. I'll gladly tell your mama I shot you for being stupid."

Robert froze.

Carter turned his attention to the other four. One had a bloody nose. "Before we haul you to jail, tell me what you've done with George."

Robert said, "Don't know what you're talking about." He shot a look at Will. "George's good buddy, Will, has been pulling your leg, Sheriff. Nothing has happened to George."

Will aimed his pistol at Robert. "I've nothing to do with this. You made sure I didn't know anything you'd planned. You knew I'd put a stop to it."

"That so?" Robert asked.

The sheriff took a step closer to Robert. "I'm not putting up with your sass. I know Will wasn't involved in this. Tell me what you've done with George, or I'll shoot you dead right where you stand."

Robert eyed him for a moment. "We don't know."

"What do you mean?"

"He's not here. He's escaped. Look over there." Robert gestured with his head toward ropes lying on the straw. "He untied himself."

The sheriff strode over and examined the rope. There was a knot, but the rope showed a clean cut. Cut by a sharp knife. Sheriff Carter burst out laughing. "You pack of fools. Did you check to see if he had his whittling knives?"

Robert's face burned red.

"You dumped him here, tied him up, and returned to get the supplies."

Silence.

"First, you're guilty of kidnapping. Then you tie him up and leave him without checking his pockets." The sheriff regarded the group of captured men. "George Hunter always has whittling knives on him. None of you are as smart as you think you are."

Carter surveyed the other four captives. "Williams. Why is your nose bleeding?"

Williams straightened. "Robert was angry at me for not checking George's pockets. Called me an idiot. I belted him one, and he hit me back."

"Why did you kidnap George?"

No response.

"Do you know what the Army will do if you steal their supplies?"

They all remained silent.

Carter called out, "Deputy?"

Deputy Benskin moved forward. "Yes, sir."

"These men are under arrest for kidnapping. Every one of them. Gather a few men to round up their horses. The rest of you tie them up. Benskin and a few others can take them to jail."

The sheriff gave a steely gaze to the captives.

"I'll contact the Army. It'll be up to them how they want to handle the theft of their goods. No bail considered until the circuit judge makes his way into town." Carter paused for full effect and added, "It could be months."

The captives uttered a few groans.

The group was secured and marched out of the shed at gunpoint by Deputy Benskin and his group. The kidnappers were smart enough to comply, leaving without further incident.

Sheriff Carter called out to those remaining, "Will, Ernst, Klaus, and the rest of you, we'll search for George. He couldn't have gotten very far with us on horseback and him on foot. Especially with that leg of his."

Outside, the remaining search party waited for orders from the sheriff.

He glanced around for a moment. "We have but a few minutes of light left. We'll need to make torches if we're searching in total darkness. We'll be blind without them."

Ernst spoke up. "I'll go back to the shed and look for materials we can use."

Klaus stepped forward. "I'll help you."

The group discussed search options and scouted nearby for George's tracks.

WHEN NO ONE else found any sign of a trail, Will stopped to think. He stared at the surrounding wilderness for a moment.

A familiar sound penetrated his thoughts, and he smiled. The faint music of running water was nearby. Davis Creek. Had to be. Will hadn't realized the shed was situated so close to the creek.

"Sheriff, I think I know which way George walked."

Carter approached. "I'm listening."

"That's my point. Listen. Do you hear that water?"

With a nod from Carter, Will continued. "George and I have always kept close to a creek bank or edge of a river when we're out hunting or fishing. It's the easiest guide to find our way back home or into town."

"Most people do that," Carter said.

"I'm guessing George would have heard the creek and followed it. He'd walk along that bank until he ran across a person, a farm, or something."

"Good thinking. We'll go as soon as we have some torches."

A few minutes later, equipped with makeshift torches, they rode. The men took different angles from the creek.

They spotted tracks in the muddier parts of the creek bed, confirming someone was ahead of them. Taking turns calling out for George, they agreed not to shoot their guns. The sounds might cause George to think his kidnappers followed him.

Eventually, one of their calls was answered by a shout.

The response sounded like George. From Ernst Hunter's reaction, it was confirmed they'd found him.

THE SEARCH PARTY brought a tired but healthy George to the sheriff's office. Some of his rescuers wanted to take him to Doc Bradley's home, but George insisted his only ailment was hunger. When they secured food from the local diner for him and many others who'd missed their supper to search, George was back to normal.

One of the kidnappers confessed to the location of Dawson's wagon and horse during his ride to jail. When Carter's group returned, another group was sent to retrieve them, including Dawson, to identify the wagon and supplies.

Once the food had been consumed, George looked around the room with a sheepish smile. "I must apologize to everyone who helped find me tonight. I thought making deliveries to the Army was a decision that affected only me. When I was tied up in the shed, I realized my actions caused grave consequences for my family. After you all turned out to find me, I understand that my decision also affected the rest of you. Thank you for answering the call to search for me. I'm grateful. I know my family would appreciate it if I pass on the sentiment that they're also grateful to you."

Mr. Hunter stepped close to George. "I'd like to lead this group in a quick prayer of thanks to the Lord."

Heads bowed.

Mr. Hunter prayed his gratitude for the fine citizens of Audrain County coming to their aid. He ended by thanking the Lord for keeping his son safe once again.

"Thanks, Ernst." Sheriff Carter said. Then he patted George on the back. "Before you all depart, I want you to hear this. I've worried about George making these deliveries. I didn't know what to do. Tonight, I figured out exactly what must be done."

He turned to George. "I'm going to appoint you special deputy to the sheriff's office of Audrain County."

George was stunned. "Deputy? With my bum leg?"

Carter chuckled. "The *special* means this, George. It will only be during the time you're delivering to the Army. From the time you leave your home until you return, you will be an acting deputy. I'm ordering you, as my deputy, to make those deliveries. Anyone who interferes will be arrested and charged. Your deliveries will be as a law enforcement officer. You'll have the protection of a badge. No longer will a regular citizen make the deliveries."

Murmurs arose from the gathered men. They'd never heard of such a thing. What was the sheriff thinking?

George turned to his father, who was beaming about the news. George was grateful for the added layer of protection to keep him safe.

Then he turned toward the sheriff. "Are you giving me a choice about this?"

"Nope." Carter surveyed the crowd. "Anybody got a problem with it?"

No one spoke in opposition.

"Then it's settled." Carter strode to his desk, opened a drawer, and handed a silver star to George. "Wear that when you're making deliveries." To the rest of the men, he said, "Go home. We're all grateful for the turnout and your help tonight."

~

GEORGE'S FATHER and Alice's father accompanied him home. On their way, the group sent to recover the wagon reunited George with Buster. He was riding double with his father when they caught up to them. George was never more grateful to be back with the plodding horse.

George petted him and said, "Walk as slow as you want, Buster. Just get me home."

When they neared the Schumacher house, light shone from the windows. It was late. Who would be awake at this hour? It wasn't long before they had an answer.

Although dark, they made out Alice's silhouette as she ran out of the front door and scurried toward them.

"You should be in bed," her father admonished.

"I couldn't sleep. I was too worried about George."

George slid off Buster and approached her with a smiling face. "No reason to be concerned, Miss Zimmerman. I'm back from my adventures in one piece."

"Please, call me Alice. After all my worrying, I think we can dispense with formal address. Don't you think, George?"

"I'm honored, Miss Alice."

Mr. Zimmerman dismounted and led his horse toward the barn. He turned and called over his shoulder, "Maybe you ought to call him Deputy George."

Alice tilted her head. "Why? What happened? Tell me everything."

George turned to his father. "You go on home. I'm sure you're tuckered out. But Miss Alice, here, deserves to hear the full story. I promise I won't be too long. And I'll take care of the animals when I get there."

He held out his hand to Alice.

She took it. "We should sit in the parlor and you can tell me all about it."

With her hand in his, he'd sit wherever she wanted him to. Even out here in the cold. For some reason, the chill wasn't numbing his fingers like it had the whole day.

12

On Christmas Day, George was up before dawn. He scrambled to dress and then raced outside to do his chores and Frankie's. Before they left for church, much work needed to be done.

Last night he'd alerted their father not to wake Frankie. Part of George's present for his brother was giving him a day off from his daily farm duties. Christmas was a good time to give the boy a break.

When George finished and walked inside, Mary and his mother stood beaming at him. He found it strange. Mornings were their busiest time, their faces serious as they focused on preparing breakfast and cleaning up. They spared no time for silly grins under most circumstances. Must be a Christmas thing.

"Why are you two so happy this Christmas morn?"

They continued to grin at him while Mary explained. "We were sworn to secrecy yesterday, but today we can tell you the plan."

"What plan?"

"Alice wants to treat you and our family to a special Christmas dinner. At her house. After church. It's a present from their family to ours."

George grinned. "A wonderful gift. I supposed Mrs. Schumacher is in on the plan too."

"They all are," Mary said.

Mama walked over to the serving dishes that covered the table. The platters held various foods and loaves of breads. "Look at all this."

"It all looks delicious."

"You're getting none of this now." She waved her hand over the food. "We've made you poached eggs and toast. That will have to hold you over until after services." She pushed a small plate toward him. "Sit down and eat. We'll need to go soon."

When George sat down, his sister Mary claimed the chair beside him. "I'm so excited. Alice has been working on her contributions for days. We're going from church services directly to their house. The feast is going to be unforgettable."

"Chicken? Ham? What's in store for us?"

Mary chuckled. "I will not tell you. Let the food be a surprise."

He nodded. "It was nice of them to think of us."

"This was Alice's idea," Mary teased. "She thinks you're pretty special, George. I think she may be sweet on you."

His face reddened. "You're trying to embarrass me. On Christmas Day. Not a charitable thing to do, Mary."

"I figured we'd also do our family present exchange there." Mama turned to Mary. "We need to stop by their house on the way to church. Drop off our contributions to the meal."

Their mother and Mary discussed the best way to load their items into the wagon. Then Mama added, "We could drop our gifts off then, too, if you have them ready. After church, we'll spend the rest of the day at their house. Eating, playing games, and exchanging gifts. It's going to be fun."

George said, "If we're not coming back here, I'll need some baskets, Mama. I'll have presents to leave when we drop off your food."

"A large basket or some small ones?"

"Give me several. I need at least one big one for Mrs. Schumacher's gift. Once I get everything packed up, I'll bring back what I don't need."

With arms overloaded with baskets, George entered the room he shared with Frankie. His brother remained buried within the sheets of the bed. With as much silence as possible, George loaded the presents he'd made. He was proud of his accomplishments and hoped Alice and her family would like them too.

An idea came to him. Once he'd filled the baskets, he gathered them and went to find Mary. He needed to ask her for a favor.

When he found her in the kitchen, he said, "I'd like to use some of your material scraps to wrap some things I've made."

Mary smiled at his request. "I suppose you'll want to tie up your bundles with string or ribbon?"

"Yes. Please."

"Bring everything to the parlor. All but your gift to me. I'll get the scraps and ribbons and help you wrap them. Otherwise, we'll never get to church on time."

Mary made murmurs of delight as they worked together to bundle the gifts. She was impressed by every present he'd made. When George explained the reason behind his gift to Mrs. Schumacher, tears filled Mary's eyes.

"Mrs. Schumacher is going to love what you've done, George. Your gift will be cherished. It gives her favorite pastime back to her."

George eyed Mary. "You think so?"

"Definitely."

"Do you like the nativity set for Alice?"

"If she loves the pieces her aunt has, then giving her a complete set will be a wonderful gift. She'll love them, I'm sure."

George evaluated her sincerity. "It's not fancy. Or expensive."

Mary sighed with exasperation. "George. Don't you know her personality yet? That girl will love that you made her something with your talented hands. Something she admires, but doesn't have. You've created the complete set for her. Believe me. She's going to love it."

FOR THE FIRST TIME, Alice sat beside him at church. It was as if her gift to him this Christmas Day exceeded the feast. She was also giving him the gift of her complete attention while they celebrated the birth of Jesus.

He loved the sound of her singing voice rising high on the hymns. It filled him with a sense of happiness he'd never experienced. Between Alice, her singing, and celebrating Jesus, he felt closer to God than he'd ever felt before. Here in God's house, he realized he loved Alice. *God, please let her love me too.*

THE FAMILIES GATHERED around two tables decorated with cedar branches. Everyone joined hands during the prayer, giving thanks for their abundant meal and the fellowship they would enjoy.

George said, "Alice, you must have been cooking for days."

Thank you for everything that you did. It was an excellent idea."

She beamed at him. "I'm pleased you're pleased."

"Mama and Mary were busy too." He smiled his thanks to them.

Mr. Hunter and Mr. Zimmerman carved the haunch of pork and leg of lamb, passing plates to the eager gathering. Next, vegetables, salads, and finally, delicious desserts were enjoyed.

Without allowing a second to digest their meal, Hans, Albert, and Frankie clamored to open presents.

After some discussion, they appointed Mary to pass out gifts. While she began distributing items, she whispered to George. "I'll do yours last."

When it came time for his gifts, George asked Mary to bring him the large basket. He wanted to start with his unique project for Mrs. Schumacher.

She was sitting on the divan, talking to Mama, when he carried the large basket to her.

"You've given me an enormous gift," Mrs. Schumacher said.

"It is almost a piece of furniture. I will need to make sure it fits for the purpose it's intended. I'll pull it out of the basket, if you don't mind. It might be heavy for your hands."

She nodded. "That would be nice."

George placed the large wrapped item on her lap.

She pulled on the bow and the material fell away, revealing a large wooden tray with legs.

George picked up the tray. "May I place this across your legs?"

Mrs. Schumacher adjusted her skirts while Mary ran to pull a book from the bookshelf.

George lowered the tray, positioning it on the outside of Mrs. Schumacher's legs. "I curved the bottom to sit on your lap in comfort. If it isn't soft enough, a pillow on your lap would lighten the weight." Then he adjusted the top of the tray into a notch he'd cut into the wood, so it held at an angle.

Mary placed the book on the angled part of the tray, and everyone murmured. A tray for holding books while she read them.

Mrs. Schumacher put her arms around the tray and hugged it. She motioned for George to lean closer so she could hug him. Then, eyes brimming with tears, she said, "I couldn't have a better gift. Thank you, George."

"I have another gift for you, but I'd like to do Alice's gift next."

"Please do."

Mary handed George the present they'd wrapped for Alice.

He walked over to Alice and handed her the bundle. "I hope you like this."

She smiled at him and untied the bow, spotting a wooden figurine. "Oh my." Her brow furrowed. "Are these from the Old Country?" She pulled out Joseph, then a shepherd and a tiny sheep. "How did you get them here?"

George chuckled. "I made them."

She stared at him, her mouth falling open. "You made these? You carved them yourself?"

He nodded, filled with pride. "It's a complete nativity set made to look like Mrs. Schumacher's set."

Tears flowed down her cheeks as she pulled up the angel and baby Jesus in His manger. "They are perfect. Made exactly like Aunt Berta's." She wiped her eyes with her sleeve, the objects still in her hands. "I can't believe it."

George chuckled. "I don't know why you are so surprised. I am German by heritage and I whittle. It was polishing them to a shine that was the hardest part."

Hans peered over Alice's shoulder and stared at the carvings. Then he turned to George. "Is good!"

"You like?" George asked.

"Is good," Hans replied.

"Then I'm sure you'll like what I made for you." George spotted Mary rushing over with a small bundle. "There you go."

Hans sat on the floor and opened his present. He shouted German words.

George didn't understand what Hans said, but it was easy to see he was happy with his gift.

Frankie and Albert jumped up and stood on either side of Hans. They were nearly as excited about the nativity set as Hans.

Mary soon placed a bundle into the outstretched hands of Frankie and Albert. "George made sure you each have your own set."

Alice passed some of her figurines to Aunt Berta to be inspected. "These are simply the most beautiful things I've ever seen. Thank you, George. Thank you."

"You don't have to share either, Alice. I made the pieces missing from Mrs. Schumacher's set for her. Now she'll have a complete nativity scene again. That's the other gift I made for her."

When their excitement dissipated, Mrs. Schumacher asked for everyone's attention. "Because this is Christmas, it's a time to appreciate our blessings and spread God's love." She pushed herself up from the couch. "I'm so grateful to each and every one of you this Christmas. For your gift of fellowship and the individual presents you've given me. More importantly, I thank you for being a part of my life. Since Otto passed, all of you have given my life purpose and filled me with happiness. Thank you."

She smiled at those gathered around the room until her sparkling eyes settled on Hans. In German, she asked Hans to approach her.

He jumped to do her bidding, an expression of curiosity on his face.

Mrs. Schumacher said several things in German, which caused Hans to beam with joy. Those in the room who spoke German nodded their approval.

Alice turned to George. "She's telling Hans that we will continue to search for his family. But until we find them, she would like for him to claim this as his home and us as his family." Alice paused to listen again. "She's asked him to be known as Hans Schumacher and she would like to informally adopt him. If his original family is not found after time, she wants to legally adopt him."

For the first time since his discovery as a stowaway in George's wagon, Hans wept. With tears flowing, he hugged Mrs. Schumacher, and the two of them wept together.

Hours later, it was time for the Hunter family to pack up and go home. George dragged his feet, watching Alice as she thanked everyone for their contributions to the meal and for their gifts. She passed out hugs, calls of 'Merry Christmas,' and kisses upon cheeks to his entire family, but spared nothing for him.

As he helped his Mama to the wagon, Alice waved him back to the porch. He got his mother settled and walked back to Alice.

"Where do you think you're going?"

He furrowed his brow. "Home."

"Without kissing your sweetheart on the cheek? For shame."

He took her hands in his. "So you're bold enough to call yourself my sweetheart?"

"A man who carves a replica of something I cherish to make me happy is worth more than gold. And this man carves a book holder for my aunt and multiple nativity sets for my family. He should understand that he's carved a place in my heart."

"Forever in your heart?"

She nodded.

He leaned over and his lips brushed her cheek. "Since I first saw you, you've had my heart. No carving necessary."

THE END

Author's Note: Historical Information

Although Missouri did not secede from the Union during the Civil War, it was a "border state," which left it divided between Union loyalists and secessionists. The Union Army occupied Mexico, Missouri, from the spring of 1861 until the end of the Civil War because the town's railroad lines were key to the control of northern Missouri.

Colonel Ulysses Grant, a regimental commander stationed in Mexico, was a popular leader. He received orders to transfer to Ironton, Missouri, and was informed of his promotion to brigadier general upon arrival. He later became the Commanding General of the Union Army and elected the 18th President of the United States.

The citizens in and around Mexico appreciated Grant because he halted the forcing of locals at gunpoint to swear their loyalty to the Union. He also stopped the military from seizing local property and supplies. Although George Hunter's mercantile deliveries could have happened because of Grant stopping supply and property seizures, both he and his deliveries are fictional.

Sheriff Alexander Carter, Sr., was sheriff of Audrain County in 1861. Because of a Missouri legislative ordinance passed in October 1861, any government official who failed to file an oath of loyalty to the state was subject to being ousted from their office. The oath required them to declare they didn't support the secessionist cause and had never previously supported the secessionist cause. They ordered Sheriff Carter to vacate his office in February 1862, for failure to file the oath of loyalty. He returned to his farm and remained a respected citizen of Audrain County until his death.

General John Pope was commander of North Missouri for the Union Army, headquartered in Mexico, Missouri in 1861. He commanded the Army of Virginia until defeated by Confederate generals in several battles. After the war, he was appointed to commands involving the reconstruction of Atlanta and the Indian Wars.

When George questions whether the "Audrain Rangers" might have had something to do with his kidnapping, this group existed. Formed by John G. Muldrow, a secessionist from Mexico, Missouri, the "Audrain Rangers" were a group of men and boys. They fired upon Union soldiers, killing some, but the group soon disbanded.

About the Author

Ellen E. Withers is an award-winning fiction writer and retired insurance fraud investigator. Her publishing credits include inclusion in nineteen anthologies for short stories and devotionals, plus regional and international magazine articles. She was nominated for the prestigious Pushcart Prize in the published short story category. She's a contributing columnist to *Writers Monthly Magazine*, an online guide for professional writers, on the subject of Writing for Contests.

Her first book in the Show Me mystery series, set in Ellen's picturesque hometown of Mexico, Missouri, was published by

Scrivenings Press in May 2023. For more information, visit her website at www.ellenewithers.com.

Also by Ellen E. Withers

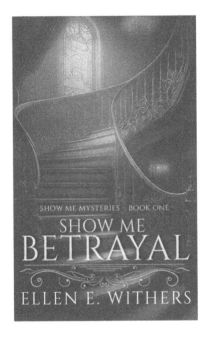

Show Me Betrayal by Ellen E. Withers

Show Me Mysteries - Book One

Two deaths occur decades apart. Is it possible these deaths are related? What motivates a killer, who got away with murder sixty years ago, to kill again? Was it uncontrollable rage or the hope of silencing someone who fit all the puzzle pieces together and deduced who committed the crime?

Set in the picturesque town of Mexico, Missouri, _Show Me Betrayal_ takes flight in words and emotions of rich characters woven together into a story you won't want to put down.

Get your copy here:

https://scrivenings.link/showmebetrayal

REJOICING with JOY

Jenny Carlisle

Rejoice!

Jenny Carlisle

"When they saw the star, they rejoiced with exceedingly great joy."
~ *Matthew 2:10 (NKJV)*

For Caddo Gap, Norman, and Paron.

Prologue

"Joy! Christmas Joy! Where are you?" Grandma's voice carried from the bottom of the stairs to Joy's favorite hiding spot in the church building.

"Coming, Grandma." She carefully wrapped the wooden figure of Mary she was holding and placed it back into the crate where she'd found it. She still couldn't believe her luck today. Imagine, a whole nativity set had been in this crate for who knew how long.

Her hand bumped one of the wise men, and she unwrapped it for another quick look. She loved hearing her grandpa preach about the baby Jesus when he was born in Bethlehem. These figures made the story come to life.

Who had made this set? Why was it hidden here?

One thing she knew—she could not tell anyone. Especially not her brother, Brannon. He was so clumsy. He would probably break it into a million pieces. But it was made of wood. Could it break?

Why had she never known this set was here? Now that she was ten, she was old enough to help decorate the house and the church building. Even though her grandpa had stood in the pulpit her whole life and she'd grown up feeling very much at home here, she'd never noticed this box. Marked "Decorations," it had been hiding below one of the four huge windows in the tower of the old brick building.

If she didn't tell, she'd have to leave it up here in the church's attic. But the box was too big to carry downstairs, and where would she hide it?

There was one person she could trust completely. Someone who would understand how important this was. Someone who would help her protect the precious set from her overgrown ox of a brother.

"Grandma! Could you come up here, please?"

1

Nine years later

J oy Fredericks squatted on her heels, glaring at the extension ladder lying on the ground beneath her. Everyone inside her house was either napping or watching football, and here she was, stuck on Grandpa's roof. One more time, she'd plowed ahead with one of her crazy schemes, and look where it took her. Was there another way down? How long would she have to yell before someone heard her? At least she could take the string of Christmas lights to the roof's peak while she was up here. No need to worry about finding a way down until she finished her work.

She climbed slowly, her toes flexing inside her tennis shoes to better grip the sloping shingles.

"Hey," a male voice reached her ear. "Need some help?"

"Not right now," she yelled down. "But I will need that ladder pretty soon."

The top of the ladder peeked over the gutter below.

"Thanks!" The word was barely out of her mouth before her lanky rescuer clambered up, joining her on the roof.

"Taking down the Thanksgiving lights, huh?" His blue eyes laughed at his own joke.

"Yeah. I thought I'd get some Christmas lights up while the weather was so nice. Thanks again. I'm Joy Fredericks." She extended her hand. His handshake was firm, and so far, he resisted the urge to ridicule her.

"Junior Caldwell. So, I take it this is the roof of your house? Or maybe you're a burglar, and I should call the cops." He stood, picking up the string of lights that rested near her feet.

"It's my grandpa's house. His display usually brings people out from miles around." She plugged the string of multi-colored lights into the extension cord that stretched over the corner of the roof. "I know he can't manage it this year, so I wanted to get a head start."

"If I help, could I ask you some questions about this little town?" Junior worked on unraveling another string of lights.

"Sure." The sun warmed her face, and she was glad she had chosen a short-sleeved T-shirt to work in, even on Thanksgiving day. With this stranger's help on the roof, she might not need to stay here long. "But me, first. Where did you come from? I didn't hear anyone drive up."

"That's my bicycle over there by the diner." Junior pointed. "I rode it from our ranch near Crossroads after dinner."

"Did you expect the diner to be open on Thanksgiving?" That may have sounded blunter than she intended.

"No. I've had dinner already. I'm just checking out the route between Crossroads and Van Buren. We're planning to sponsor a charity bike ride in the springtime. Roads with little traffic are best." Junior handed her the next string, waiting for her to plug it in.

"If you're looking for a place with no traffic, you found it.

The church and the diner are the only places still open. So, Sunday mornings and weekend evenings are the big days. Even those aren't huge." Joy stood taller as she surveyed the closed-up gas station and the other empty buildings leading up to the old school building on the hill.

"It's been a while since I've been out here. When I was a kid, we used to come to a live nativity scene at that church. I was always disappointed there was no snow in Snowville." Junior pointed in the general direction of the brick sanctuary.

"Yeah. I can only remember one or two times we had snow during the nativity. If we have any, it's after Christmas. Sometimes I wore shorts and a T-shirt under my angel robe. Last year, I did have to add a sweatshirt under Mary's dress." Joy tacked the lights down with a staple gun.

"Hey, I don't think Jesus would care what His mom wore. Those pageants were always great. I remember the animals most. Didn't you have a camel once?" Junior handed her another string of lights before following her down the back of the house.

"Yeah! That was quite a deal. There was some exotic animal refuge up north of here. I think the guy wanted us to pay him. We've always been volunteers. He only brought the camel once."

Joy watched as Junior stood, peering over her community. The wind ruffled his wavy blond hair when he removed his baseball cap to place it more firmly on his head.

"I guess that's all I need to do up here for now." Joy walked toward the ladder. "Thanks again. The diner will be open tomorrow, so you can come back if you want to talk to Big Ed about your fundraiser."

"Sounds good. I might do that. Maybe I'll drive my pickup next time." He turned in the direction of the old schoolhouse. "So what's the story? Why did the school close?"

"The state said we weren't getting a proper education with so few students. They didn't ask the kids. We loved the individual attention. And the food in the cafeteria was to die for. My grandma was one of the cooks. Most everyone who graduated got a scholarship to college if they wanted one. But, it closed, and we were loaded up on school buses for the long ride to the big, impersonal school in town." Joy hung the staple gun on her toolbelt.

"Oops. Didn't mean to hit a sore spot." Junior took a step toward the ladder.

"That's okay. The timing was rotten, though. If it stayed open for one more year, I could have graduated here. Instead, last May I walked across a huge, cold stage with a bunch of strangers. My dad and I have been trying to make good use of the building. We started a community organization that keeps the lights on for a few events. But hardly anyone shows up." Did this stranger care about sad little Snowville?

"Get a load of that gym." Junior pointed. "Looks like it's in great shape."

"Not bad for almost a hundred years old." Joy climbed down the ladder first. Junior scrambled down quickly, right after her. This afternoon had turned out to be much more interesting than she had anticipated.

He reached down to touch a pile of boxes at the foot of the ladder. "Looks like you've still got quite a job ahead of you."

"I need to sort through that stuff to see what goes on the house and what goes inside." Joy retied the bandana that held back her wavy brown hair. "This one goes in, for sure." She picked up the small plastic tub that contained her favorite nativity scene. This would be the first year Grandma wouldn't be here to see it displayed. Maybe Joy would leave it in the box.

"Let me help. I'm not in a big hurry. I have a headlamp for my bike if I don't get home before dark." Junior took the container from her. Joy used her foot to push a cardboard box full of greenery under Grandpa's front porch roof.

"Come on in. You'll need something to eat before you ride all the way home. I owe you at least a sandwich for rescuing me before I had to admit to everybody else what a dunce I am." Joy ran ahead, bouncing up the Craftsman-style front porch steps in front of her parents' house, next-door to Grandpa's.

"Okay. You convinced me. Riding all this way by myself was not the world's smartest move." He juggled the box from one hand to the other as he navigated the steps.

"There you are, Christmas Joy." Grandpa opened the front door. "I thought I saw you on my roof."

"Just getting a head start on your decorations." Joy held the door open for Junior.

"Grandpa, this is my friend, Junior Caldwell, from Crossroads. He is on a long bicycle ride and could use a sandwich to take back with him." She heard herself introducing this guy as if she'd known him for a long time. It seemed that way, honestly.

"Caldwell. Like the Caldwell Rodeo?" Grandpa followed them into the entryway. "I hated that they went under. Great entertainment."

"Thanks." Junior held the box toward Joy.

"Hey, you brought your old nativity scene from my house. Where should we put it?" Grandpa grabbed the box from Junior. Unfortunately, it immediately crashed to the hardwood floor, spilling the contents at their feet.

"Grandpa!" Joy cringed. She hadn't intended to sound so harsh. Grandpa stepped back, wobbling a little before leaning against the door frame.

"Honey, I am so sorry. Here, let me help." Grandpa bent his knees, reaching toward the floor, but Joy caught his arm.

"No, Grandpa. It's okay. I can get it." She blinked back

tears. The trembling that had become more prevalent lately was only part of the reason he was moving from his own house to an assisted living apartment in town.

"Joy, you haven't introduced the rest of us to your friend." Mom stepped in from the kitchen.

"This is Junior Caldwell. He's from Crossroads. He rode up here on his bicycle." Joy nudged Junior, who was reaching under the entryway table for a wise man.

"Well, come on in. Joy can pick up those pieces. They have survived much worse over the years." Mom led the way to the kitchen, where her brother already assembled a sandwich.

Joy retrieved the pieces of the nativity scene from the entryway floor. She was glad Grandma had helped her wrap each piece in bubble wrap before packing the set away last year. That extra bit of cushion had protected them once again. She placed each one back in the plastic box. Mom had a much newer set that she would display in the living room. Maybe she'd clear a spot on her dresser for this one. She wondered again about the story behind each mismatched figure. How many hands had held the precious pieces, wrapping them carefully before they were packed away again?

Junior stood next to her with a brown paper sack.

"Did Mom fix you up?" Joy placed the plastic crate in a chair just below the hat rack.

"She wanted to send more food with me, but I told her I could only carry so much in my backpack." Junior squatted near the doorway to the living room. "What's this?" He held up a piece of white cloth wrapped around a wooden clothespin.

"Oh. That's my homemade baby Jesus. The more official one has been lost for a couple of years. Grandpa promised to carve me a new baby, but ..." She took the makeshift figurine from his outstretched hand.

"Life happens." Junior smiled at her. "This one serves the purpose, I guess."

"Yeah." Joy placed the clothespin baby in the top of the box. "I guess you want to get started back before dark." She opened the front door, walking out to the front porch.

"I'll be back tomorrow to talk to Big Ed. This would be a good place for our bike ride to stop for lunch." Junior punched the brown sack into his backpack.

"Great. I'll be around. I can clue you in on what to order. But everything Ed makes is delicious. Besides the live nativity scene, his diner is the only thing that keeps Snowville, Arkansas, on the map."

"Okay, then. It's a date." Junior mounted his bicycle and headed to the two-lane highway in front of the diner. "See you around noon tomorrow."

Joy looked up the hill toward the empty schoolhouse. No kids playing on the old metal slide or launching feet first into space on the swings. No matter how many Christmas lights she installed on Grandpa's house, life would never be the same around here. Her mom and dad didn't let Grandpa stay in his house alone, so it sat empty most of the time. She wished he could be content living with them, but he didn't seem happy anywhere now.

Without Grandma's presence, all the spirit seemed to be gone from the family's celebration. Loneliness was building in this little town.

She forced a smile as she waved at Junior. His red ball cap faded into the distance. He had promised to return, but only a few people ever did.

2

Junior pulled into a parking space on the gravel lot in front of Ed's Diner. It was hard to believe this was the same place he'd seen yesterday when he'd helped Joy climb down from her Grandpa's roof. Two older couples strolled from their cars to the front door, and a young woman corralled two toddlers as a man lugged a baby carrier from a muddy SUV.

Good thing he'd set aside some time for this lunch visit. Anyone in a hurry should probably not choose Ed's on a day like today. Who was he kidding? He didn't have much on the agenda at home either. He wasn't interested in Black Friday shopping, and his dad had winnowed their cattle herd to almost nothing. If it wasn't for the horses and goats his sisters left when they married, their place wouldn't seem much like a ranch.

He pulled out his cell phone. Noon on the dot. He hadn't underestimated the time it took to drive to Snowville from Crossroads. There was something about Joy that made him hope yesterday's visit might be the first of many.

"Welcome!" A dark-haired woman opened the diner's front door and stepped out with a fresh green wreath propped against her pregnant belly. "Come right in and sit wherever you like. I'll be right with you."

"Hi!" Joy followed behind with a stepladder. "I've got to help Lisa attach this wreath to the front of the building."

"Need some help?" He had a feeling it was useless to ask. This girl looked determined to complete her task.

"No, thanks. We've already got the hook in place. I'm just going to climb the stepladder. I'm not letting Lisa do anything like that until after her baby gets here." She smiled at him. "And no comments about me and ladders if you please. I've always heard you must get back on the horse after getting bucked off."

"I'm not saying a word." Junior stepped back, holding both palms out in front of him.

Joy ran ahead of Lisa and placed the ladder in the flowerbed below the diner's window. She scrambled to the top step and held the handle with one hand, reaching for the wreath with the other.

Junior tucked his hands in his back pockets, resisting the urge to run over and help. No need to insult their abilities.

"Thanks, friend." Lisa held the stepladder as Joy descended. "I need to go in to make sure the servers don't need anything."

"Yeah. I'll help with the other wreath when you're ready." Joy hugged her before folding up the stepladder.

"Good job. I'll take this inside for you." Junior was a little surprised by the weight of the sturdy three-step stool.

"You can stash it inside the door." Joy stepped past him.

"This is the lunch rush, I guess." Junior propped the ladder behind the hostess station and followed Joy to a booth.

"Yep. Normally it's like this on Saturday, but I guess Black

Friday qualifies. Have a seat. I'll go wash my hands and be right back." She rushed toward the back of the diner, waving at several of the patrons on the way.

Junior slid into the booth. Delicious smells made his mouth water as he read through the items on the menu. Whatever he ordered would be much better than the turkey sandwiches and leftover dressing they'd be eating back at his house. Back home in Crossroads, he could always find something good at Amy's Diner. This place just might be Snowville's version. Bells jingled behind him. He turned to watch a dark-haired man in his mid-twenties enter the diner, pushing back his cowboy hat.

"Hey, Brannon." Joy greeted the man as she approached Junior's booth.

"Let's get after this." Brannon walked back toward the door. "I don't have time for lunch. I've got to get back to the shop."

"Good to see you, too, big brother." She settled across from Junior. "You are not in too big a hurry to enjoy Big Ed's good cooking. Sit down."

"Okay, but if you want this Christmas tree thing to happen, I don't have all day. I've got to go home to change the oil in my wife's car while little man is napping." Brannon took his hat off and slid in next to Joy. "Sorry, man. I'm Joy's brother, Brannon Fredricks." He held his hand across the table.

"Junior Caldwell." Junior returned Brannon's firm handshake. Funny, his face was familiar. The guy had a good grip.

"Caldwell." Brannon's face lit up. "Yeah. I thought I recognized you. You look different without the makeup."

"Makeup?" Joy laughed.

"He's a rodeo clown!" Brannon waved at Lisa, who walked over with an order pad.

256

"Used to be." Junior hoped his cheeks were not as red as they felt right now. "And you rode broncs, right?"

"Still do when I'm not working. As Lisa started writing, Brannon pointed to the item he wanted on the menu.

"You're waiting tables?" Joy craned her neck to look past her friend.

"Two servers called in, and we're slammed," Lisa explained.

"That stinks. I'll make it easy on Ed. Just get me a BLT." Joy eased away from Brannon in the booth.

"I may not be as easy. I've got to have the Pulled Pork Sandwich and Cajun fries." After all, Junior needed to see what Ed's cooking was like. That was the reason for his visit. Watching his new friend Joy trying so hard to be helpful was fun too.

"Of course. You want slaw on the sandwich? It also comes with a side dish." Lisa smiled.

"If you didn't put slaw on it, I would have added it. Let's try the potato salad for the side." Junior folded the menu and held it in Lisa's direction.

"Lisa, this guy wants to talk to Ed about a charity bicycle ride he's organizing." Joy nodded toward Junior.

"It may be a minute before he has time to talk to you, but I'll tell him." Lisa walked away quickly, tearing off the ticket with their orders and clamping it to a clip behind the counter.

"So, you're organizing bike rides instead of being a professional bull-fighter?" Brannon leaned back, chewing on a toothpick.

"No way my dad would approve hitting the pro circuit until after I graduate from high school this coming year. The bike ride is just a way to raise money for a friend who needs lots of medical treatment." Junior nodded at Lisa as she placed his Coke in front of him.

"Oh, yeah." Brannon sat up. His voice was softer as he spoke again. "So, how is the Billings kid? Isn't his name Cody?"

"Yeah. He's better every day. Just a lot of expense. Therapy, equipment, modifications to his house. It just goes on and on." Junior tied the paper from his straw in a knot. The truth was, he missed hanging out with Cody. With all the appointments his buddy had these days, finding the time was difficult, especially with all their senior activities.

"You're a good friend to take on something like that." Joy met his glance with a calming smile.

"Trying." Junior swallowed a lump in his throat. Someday, he would be able to talk about Cody without getting emotional.

"Well, you came to the right place for food, anyway." Brannon broke open one of his catfish fillets with a fork and placed a piece on Junior's plate. "Sink your teeth into this, my friend."

Junior placed the warm, salty bite into his mouth. Catfish was today's special, and apparently, for good reason. This was the lightest, most flavorful fried catfish he'd had in a long time. His barbecue sandwich was equally delicious. He might make the drive to Snowville more often.

"By the way," Joy said as she finished her sandwich and wiped her mouth with a napkin. "I'm not sure why you want my help with the Christmas tree. *That* is your job, big brother."

"Watch out. First year in college, and she already has her main purpose in life. To make sure everyone knows what their job is." Brannon popped a hushpuppy into his mouth.

"You've had the tree picked out for months, and today's the day to get it." Joy pulled out the calendar on her phone. "The lighting ceremony is this Sunday, and then we concentrate on the live nativity."

"See? The infamous calendar. Better see where you fit in, Junior." Brannon picked up his hat. "Come on, sis. Let's go."

"I'd like to help Lisa out in the diner, at least through the lunch rush." Joy stacked her plates.

"Hey. I don't have anything going on today. If you show me where this tree is, I could help bring it into town." Junior placed his fork across the plate. Joy's Christmas spirit was contagious. It was an unusually warm November day, so there was no good reason not to offer his help.

"Oh. No. I didn't mean ..." Joy lifted her hands in front of her.

"Really. It's fine. Maybe Ed will be ready to talk to me when we return." Junior pulled some cash out of his billfold and placed it under his plate.

"Okay, clown face. If you can dodge charging bulls in the arena, you can tromp through some brush to haul in a tree." Brannon settled his hat on his head. "You're paying for my lunch, right, sis?"

"Sure. Now you two get out of here." Joy slapped her brother's arm.

Junior laughed. This out-of-the-way town was feeling more and more like home all the time.

3

J oy stopped to look out the diner's front window before taking another table's order. She didn't mind helping Lisa but couldn't help wondering how Brannon and Junior were coming along with the Christmas tree. Had a stranger ever fit into their little town so quickly? Why was this one so eager to buy into her vision for Christmas in Snowville? Did he have some hidden agenda? She didn't know him well, but that didn't seem likely. This lively rodeo clown gave the impression of being an open book.

"Miss." A customer at a nearby table begged her attention. "Could I get some more sweet tea, please?"

"Of course." Joy bustled off to pick up the glass for a refill. Dreaming about the community celebration was not helping Ed and Lisa's business today. Or was she thinking about a particular curly-headed stranger?

After she delivered the refilled glass of tea, she stood quietly as a young family made up their minds about lunch. The sun glinted off the steeple of the community's church building, and her mind strayed again to getting firm commitments out of the participants in the live nativity.

Ed and Lisa's almost one-year-old son to was too old to play the part of Jesus, but since Lisa was expecting her second baby, she would create precisely the right image for Mary with her concerned husband looking on and a doll playing the new baby's part. Joy's mom had agreed to handle babysitting for "Little Eddie" while serving hot chocolate inside the fellowship hall.

"Okay, two specials and two orders of mac and cheese?" Luckily, Joy heard the customer's final decision in the middle of her daydreaming. "I'll be right back with that."

On her way back from delivering the order to Ed, Lisa's mom, Mrs. Gray, touched her arm.

"I've got three shepherd's costumes finished." Joy stopped to greet this treasure who had the kindest eyes and softest voice ever. "The kings' robes are good, so I'm checking over the angel outfits next. A couple had some big rips in them."

"You're such a blessing." Joy leaned over to hug her shoulders. "Now, if I can just find volunteers to wear them."

"I have faith in you." Lisa's mom smiled. "Our little town can always rely on Joy just in time for Christmas."

Joy waved at Lisa, who was placing an order up in the window behind the counter. She was glad someone had faith in her. She only hoped she could live up to that trust.

JUNIOR STEPPED out of the way as Brannon took one last swipe at the trunk of the enormous cedar tree, which fell with a soft thud.

"We may need to trim some bottom branches, but I think

this is a pretty good one, don't you?" Brannon wiped his forehead with a bandana he had pulled from his back pocket.

"Should make quite a statement in the town square." Junior fastened a loop around the tree trunk, careful not to crush too many branches.

"I keep thinking every year, this will be the last time. Dad's been indulging Joy's bossy nature since she was in middle school. Someday, she will get the message that Snowville is done with all this fuss." Brannon walked to the top of the tree. "This will be the easiest way out to the road." He pointed to a different path than the one they had used to enter.

"Really? You don't think anybody cares anymore?" Junior pulled his leather gloves on in preparation for lugging the prickly tree.

"Oh, I guess some old-timers still remember the big celebrations when we were kids. But most of the younger ones have moved on, especially now that they live in town for their jobs." Brannon replaced his baseball cap with the bill toward the back and grabbed the top end of the tree.

Junior concentrated on the path ahead. It was good of Brannon to volunteer for a job he didn't believe in. The bond between these siblings must be strong. Was Joy alone in her quest to keep the Snowville Christmas celebration happening?

He brushed back a scrubby bush and plowed ahead with his half of the heavy tree. He understood how hard it was to let go of old traditions. The family's rodeo had been a significant part of his life for so long. When his dad and uncle decided to end it, the transition had not been easy. Joy was fighting a similar battle now. Maybe that's why he felt an instant connection when he found her stranded on her grandpa's roof.

"Ugh. I didn't realize there was such a big hill next to the road." Brannon tugged on the cut end of the tree.

"Here, let me help." Junior ran up to the top of the rise and used the rope he had tied around the tree to help hoist it nearer the open truck bed. "Your sister is going to owe you big time." He smiled, thinking of his two sisters and the favors he'd done for them. As the baby of the family, the truth was that they had helped him out more times than he could remember.

"Thanks!" Brannon heaved the tree into the truck bed with the top branches hanging off the end of the open tailgate. "Think we can tie it in, or should we close the tailgate?"

"I can ride in back with it no farther than we're going. Shouldn't be any harder to manage than some of those bulls I used to hang out with." Junior hopped up, wrapping the rope around the tree trunk and securing each end to the tie-downs in the truck's bed.

"Okay, buddy. But this might take more than eight seconds." Brannon laughed as he climbed into the driver's seat.

Junior settled into the only available space in the pickup bed, glad for the leather gloves that allowed a firm grip on the trunk of the cedar tree. He had a reputation in his family for tackling the most unusual tasks, but this was a first. The prickly branches rubbed up and down the legs of his blue jeans. The majestic tree would be a great centerpiece for the community's celebration. Even after two days, he understood that pleasing Joy made everyone in town happier.

The truck bounced over rocky side roads until they finally reached the paved highway through Snowville. Junior spotted Joy outside Ed's Diner, opening the door for an older couple.

"We need to deliver this to the town square," Brannon yelled from the cab.

"Gotcha." Junior waved at Joy with the hand not holding the tree down.

The truck stopped next to a statue in the square. Junior moved behind the cab's passenger side and vaulted to the ground.

"We're headed for that bucket of sand. Dad will help me get it straight. But, for now, we need to keep it moist." Brannon began tugging at the top branches. Junior grabbed the other side, and they wrangled the monster to the bucket. Brannon guided the cut end of the trunk into the wet sand and stepped back, wiping his forehead with a bandana.

"Thanks for your help, man. This was much easier than it would have been with my sibling fighting me every step of the way."

"Sisters." Junior laughed.

"Come on back to Ed's. Lisa makes a mean milkshake. I owe you at least that much." Brannon climbed back into his truck.

"Yeah. I'll be there." Junior waved. "But I'll walk back. Not too far."

Brannon drove the short distance and parked in front of the diner. Junior walked past a boarded-up post office, a bank, and a three-story building that must have once been a hotel. When his family had been here, he'd never noticed all of this. It was easy to see why Joy was discouraged. He passed the church, Joy's Grandpa's house, and her parents', then jogged the last few steps to the diner.

"Hi," He greeted Joy as she waited for him inside the door. "Is there somewhere I can clean up? I look like I just rode bareback on a Christmas tree."

"Sure!" She laughed and pointed toward the restrooms at the rear of the diner. "Thanks for your help."

Her dark hair shone in the sunlight streaming through the big plate glass windows. Even in casual clothes, she stood out. He resisted the urge to look back in her direction after he passed by. Something about this girl had him all undone.

"Here you go" Lisa handed Ed the upcoming year's calendar as he sat across from Junior at a back table.

Joy looked straight ahead as she passed them with a tray of empty glasses and silverware.

"I'll be sure to have extra catfish and pulled pork on hand that day." Ed said, making notes on the calendar. "Anything else you might need?"

"It's still a ways off," Junior responded. "I'm following you on social media. I'll send you a message if I think of anything else."

"Here." Ed stood up to pull a business card out of his back pocket. "Call me anytime. I should see you between now and then, right?"

"Definitely," Junior stood up. "This may be one of my new favorite hangouts!"

Joy picked up the piece of pie her customer had ordered. She saw Junior's smile reflected in the mirror behind the counter and smiled back.

"So, when's the Christmas tree lighting?" Junior asked as she passed him.

"Sunday night, six o'clock." Her cheeks flushed. Was he thinking of coming?

"Will you be busy after, or could I interest you in dinner?" He lowered his voice, moving closer to hear her answer.

"The decorating will be done before I go to bed tomorrow. All that will be left for Sunday evening will be flipping a switch. Dinner sounds great." She probably would have warmed up whatever Mom fixed after church. "If you have time, I can give you the VIP tour of the town when the ceremony ends."

"Sure. How long will that take?" Junior smiled and winked.

"It's a small town. Shouldn't take more than a few minutes." How long had it been since someone had asked her for a date, then winked when she accepted? This guy was nothing if not unique.

He waved and pushed the diner door open. His blond, curly mop bounced as he jogged to his pickup. Joy smiled. He was leaving with a promise to return once again.

"Hey, Joy." A young man called to her from the corner booth.

"Hi, Jon. How's that lovely little family of yours?" She stepped over to his side.

"They're good. My wife has them lined up to wash their hands before we order lunch. I wanted to tell you something while they're gone." He lowered his voice, focusing on the hallway that led to the restrooms.

"Yeah?" Joy couldn't help wondering about the urgency of this message of his.

"My Mom and Dad have surprised us with a Christmas vacation at Disney this year. The kids don't know. Unfortunately, we will be gone for all the live nativity performances. As his wife emerged from the hallway, he put his finger across his lips.

Joy stopped at another table to wipe up a mess. Her stomach lurched. One Christmas vacation took away a shepherd and two sweet little angels from her crew. She'd have to make a list of church members with children and talk to them on Sunday. Tomorrow would be spent making phone calls to line up the animals to make the scene more realistic. She knew that stressing about this wouldn't help. But worrying seemed to be the only thing she did well these days.

4

"Hey, buddy. Are you decent?" Junior rapped on Cody's door and pushed it open.

"Decent?" Cody laughed. "Is that like, just okay? Then, no. I'm never decent. I'm exceptional."

"Yeah, yeah." Junior crossed the room and plopped into the swinging chair in the corner. "Whatever. Just trying to be polite."

"Well, don't. It's totally out of character. So, tell me about this trip to Snowville yesterday. Was it snowing?" Cody spun around in his wheelchair.

"I don't think it will ever snow there, even if it is knee-deep here. That town needs a new name." Junior picked up a tennis ball from Cody's dresser, tossed it, caught it, and tossed it again.

"The big thing—will it be a good rest stop for the bicycle race?" Cody moved forward, catching the tennis ball in mid-air.

"Yeah. The diner there has terrific food, and it all looks pretty accessible. I've been wondering, should I have planned something else to raise money? Something you could participate in?" Junior pushed the hair back from his forehead.

"Hey, I've been researching recumbent bikes that operate solely with hand controls. My therapist thinks I should be good to go by then. This is happening during spring break, right?" Cody tossed the ball to Junior and picked up a barbell, raising it and lowering it with his right forearm.

"Seriously?" Junior stood up. "That would be so cool, man. I was hoping you'd be riding a regular bike by then."

Cody moved the weight to his other hand and rested it on his knee. "Thanks, buddy. But, you know, it's been a whole year since our bull wreck. I can't use the words 'give up' around my family, but I know I won't be walking again. My whole focus now is upper body strength. That's why I've avoided using a power chair. My arms are getting super strong just from navigating around in this thing. I'm getting really good." He rolled into the center of the bedroom and executed a quick circle.

"I know, dude. You are buff, for sure." Junior clapped his friend on the shoulder. "I hope I can get everything lined up by then. My sisters keep reminding me about our contest before our rodeo went belly-up. They say this bike rally is too much for a senior in high school to coordinate."

"What do they know?" Cody said. "My friend Junior is the king of checking off all the boxes, covering all the bases. You have never let negative talk hold you back."

"Look who's talking. Mr. Positivity. Sometimes I'm not so sure. Remember, we've both got to graduate this year too."

"Aww. That's a breeze." Cody laughed. "We both signed up for the easy stuff for our senior year. My only issue is staying awake while I'm in class. I can handle the work they assign, no problem-o."

"I wish it was that easy for me. I stay awake, study all the time, and still have issues. Especially with math." Junior pulled his school iPad out of his backpack. "That's why I'm here. I need you, Einstein."

"We usually don't worry about homework until Sunday night. Today is just Saturday." Cody reached for his computer.

"I'm busy Sunday night." Junior blushed.

"Oh yeah? There's more in Snowville than good barbecue. My clown-faced buddy is smitten by an older woman." Cody leaned over to poke Junior's arm.

"She's just a freshman in college. Not that much older. You'd like her, dude. Anyway. Let's work on math so we can put it behind us for the weekend." Junior logged on to his tablet.

"Yes, sir." Cody saluted. "You've got more important things to think about."

Junior tried to listen as Cody explained the math problems they were working on. This subject was pulling his grade point down. How important were grades anyway? He couldn't get too excited about college. He'd like to be a coach or activity leader for younger kids. Did he need good grades for that? His mind kept straying to Joy and her clear vision for revitalizing her little town. If only he had such a clear goal in mind.

"So, do you get it?" Cody was speaking to him.

"Yeah, yeah." Junior tried to focus on the problems again. It was no use. What kind of decorations would be on the Snowville Christmas tree, and how would they get lights all over it for the lighting ceremony? Would Joy have to decorate that massive thing all by herself? It was no use. He was not getting any math homework done today.

A text message popped up on his phone—his sister, Hope.

Did you feed my goats?

Of course.

You're a pretty good brother, I don't care
what anybody says.

Shh. I have a reputation.

The old clown comebacks just wouldn't quit.

"Is that your new girlfriend texting?" Cody asked, turning off his iPad.

"No, my old sister. Well, not the oldest, the one who lives on top of the hill." Junior pointed behind Cody's house. "She could easily come down from her perch and care for her own goats."

"Nah. That's why your mom had three kids. You are the goat-keeper for life, man." Cody laughed.

"Whatever." Junior picked up a pillow and walloped his buddy with it.

"Oh, it's on now." Cody retaliated with his own feather-filled weapon.

Junior took a deep breath. Who cared if he never decided what to study in college? If his buddy was around to keep him on his toes, he'd be just fine.

JOY SURVEYED the city square from her perch atop the ladder. Another sunny day for tree decorating. *Thanks, God. I do appreciate it.* The glittery star that had been used since she was in kindergarten made its way through the hands of every member of her family. This assembly line method of adorning the community tree was one of her favorite parts of the Christmas season. It was hard without Grandma, but Brannon's wife Ashley filled her spot in the human chain.

Ashley wrangled the tinsel-covered wooden contraption and handed it off to Brannon, who made his way up the ladder.

This part was a little scary for Joy. She couldn't help reviewing the weight limits she had seen printed somewhere. Dad assured her it was sturdy enough as long as Brannon stayed clear of extra milkshakes for a week or so beforehand. *Hmmph.* Everyone was a joker around here.

"Okay, sis. Here you go." Brannon pushed the star closer. She rechecked her feet and turned toward her brother.

"Easy, peasy, right?" Her heart pounded as she gripped the prickly strings of lights firmly and turned back toward the tree. The newly reinforced cone that would slip over the tip-top of the evergreen looked ready. From the next to the top step of the ladder, she leaned and pushed the star down over the branches Brannon had duct-taped together. Then, with a big sigh, she pushed the electrical connection into the plug. She squinted in the sunlight, spotting a glimmer of light from the star. *Thanks again. God.*

She moved to a lower step and waited, watching for Ashley, who would be carrying a box of metal ornaments created by a local craftsman. The snowmen, stars, and Santa faces added a sparkly touch to the top branches, even in the daytime. Brannon teased that Joy was the only one who still cared about the community tree, but there was evidence everywhere that many others were involved.

The hooks crafted by the tinsmith clamped easily around the branches. Joy made her way down, where even Brannon's three-year-old son, Shelby, was busy finding the perfect spot for an ornament. She glanced out to the parking lot, hoping to see a familiar curly blond head. Junior would fit right in with this crew. He had promised to be here Sunday night. So far, he'd followed through with all of his promises, so she would have to be patient.

"Okay, everybody. Dry run on the lights." Dad hollered from the lectern on the small stage where Grandpa would hit the official switch on Sunday night. "One, two, three." White lights sparkled against the dark branches of the tree.

"Looks good in the daylight." Joy gave him a thumbs-up. "We might want to turn them on again after dark tonight. We probably wouldn't notice if a few random bulbs were burned out while it's still light."

"Thinking of everything is my little sister's superpower." Brannon pushed his hat back as he stared at the tree.

"Whatever." Joy bumped her hip into his, throwing him off balance. "Thanks for getting this tree, dumbo. It is one of our best in a long time."

"You're welcome. It's a good one, for sure. Your new buddy was a big help when we brought it out of the woods. I'm not sure you and I could have wrangled it."

"Yeah. Junior seems like an okay guy. Funny how God just seemed to send him along at the right time." She stood back, examining the tree and the big star at the top. Once again, all the effort of her friends and family would be worthwhile. The centerpiece of Snowville's celebration was almost perfect.

As the assembly line method of decorating the tree continued, Joy spotted her grandpa standing silently near the front door of his house. His hands shook as he zipped up his jacket. Unlike some elderly people, Grandpa's mind was still sharp. If only his body would cooperate. She knew he wasn't excited about the coming move to a facility in town, but living here was becoming harder and harder. Trips to the doctor were an all-day excursion and exhausting for him. Finally, he flicked a tear off his cheek and moved slowly toward the Christmas tree. Joy swallowed the lump in her throat, moved closer, wrapped her fingers around his.

"What do you think?" She asked.

During his first year as minister of the town's only church, the community Christmas tree had been his idea.

"Best tree ever." He smiled and squeezed her hand. "I remember when your grandma and I made some ornaments. Quite a deal to make them big enough and sturdy enough to hold up to the crazy Arkansas weather."

"For sure. This tree is so big. We may have to add some more." Joy looped her elbow in his, providing more stability for him as they stood, watching the decorations going up.

"Thanks for making sure we keep doing this every year." He caught her eye and winked.

"It takes the whole community." Joy blushed.

"Yes, but our Christmas Joy is the real spark behind it. God had a purpose for sending you to us on Christmas day." He pecked her softly on the cheek.

"The tree is great. But the important thing is the live nativity. I hope that comes together this year." She leaned her head on his shoulder.

"The Father has a plan. It all came together in Bethlehem and will also come together in Snowville. Trust Him." Grandpa spoke louder, more firmly than he had in weeks.

"I know. Thanks, Grandpa." She guided him to a park bench where he could watch the rest of the decoration process. "Looking forward to you throwing the switch tomorrow night."

"You bet. Wouldn't miss it." Grandpa released her arm and sank onto the wooden bench.

Joy switched on the battery-operated string of lights illuminating the antique nativity scene on her dresser. She turned off the overhead light and stretched across the end of her bed. Mom had taken care of the cleanup after supper and persuaded Joy to relax.

The ancient figurines stood quietly inside the stable Grandpa had crafted for them years ago. Her stomach quivered as she recalled the day she'd opened the old crate in the attic of the church building. When she and Grandma had shown the box to him, he said he remembered seeing it when he first took the job as minister. The congregation's focus had been to ensure the building was safe and secure for worship, with little thought to decoration. The crate had been moved a time or two but never opened.

The beautiful expression on the tiny face of Baby Jesus had convinced her that she must share the set. Just like the shepherds who immediately left the manger to spread the word about the newborn King, Joy had known she could not keep the discovery to herself.

The craftsmanship of the original woodcarvers was amazing. The set must have been special to many people who protected it for over a hundred years. All through her teen years, she had loved unboxing the set and finding the perfect way to display it. If only Brannon hadn't lost the little baby. She'd had trouble forgiving him for that.

Joy's cell phone beeped, notifying her of a message from Junior Caldwell.

What's up? Did the tree get decorated?

She smiled. Hadn't she told him it would be done before she went to sleep tonight?

Of course. Looks great.

Can't wait to see it all lit up.

See you tomorrow.

He sent her a thumbs-up emoji.

The clothespin figure that held the spot for the baby Jesus caught a glimmer of the twinkling lights inside the tiny stable.

"Good night," she whispered to the carved figures.

This was shaping up to be a unique Christmas season in Snowville. She stood, catching a glimpse of her reflection in the mirror. The hopeful expression on her face was new, but she liked it.

Thanks, God. I can still use your help making sure the live nativity comes together. I know Your plan is perfect.

"How's that homework coming?" Dad poked his head into Junior's bedroom.

"Just fine." Junior closed the website for a local stock provider. This one didn't have anything exotic like camels, but he was determined to find one.

"Have you decided on a topic for your research paper?" Dad stepped inside and leaned against Junior's dresser.

"Not exactly. I want it to have something to do with accessibility in sports venues. I don't want it to be boring." Never mind that he had only been thinking about Joy's live nativity all night. Dad didn't need to know that.

"Well, make sure this is your topic, not Cody's. I know you want to help him, buddy. But after graduation, you two will have your own trails to ride. So you need to have a plan for your own career, your own life."

Dad's argument was getting old. Of course, Junior knew he would have his own life to live. But no one understood how vital it was to ensure that anyone who wanted to live an active and healthy life got that chance. He might have headed down this path even before Cody's accident. That night just over a year ago made him more determined than ever.

Something told him Joy would understand. Her goal of keeping Snowville's holiday celebration alive was about more than Christmas. It was obvious that revitalizing the lifeless community was the only thing that would ever really make her happy. They both had big dreams and a big job convincing others about their importance.

His cousin Kayla shared the vision for making life more enjoyable for Cody. He'd started to notice admiration in her eyes when around his buddy. When she'd won the Arkansas Teen Rodeo crown, she'd talked about making rodeo arenas more accessible. So maybe he'd start with that topic. He knew about rodeos, that was for sure.

He opened his laptop again and googled accessibility at rodeos. His search led him back to stock contractors. Here was one that talked about exotic animals—even camels. He was back on the Snowville track again.

That big cedar tree he and Brannon brought out of the woods must look great by now, standing in its place of honor in the town square. What would the weather be like for Sunday night's tree lighting? He looked up the forecast. There might be some rain Sunday morning, but then, clear and cold. Perfect. Thankfully the heater worked in his new pickup truck. Where should he take Joy for dinner after the ceremony? The Christmas lights in Crossroads would also be making their debut this weekend. Maybe they'd just come back here for a bit.

Research paper. How would he ever get his topic narrowed down if his mind kept straying back to a certain pretty young lady? It was a losing battle. At least tonight.

Hey.

He might as well text her.

I may or may not have a lead on a camel
for your live nativity.

Joy didn't waste much time responding.

Really?

Yeah. What other animals do you need?

I have a donkey and some cattle. Do you
have any sheep connections?

She must have forgotten about the mutton-busting event
at the rodeo. He knew lots of people with sheep.

Baaaa.

He couldn't resist.
She sent a gif of sheep laughing.
What research paper? Texting with Joy was a lot more fun.

5

"Would you all please bow with me as we have a word with our Heavenly Father?" Dad was in full preacher mode at the lectern in the city's gazebo.

A damp breeze tickled Joy's cheek. She looped her arm through Junior's. Then, eyes closed, she bowed her head.

"Father, we come to You today to dedicate this community's celebration to You. Our hearts are filled with happiness during this time of year as we remember Your perfect plan. The world had been waiting. The faithful were probably doubting. That tiny baby You sent to Bethlehem amazed everyone who saw Him that night. The angels announced His arrival, and the shepherds spread the word, as His young mother pondered it all in her heart."

Junior clasped her left hand in his right one. Her heartbeat increased as she resisted the urge to open her eyes and look at him.

"Please help us to remain excited to spread the word about this most precious gift. Please help us tell the whole story, including your Son's death and resurrection. Your plan is perfect, and we are so grateful to You. Thank You for loving us so much. Amen."

Joy opened her eyes and turned to face Junior. He smiled silently.

"Now, I am honored to ask my dad, Norman 'Freddy' Fredericks, to throw the switch, lighting this beautiful tree."

"Merry Christmas, Snowville!" Grandpa shouted, pulling down the oversized lever with both hands.

"Ahhh!!!" The small crowd sighed in unison, then clapped and cheered as the lights on the tree and the well-placed floodlights below it glowed bravely in the clear night air.

"Hey! It looks great." Junior pulled her closer. "You did an excellent job decorating it."

"It was a community effort. And it wouldn't be standing there without you." She faced the tree again, spotting the handmade ornaments that Grandma had made. Though only reflecting the lights on the tree, the shiny aluminum stars seemed to cast their unique glow.

"It does look good, doesn't it?" She smiled up at him.

"Now, join us in a song, please." Dad returned to the mic.

"Oh come, all ye faithful ..." Joy sang proudly. The tree lighting was a success. Now, if she could get all the details for the live nativity ironed out, she'd feel much more like celebrating. The breeze picked up. She wished she'd worn her winter headband. No problem. Cold weather puts everyone in the mood for Christmas, right?

"Amen!" Junior concluded the last line of the hymn with an emphatic declaration. "What's next on the agenda?"

"That's pretty much it." Joy left their elbows interlocked. "Now for the tour of our fair city."

"I'm at your disposal, *mademoiselle*." Junior bowed from the waist.

"Okay. There's nothing that grand about it." Joy laughed.

"We don't have streetlights, but most places are decorated so it won't be completely dark. Follow me." She turned to walk up the hill toward the old school. Her tennis shoes bounced up the asphalt street, past a couple of abandoned houses and an old lodge hall. Not many people were as interested in this old place as she was.

"Can we go inside?" Junior stood next to her on the concrete front steps.

"Sure. But if you tell anyone how we got in, I'll have to kill you." Joy ran to the side of the building, facing away from the street. She reached over the top of a door and found the key always hidden on top of the door jam.

"My lips are sealed." Junior laughed. "But are there lights inside?"

The words were barely out of his mouth before Joy reached to the left of the door and switched on the lights in the main hallway. She pushed the front door open and stepped inside, inhaling the unique scent of floor wax and paper dust that had probably inhabited this place for decades. A quick shake of her head helped dispel a familiar twinge of sadness. Abandoned, just like her town. Lonely, just like she often felt.

"Wow." Junior stood behind her. "This is like an old movie or something. A real treasure."

"The district hasn't decided what to do with the property, so Grandpa volunteered to keep it clean and maintained for them. Our community organization has talked about holding classes of some kind here. Maybe the cooperative extension group or CPR classes. It's all in the talking stages, and since I go to college during the day, I can't be too involved right now."

Junior opened one door after the other, peering in and stepping back out again.

"It's a great asset. I know you will come up with

something." He was now at the other end of the long hallway, pushing against double doors.

"That goes into the gym. Give me a minute." She found the key on a nail behind the fire extinguisher next to the door.

Junior pushed past her and stepped inside. Joy reached to the left and flipped up three double switches. The lights overhead sizzled and crackled as they warmed up, growing brighter and still brighter.

"Joy!" His voice rose an octave as he peered up into the steel rafters overhead. "This is amazing. I was picturing small and dingy. This is neither!" He jogged across the basketball court and scampered up the steps of the bleachers.

Joy laughed. She had met athletes who enjoyed being inside a gym, especially those who were good at playing basketball. But Junior's reaction was incredible. What had him so excited about this place?

For the moment, he wasn't giving her any clues. He stood at the top of the bleachers, hands on hips, turning his head one way and then the other. His lips moved, and he nodded, maybe counting ceiling tiles.

"We can come back sometime, maybe get a game organized." She hated to break the spell, but she hadn't intended to stay here all night.

"Yeah, yeah." He shook his curly head and scampered back to join her on the gym floor. "I have just never seen anything like this. The ceiling is so tall, and the floor is extra big. You could almost turn the basketball court sideways and fit another one next to it. Whoever designed this place had a bigger vision in mind."

"Funny you should say that." Joy searched her memory for an old conversation. "Grandpa said that the school board had discussions about expanding, maybe even adding a second floor to this place. But, the highway was rerouted, and the town stopped growing. The school was struggling to stay afloat, so plans were dropped."

"Well, you never know." Junior took one last long look around. "But you probably have more to show me. I have a crazy fascination with gyms. Someday, I'd like to be a coach. Maybe not a basketball coach, but more like an activity director. Helping folks of all ages stay physically fit. The wheels in my head start turning when I come into a spot like this."

"That's so cool!" Finally, she was starting to understand. "I have no doubt you will make that happen someday."

The wind rattled the windows near the top of the massive room. Lights swayed and flickered.

"We'd better move along. The weather may be getting nasty before the night is over." She led the way to the door leading back to the main school building, turning off light switches as she went. What fun to find that this guy from another town shared her fascination with old places like this. Not many guys his age had such definite dreams about their future. There was more to this rodeo clown than most folks saw, that was for sure.

JUNIOR ZIPPED up his jacket and jogged to keep up with Joy as she made her way down the hillside in front of the old school. He hadn't pictured any of this happening after the tree-lighting ceremony. They passed the brightly lit tree, and she waved at some people still milling about nearby, sipping hot chocolate provided by her mom and dad.

"The best view of the town is this way. We should be able to see pretty much everything from up here." She opened the unlocked front door of the church building, and they stepped into the comfort of the heated sanctuary.

Dim lights accented the ceiling and the area near the altar. Wood paneling dominated the room, interrupted by several tall windows on each side of the double row of pews. This was another place in Snowville that obviously hadn't changed for generations. Though very different from the relaxed atmosphere of his dad's cowboy church, this place was comfortable and welcoming. The large wooden cross hanging in the center of the front reminded him that he was in the right place.

"What do you think? Pretty outdated, huh?" Joy ran her hand across the smoothly polished back of a pew.

"No need to change anything when it's this beautiful." Junior meant what he said. Nothing stodgy here. He knew that all visitors were made to feel at home.

"We like it." Joy's voice was quiet. "But what I want to show you is this way." She took his hand and led him down the center aisle, then to the left in front of the pulpit. She opened a door that covered a narrow staircase. "I'm not sure there was ever a bell up here, but there's always been a light."

She flipped a switch and started up the stairs. Junior followed, watching his footsteps as they climbed up, up, and up.

The room at the top of the stairs was perfectly square, with a window on each side. One padded bench sat next to a wall, and boxes of different sizes lined the rest of the space.

"Just a storage room." Joy opened and closed a lid on one of the boxes. "When I was ten, I came up here and opened every single box. That's when I found the oldest one, under the bench, against the wall where no one had looked for years."

"What was in it?" He could picture her, probably with braided pigtails, curiously opening the old crate.

"A really old nativity scene." She stood looking at the spot where the box must have been. "I sat here for a long time, just looking at each piece. I thought about just packing it up and leaving it here."

"But that wouldn't be right, right?" Junior prompted her.

"It was wrapped in old newspapers that were about to fall apart. Grandma helped me take the figures down the stairs a few at a time."

"Why didn't you use the box you'd found them in?" Junior asked. He inched closer as she continued the story.

"It was an old wooden crate that was falling apart. I couldn't risk dropping the pieces on the way down. So, I took down the three wise men, the shepherds, the sheep, and the angel—finally, Mary, Joseph, and the baby. Then I just sat beside them on that pew for the longest time. It was amazing to think I'd found something no one else knew about."

Junior stood very close to her now. Her eyes looked past him to the flickering lights of the town. He touched her hand, wrapped her fingers in his. He didn't want to disturb this very special memory for her.

"That nativity scene just meant so much. It was a connection to the people who had lived here before. A connection to that other little town where Jesus was born." She stopped talking and turned toward him. "Silly, huh?"

"Not a bit." He wrapped her in a hug. He'd found his own treasure here in this little town.

"Well. That's the tour." Joy stepped away, clearing her throat.

"It's beautiful. Just like you said." The lights from the houses and businesses flickered between the waving pine branches.

"Yeah. It's pretty special." She leaned against him.

"Hey, it's not even eight o'clock. How about taking a ride to see what my hometown looks like all lit up for Christmas?" He still held her hand. "We might even get a piece of pie while we're there."

"Sure. But I can't stay gone too long. I've got class tomorrow." She smiled.

"Yeah. Me too. I'll bring you right back." It was still early. Too early to try for a quick kiss. Best not to rush things. Junior stepped back, peering out each window before they started down the stairs. Joy was halfway down the rickety staircase before he started.

"I'll get the lights from down here. We leave one on all night up there." She shouted from the bottom of the stairs.

"Gotcha." Yes. The heart of Snowville was definitely in the right place. Junior was beginning to think his was too.

6

"Wow, look up there." Joy pointed from the passenger side of Junior's truck. "We don't come this way often. I don't think I've noticed that cross before."

"Yeah. Isn't it great? That's next to my sister and brother-in-law's place on the mountain behind my house." Junior nodded with evident pride. "I helped them rig up the floodlights. It makes a pretty good landmark around here."

"I guess so!" Joy's mind immediately went to the cost factor. What must it cost to keep a light like that running year-round? She knew Junior's family had run a rodeo for years, but that didn't seem like a highly profitable business. Did they have support from the community of Crossroads for this?

"So, in just a little bit, we'll be coming into town down the main highway through Crossroads." Junior kicked into tour guide mode. "On your left will be the Billings Boys car dealership. Home of the most community-minded enterprise in this county. Well, there is also a casino at the other end of town. They are big, too, I guess."

"Yeah. I've heard of both of those. Your town has had a real growth spurt lately." Joy remembered seeing commercials on television touting the success of many places in Junior's hometown. Her little town couldn't compete, and in a way, she was okay with that.

"Our main focus tonight will be the old downtown area, where crews have been working for weeks to install the retro-looking lights that hang completely across the streets." Junior slowed his truck and stopped at a red light.

A red, green, and gold glow greeted them as the stoplight changed, and Junior drove slowly forward. Joy was transported back several decades as the cold breeze prompted the strings of stars to wave and sparkle.

"Ah. Maz. Ing." She lowered her window and leaned out for a better view. "And every store along the way has lights as well."

"Yep. As my dad says, 'She's a showplace.'"

Junior made a loop around the town's courthouse square and pulled into a parking spot.

"Want to walk around a bit?' He turned off the engine and smiled in her direction.

"Of course!" Joy pulled her coat around her, zipping it against the increasing wind as Junior opened her door. Trees above their heads supported strings of lights in all colors. The courthouse itself was outlined in white, with a brilliant star topping the clock tower. Again, her mind drifted into the practicalities of this display. How long did it take for crews to accomplish this monumental task? Did the city use paid workers or volunteers? *Breathe, Joy. Just enjoy this.*

Junior took her hand and led her through the display. Children ran past them, shouting their pleasure as they found their favorite features. Small wooden buildings housed dioramas of Santa's workshop, a post office, and even a train station, complete with a tiny engine and caboose.

"Oops." Junior blocked her gently before she walked into a photo taken by an eager set of parents. "Don't want to photobomb their family pics."

"Of course not. But we need a selfie or two of our own!" She pulled her phone out of her coat pocket. "Are you okay with that? I'll only send them to my parents and maybe Brannon. They would love this."

"Sure. Text them to me too." Junior poked his head through a hole in a life-size wooden figure of a Grinch.

Joy laughed and snapped the picture. "Somehow, that doesn't fit you at all."

"Hey. We all have our moments. God loves grinches too." He gave her his best goofy grin. "I don't know about you, but I'm starving. I know a perfect place a block or two away with great food, and they stay open late for Christmas light lookers."

"Lead on!" She grabbed his hand and followed. Nope. Not a grinch at all. She didn't remember meeting a more joyful person than Junior Caldwell.

JUNIOR PUSHED the glass door open at Amy Lou's and flinched when the jangling bell announced their arrival. No way was he ashamed to bring his new friend here, but in this small town, eating at the local diner was akin to bringing your date home to meet the parents.

"Sit anywhere, honey. You know the drill." Candace waved at him with the rag she was using to wipe down a table.

Junior led the way past all the booths in front toward a table for two in the back of the diner. He smiled at Joy as they passed a familiar blue jean jacket at the counter.

"Hey. Stop just a sec." He touched her shoulder gently.

"Sure." She turned to face him, her cheeks glowing from the cold air they'd just left.

"Dad." Junior tapped the back of the jacket, just under the fleece collar.

"Oh, hey, son!" Dad turned their way. "Back from Snowville?"

"Yeah. I'd like you to meet Joy Fredericks, the main cog behind their Christmas celebration." He nodded at Joy. "Joy, this is my dad, Calvin Caldwell, Sr."

"Very nice to meet you, sir." Joy extended her hand, still covered by a white knit glove.

"The pleasure is mine, young lady." Dad shook her hand. "Junior, don't forget, you've got school tomorrow. Semester tests start soon."

"Yes, sir." Junior stepped backward for a moment before guiding Joy toward the table he had spotted. Another reminder from Dad that he was still a child. Oh, well, the curse of being born as the last of three siblings. Nothing new.

"Are you hungry?" He pulled out a ladder-back chair and ensured Joy was seated before walking to the other side of the table.

"A little." Joy removed her gloves and stuffed them in her pockets. "Mom fixed her traditional sloppy joe supper before the tree lighting, but that cold air makes my belly thinks it needs something else."

"Cold air, warm air, no difference for me. I'm always hungry." Junior quickly glanced at the menu to be sure nothing had been marked off. "They have great burgers and fries and stuff. Or, if you want dessert, the pie is famous around here."

"Pie sounds great." Joy tapped her fingers on the table. "And maybe something hot to drink."

"So, what do you think? Does the Crossroads Christmas

289

display meet your approval? Too gaudy or just right?" He watched as Candace approached and nodded her way.

"It's fabulous. Bigger and more involved than ours, but you have lots more people here."

"Welcome to Amy Lou's, ma'am. What can I bring you?" Candace stood next to the table with her order pad.

"I hear good things about your pie. And I'd like a cup of coffee with cream and sugar." Joy tented her fingers.

"Coconut cream, chocolate, or," Candace craned her neck, checking the pie cabinet behind the counter, "Apple?"

"Apple sounds perfect."

"And for you, young Mr. Caldwell?" Candace smiled at him.

"Your chili burger, please. With fries. I'll let you know about the pie later." Junior replaced the menu behind the napkin holder.

"And a large Coke, right?" Candace nodded as she walked away.

"Sometimes you want to go where everybody knows your name, right?" Joy laughed.

"I guess there are good and bad points to that." Junior's cheeks warmed. "All of these people think they know me a little too well. They probably have my whole life figured out by now."

"It's good to have some support. But you can always surprise them." Joy stirred sugar into her coffee. "From what I've seen, you can do pretty much whatever you set your mind to."

"Great judge of character." Junior laughed. "What did you say you are studying in college? Psychology?"

"I'm taking basics now, so I will have to do some of that. But my major will be Business and Economic Development." She unzipped her coat and settled back in her chair.

"Of course. I'm sure you'll put little Snowville on the map and move on to bigger things." He tucked a napkin in his shirt collar before taking the first bite of his messy burger.

The bell on the door jangled again, and he was only a little surprised to see more members of his family walking in.

"Hi there," His sister, Hope and her husband, O.D. Billings, stood next to Junior and Joy's table.

"How are you doing, little brother?" O.D. patted Junior's shoulder.

"Hope wouldn't cook for you?" Junior stood to shake O.D.'s hand, then reached around to give Hope a sideways hug.

"She did. It was actually pretty good too. So, I brought her out for some dessert." O.D. winked at Hope.

"Joy Fredericks, this is my sister, Hope, and her husband, O.D. Guys, this is Joy from Snowville." Junior turned toward Joy.

"Welcome!" Hope reached for Joy's hand. "I remember coming to your town when we were kids. It's gorgeous out there."

"Thanks. Yes, we love it. Unfortunately, not many folks know about it, except at Christmastime." Joy nodded and waved at them. "Very nice to meet both of you."

Dad stood behind O.D. with his coffee cup. "Hey, let's grab the round table in the corner." O.D. started toward the back wall. "Junior, do y'all want to join us?"

"No, thanks. I'll have to get Joy back home in a bit. We'll see y'all later." He sat back down. It might be best to avoid 'family overload' on their first real date.

JOY RELEASED Junior's hand as they squeezed through the crowd on the opposite side of the courthouse. A moist breeze tickled her cheeks. Hopefully, the temperature would remain above freezing until Junior had her safely back home again.

With his Razorback red toboggan on his head, Junior didn't stand out in the crowd like he did when his curly blond hair was shining. She caught up with him as he stopped in front of the large church across the street from the government building.

"One last stop." Junior turned to reach for her hand. "The church has a pretty cool manger scene."

Joy took a deep breath. The life-sized figures showed beautiful craftsmanship in the skillful wood carving. Facial features had been carefully added, and the calm expressions of the Mary and Joseph figures reached into her heart.

"Incredible." She was reluctant to break the silence but knew Junior was waiting for a reaction.

"This has been here all my life. Before the days of video cameras, the men of the community used to stay up here 24/7 to watch for vandals. Some people will go to any lengths to have the baby Jesus in their lives." He looped his arm through hers.

"So, it's been stolen?" She couldn't imagine why someone would do this.

"Yeah. I think years ago, it was just a prank. Whoever took it always brought it back the next day. As I said, cameras ended that because the police know everybody, and one look at the video was all they would need."

"I wish I had a video to help me find our baby Jesus." Joy turned to walk toward Junior's nearby pickup truck. She should have gotten over Brannon losing the beloved figure by now. Why couldn't he have just left it alone?

"You ready to head home?" Junior opened the passenger door.

"Yes. Thanks for showing me around. Your town does a great job with Christmas." She did enjoy the trip, but in a way, it made Snowville's celebration seem paltry in comparison.

Junior was quiet as he navigated through the busy streets around the courthouse.

"So, what did happen with your nativity scene?" Junior asked as they reached the city limits.

"Well, my brother started a little tradition when we were kids. He created a scavenger hunt for me, hiding the pieces of the nativity scene and giving me clues to find them." Joy removed her gloves and hat as Junior's heater warmed the truck's cab. "As we got older, he reduced it to just hiding one of the figures."

"Sounds like fun." Junior accelerated as the highway changed to a four-lane road.

"It was, I guess. But the last time, he chose to hide the baby Jesus figure." Joy said. "That worried me, but it was out of my control. He was grown and married by then but still liked the tradition. I couldn't ruin his fun, so I went along."

"So, did he forget where he hid it?" Junior asked.

"Not really. It's just that we had a little too much excitement on the day of the scavenger hunt." Joy tried to decide how to summarize the events of that day.

"Yeah?" Junior sounded intrigued.

"Brannon had bought the old gas station in town from Bob Baker. He intended to start a car repair business there. We didn't have much traffic on the highway, even back then, but he thought he would have some regular customers."

"Sounds like a great idea." Junior turned on his windshield wipers to battle the increasing rain.

"That day, a huge tractor-trailer tried to take the curve in front of Bob's gas station way too fast. As a result, it plowed into the building while we were finishing Sunday dinner at Grandpa's house." Joy's heart raced as she remembered the chaos of that day.

"So, I guess that became more important than the scavenger hunt," Junior prompted.

"To say the least. Luckily, the truck driver was okay, and we were blessed that he missed the gas pumps. That could have been the end for most of the buildings in town."

"Wow!" Junior glanced her way. "But why didn't Brannon tell you where he had hidden the baby?"

"He did. It was inside the gas station. We searched through the rubble in the damaged part of the building but never found it." Joy leaned forward, peering into the rainy night.

"Maybe it will turn up. What does your brother plan to do with the old gas station?" Junior asked.

"Luckily, he got an insurance settlement from the truck driver. He used it to take the old gas pumps completely out. He said he didn't want to risk an explosion while the thing sat vacant. So, he just did the bare minimum to repair the building. I don't know if anyone will ever want to buy it. He said that just convinced him to start a business in town." She didn't have anything else to add. That story ended like many others—with a business closing and someone leaving Snowville behind.

"Oh, well, people don't mind driving into town for gas. Big Ed's Barbecue and your live nativity scene are the real draws for your town anyway."

Joy looked as they passed another large display of twinkling lights before turning onto the highway that led back home. This had been a fun outing, but she couldn't help comparing their handful of buildings to how wonderful Crossroads looked tonight.

"I hope I haven't kept you out too late on a 'school' night," Junior patted her hand.

"No. This was lots of fun." As Junior's pickup navigated the curvy road to Snowville, her mind churned with the details of her town's coming celebration.

An alert caused her cell phone to buzz in her pocket.

Sorry, Joy

The text came from a farmer who lived near their house.

Our donkey won't be at your Live Nativity
this year. Her baby is coming any time
now, and we can't risk it.

"Wow." Joy stuffed the phone back in her pocket.

"That didn't sound like a good 'wow.'" Junior slowed as they passed the first buildings in Snowville.

"I don't know why I still bother. What's a nativity scene without a donkey? I think we're down to one cow and a goat. The sheep are not even guaranteed." She leaned her head against the cold glass of the passenger's window.

"You certainly can't trust a sheep without a guarantee." Junior grinned.

"It's just so disappointing. No one else seems to care about this." Even her new friend thought it was a joke.

"I still have connections with stock contractors." Junior reached over to pat her hand. "Let me take care of getting a donkey and some guaranteed sheep."

"Really? You'd do that? But remember, we can't pay." She watched his face for signs that he was only teasing.

"No problem. I have a couple of resources to draw on. Trust me. Now, what are the dates for this extravaganza?"

He seemed sincere.

"It will be the two weekends before Christmas, starting at five o'clock on Friday, Saturday, and Sunday night. Six performances in all." Joy still held her phone in her hand. She hadn't even replied to the guy with the pregnant donkey.

"Totally doable." Junior stopped his pickup in front of her parents' house. "We'll talk before then, right?"

Joy forced her bottom jaw up. No use looking like a total idiot.

"Of course. Of course, we will. Thanks so much, Junior."

He bounced around to her side of the truck and opened the door.

"*Brrr.* I guess you'd better get inside. As my Granny would say, 'that wind is chillin' me through and through.'" He reached for her hand, and she allowed him to help her out of the truck.

"Hey, is that what I think it is?" Junior tilted his head and peered at the large tree behind her house.

"Yeah. Brannon's old treehouse. It is pretty cool, I guess. After he moved away, it was a good quiet spot for reading." Joy watched the glint of the vapor light in the yard as it reflected off the old tin roof of the little structure.

"I'd love to see it. I never had one since my siblings were girls, and my dad was always busy with the rodeo." Junior said.

"Brannon used every spare scrap of wood that Dad would let him have. They are both pretty handy. I guess they enjoyed building it together. I'd love to show you, but let's wait until daylight. Dicey getting up there, now." Joy smiled.

"Yeah. We'd have to use a ..." Junior whispered behind his hand "*Ladder.*"

"Oh, stop." Joy's eyes sparkled as she laughed. "Next time."

"Good night!" He squeezed her hand and ran back around to the driver's side. She wouldn't have objected to a little peck on the cheek. This guy was certainly not typical.

Grandpa's Christmas lights flickered over her shoulder as she watched Junior drive away. Nope, nothing typical about this Christmas at all.

7

"Everything okay in Snowville?" Dad's voice echoed through the quiet living area when Junior kicked off his boots in the mudroom.

"Yeah." Why did Dad insist on waiting up for him? He was a senior in high school, for cornbread's sake.

"Son." Dad stood and switched on a light over the kitchen island. "I don't like to keep harping on things over and over. But tomorrow is a school day. You have a few more days to improve your semester grades. Wouldn't tonight have been a good time to study instead of gallivanting around with your new girlfriend?"

Gallivanting?

"Yes. sir." He had learned it was better not to argue. "I really think my grades will be fine."

"Fine?" Dad refilled his coffee cup. "Last time I heard, they were far from fine. You haven't firmed up any college scholarships that I know of. I don't know what you expect to do when high school is over, but it won't be easy without a good education."

298

"I don't know if I'll need a lot of college. I've been talking to the people at the Boys and Girls Club. I am pretty sure they will hire me to be an activity director. I've been volunteering there ever since the rodeo ..." He knew Dad didn't like to hear him say the words 'went under.' Dad had been ready to move on when he sold his interest in the only business the Caldwell family had ever known. Trouble was, Junior had not been the least bit prepared.

"I think you'd better check with them a little further." Dad sat down on one of the tall barstools. "Most positions like that require a degree. Moving from leading dodgeball games to supervising people is more involved than you think."

Junior hadn't given this much thought. Dad was probably right.

"Well, anyway. I guess I'd better get to bed." Junior walked across the kitchen toward the hallway that led to his room. This house was so big these days. And so quiet without the never-ending chatter he could always get started with his sisters.

"Okay. Son, I want you to take these last few days before Christmas break a little more seriously. No more running off to visit friends on a school night."

"Good night." Junior made an effort not to slam the door of his bedroom. But, if he heard one more suggestion about what not to do on a 'school night,' he would scream.

He pulled up the email address of the stock contractor he'd been talking to about Joy's live nativity.

"I found out what nights we'll need the donkey and the sheep." Then, he resumed the email thread. "I need a quote on how much you will charge to bring them to Snowville. And, let me know about the possibility of the camel."

Now to get some buy-in on the Billings' Boys sponsoring whatever this would cost. He really couldn't expect it to be free of charge. It would help if he promised to supervise at least some of the animals himself. No need asking the man to bring a whole crew along with the animals. That would increase the price.

What was that marketing guy's name at Billings? No, he'd send O.D. an email. At his work address. It was a 'school night,' after all. He shook his head. Now he was doing it to himself. He gathered what he needed to shower and headed back down the hall. Only a few more hours until school would start. He probably did need a little sleep.

At the end of the hall leading to the living room, he caught a glimpse of where his mom had always installed the family's Christmas tree. Dad had purchased an artificial tree last year, the first year without the heart of the family's celebration.

Junior should probably cut a real tree this year. Decorating the tree had always been a special mother-son time for them. His sisters lost patience with the old traditions as they got older, but Junior treasured those times. When Mom got sick, they encouraged each other by preparing for the holidays. With Mom gone, there was an empty space inside him. Supporting Joy's Snowville celebration was helping to patch that hole. Nothing would ever be the same, but maybe new traditions could take hold and help him heal.

He shook his head and pushed the bathroom door open, flipping on the light switch inside. He needed to take things one at a time. For now, he needed to get a shower and get to bed. Tomorrow, after school, he'd get the stock for Snowville's live nativity nailed down. Then, hopefully, whatever happened at school would be over quickly.

～

"EVERYTHING OKAY IN HERE?" Joy's mom peeked into the bedroom.

"I'm just reading a little bit before bedtime." Joy marked her spot in the Bible. She'd decided to read one chapter of Luke's gospel each night leading up to Christmas. Luke's style was easy to understand, and it made the scenes surrounding the birth of Jesus so believable.

"Well, don't stay up too late. You've got class tomorrow, right?" Mom reached out to touch the stable that sheltered the antique nativity scene on Joy's dresser.

"My first class is at ten, so no hurry." Joy smiled. Maybe she should have moved to a dorm when she enrolled in the university. The commute to campus was only about an hour, and she loved being here at home before and afterward. But Mom was having trouble seeing her as an adult, even now.

"Good night, Mom." She snuggled deeper into her bed and resumed reading about the shepherds and the remarkable scene they had witnessed.

"Night, sweetie." Mom closed the door softly.

The tiny white lights she had threaded through the nativity scene twinkled. This little set had seen so many Christmas celebrations. Except for that long stretch when it rested in a box in the attic of the church building. She examined the face of the Mary figurine. If only she could feel the peace in her heart that this wooden sculpture exuded. Christmas still happened, even when the set was forgotten for all those years. It would still happen now even though the little figure of the baby Jesus had been replaced by a clothespin.

Joy took a long, deep breath. If only she could find that figure and return it to its rightful place. That might be asking too much. Maybe she just needed to concentrate on the live nativity. After all, that tradition had continued through all sorts of problems. *Lord, help me ensure this celebration happens in Snowville this year. Amen.*

She walked to her bedroom window and pressed her face against the cold pane. In this position, she could spot the star on top of the community Christmas tree. With the help of the whole community, that tree was shining brightly. With the help of a certain ex-rodeo clown, she believed the live nativity would happen too.

After finishing the Second Chapter of Luke, she turned to the spot Grandma had marked in her Bible: Matthew 2, verse 10. This verse inspired her parents to choose her name when she was born on Christmas day almost nineteen years ago. "When they saw the star, they rejoiced with exceeding great joy." A tiny tear slid down her cheek. She had always wondered if her parents decided on her name or if Grandma suggested it. Either way, her heart ached with the responsibility her name brought. No matter the difficulties, nothing could hinder the celebration of the birthday she shared with Bethlehem's most famous citizen.

Christmas would happen in Snowville. She would make sure it did.

8

J unior heaved a huge sigh as he turned the paper over and placed his pencil next to it on his desk. This final test had been tough. How much would he use math in the future anyway? Hopefully, the score would be good enough that he wouldn't need to repeat this class next semester. He had picked up an extra elective—health and physical fitness. If he had to be in school for a few more months, he wanted to ensure his time wasn't wasted on math.

"How'd you do?" Cody asked as they exited the classroom a few minutes later.

"I don't know." Junior was tired of talking about tests. "Hey, dude. After we get you situated at the lunchroom table, I want to go outside to text Joy."

"Go on out. I can handle this myself." Cody rolled past him, spinning around in the hallway a few steps ahead of Junior.

"Show-off." Junior laughed. "But, yeah. If you're sure you've got this, I'll go send my text now and then come back inside to eat."

"Yeah, yeah. Talk to your Snowville cutie. I'll be fine." Cody took off again, and Junior ducked into the courtyard next to the cafeteria.

> Finals today?

Joy had already sent him a text to get the conversation started.

Junior typed quickly.

> Yeah. Such a pain.

> Hey, at this point, those scores are important. Could determine which college you get into.

Which college? Did she assume he was going? He didn't know for sure, even now.

> Not sure I need college.

He was glad he could be honest with her. His Dad never liked hearing those words from him.

> There's a lot of good stuff in college. I'm super glad I'm doing it.

Joy was responding quickly. He was glad he had caught her during a break.

> You're probably really good at all of your subjects.

She just had the look of a brainiac.

> They're not all easy. But it opens so many doors. Hopefully, things work out for you.

Junior contemplated this for a minute before responding. Joy thought he needed to be in college. Had he ever known a girl who seemed that interested in his future? This was an exciting change.

> We'll see. Well, I gotta go get some
> lunch. Talk to you soon.

His text conversations with her were longer than most he'd had with other people. It was good to have someone to talk to.

> Call me tonight?

> Sure.

That would give him something to look forward to. He could make it through the rest of the day, now, final exams and all.

Joy wiped a few stray raindrops from her windshield as she drove home from college to Snowville.

Mom and Dad were still working in town, so she was the one who checked on Grandpa every afternoon. He enjoyed puttering around in his house for a few hours each day, but Mom wasn't confident enough to let him stay alone too long. Thankfully, Joy only had a few more days of college classes until break. They were nearing the time Grandpa would move into his room at the assisted living center.

Joy stopped her car in front of Grandpa's house and sent up a quick prayer. *God, help us all prepare for the changes coming soon. It will be so lonesome around here without Grandpa. Please help me trust Your plan for him.*

"Hey, there." Right on cue, Grandpa walked out the front door, holding something in his hand.

"Hi, Grandpa." She walked closer and wrapped his bony shoulders in a hug. "What's that?"

"I found a treasure today." He sat down in his favorite rocking chair on the porch. "Pastor Schumacher's Bible."

"Wow. That's wonderful." Joy pulled up a stool and sat in front of him. "You never met him, did you?"

"No. After he passed, the congregation did their best to stay together for a few years. He and his wife are both buried in the town's cemetery. But, when they called me, there were only a few members, and none were related to him." Grandpa turned the pages carefully to the middle. "Here is their family tree. Do you think you could help me find his kids or grandkids? They need to have this."

Joy examined the names of the Schumacher's children and a few grandchildren. With the help of ancestry websites, tracking at least one of them should be no problem.

"Sure, Grandpa. I'll do that for you." She took the Bible from Grandpa and gently thumbed through the pages. It was always interesting to look for passages marked and notes in the margin. Most of the scribbles seemed to be references to other scriptures. Grandpa's Bible probably looked much the same. She admired anyone who could stand before a group and bring these words to life. Her eyes misted as she remembered the last full-fledged sermon Grandpa had preached before handing over the pulpit to Dad. What a blessing to have two such incredible men in her family.

"Are you ready to go to our house for supper?" Joy returned the Bible to him.

"Soon," Grandpa turned toward the front door of his house. "Come in for just a minute."

Joy followed him, taking a deep breath as she stepped into the living room. Very little had changed since Grandma passed away. Each picture on the wall, the hand-crocheted doilies, and the books still in place on the bookshelf gave the impression that Grandma might walk in from the kitchen at any moment.

"Grandpa, are you sure you don't want to move in with us instead of going to the assisted living place in town?" Joy swallowed hard as she asked the question burdening her heart.

"You know, your mom and dad have asked me that question about once a week since we started talking about this." Grandpa sat in his favorite rocking chair. "I thought about it. They even said that a home health aide could come to stay while they are at work and you are in college. I think a fresh start would be better."

"A fresh start?" Joy still had a hard time accepting this.

"Yes. I'll take a few things from this house to remind me of home. But living with you and your mom and dad wouldn't be like having my own place. Besides, since Brannon and his family live in town, and your mom and dad work there, I figure I'll see all of you almost as much. And I won't be burdening any of you with the medical and housekeeping chores. I remember what it was like to be a caregiver for your grandma." His voice was firm. There was no doubt he'd made up his mind. "But listen. This is why I asked you to come in."

Joy settled on the couch, leaving Grandma's chair vacant.

"This big place is way more than I can take care of. We all know that. When your dad took over the pulpit, I bought it from the church since he had his own house already."

Where was this leading? Instead of venturing a guess, Joy just listened.

"It's a wonderful house, and it shouldn't sit here empty." He paused, standing to look down the long hallway. "I think it would make a great place for folks to visit when they need a break from the city. Your grandma and I were talking about this before she got sick." He turned to face Joy, and his face lit up.

"Do you think you could turn it into one of those 'sleep and eat' places? I know you might not want to stay here forever, but you could hire someone to run it while you are gone ... Well. I guess it's crazy. But you are the one who has the vision for this little town, and I ..."

Joy swallowed hard.

"You mean a bed and breakfast?"

"Yeah, that's what they call them. Not a hotel, just a house where a couple or two can visit or a family can stay. Either they can cook for themselves, or whomever you hire can supply the meals. Grandma and I stayed in a place like that in Eureka Springs a few years back." Grandpa sat down again and used his right hand to stop his left from trembling.

"What a great idea!" Thoughts were bouncing off every part of Joy's brain. Some upgrades would be needed before they could attract guests. Maybe a new bathroom or two should be added. Should she live here while she finished college?

"I hoped you would say that!" Grandpa laughed. "Your Mom and Dad may take some convincing, but we can talk it over at supper."

"Grandpa, you are the smartest, best man I have ever met." Joy hugged him tightly.

"High praise! But I won't disagree with you." He stood up and walked toward the door. "Now, let's prepare our speech for the rest of the family."

Joy glanced at the empty place in front of the picture window where Grandma had always placed their Christmas tree. Maybe she'd make sure there was one in that spot next year. How exciting! Surely, Mom and Dad would agree. It was better than just dusting and vacuuming this place every week or so. If she lived here, she could oversee the revival of Snowville.

Wow. Too much to think about right now. *Lord, help me keep my feet on the ground. I need to take one day at a time. After all, I still don't have the live nativity nailed down. Can I take care of a whole house and run a bed and breakfast? Does Grandpa have too much faith in me? I'll need Your help for sure. Amen.*

She followed Grandpa as he strolled to Mom and Dad's house. Funny, she already thought of the house she'd grown up in as their place, not hers. Would Grandpa and Grandma's place feel like home to her before long? She took a deep breath. First things first. Finish the semester at school, make sure the live nativity happened, then think about this bed and breakfast idea. It wouldn't be easy to keep all these wheels in her brain moving at the right speed and in the right direction.

She steadied Grandpa as he navigated the steps to their front porch. Inside the door, he headed for the half bath.

A text from Junior popped onto her phone.

What's up?

Ha! You won't believe it when I tell you.

JUNIOR LAUGHED as he sat on his bed and waited for a gap in Joy's texting to formulate a reply.

Wanna just call me?

She typed "LOL," and then his phone rang.

"Hi. I guess this is easier. Can you tell I'm excited?" Joy squeaked.

"Yeah. But I get it. If I had a possible line on a new house of my own, and maybe even a business after college, I'd be happy too. What will your parents say?" Junior tried to generate some calm.

"Oh, you know. They'll say we'll all have to talk about it. So don't get in a hurry, all that stuff." Joy sighed.

"Well, I can see that too." The role of a diplomat was new for him, but he thought he was pulling it off. "So, to change the subject for a minute, I have a question for you."

"Sure. Is it about the live nativity?"

"No. Not at all. It's a school thing. I need to give my teacher a topic and an outline for my final English paper tomorrow, and I'm doing some research online. Can you tell me when the Snowville gym was built?" Could he get her to refocus for a minute to help him with his research?

"Nineteen twenty-eight. I remember because Grandpa said they had talked about how glad folks were that it was paid for before the big crash of Nineteen twenty-nine. So, you're doing a paper about the Depression Era?" Joy's voice seemed a little calmer now.

"No, I'm not into history. I think my paper will be about making facilities accessible for disabled people. I will need to know what their laws said back then compared to what is required now. That gives me a place to start." Junior tapped a pencil on his chair as he paced around the room.

"Cool! Let me know what you find out. I'd love to see that old place brought up to date someday." Joy said.

"Back on the subject of the nativity scene, I think I can take care of the livestock for you. You worry about the people." Could she really trust him to do this for her?

"You don't know how much pressure that takes off me. Thanks so much." He could hear the smile in her voice.

"Oh, and I guess you can put me down as one of the shepherds. I'm sure I'll need to help keep the animal actors corralled." He found an extra blanket on his bed and draped it over his head and shoulders. Yeah, he'd make a great shepherd.

"Okay. There was a day or two when I wondered if Christmas would even happen this year. Thanks for coming along to help."

"Christmas always happens." Junior dropped the blanket and stood straighter. "Jesus is always around, even when we can't see Him." Was that out of line? Too preachy? No, she was a preacher's kid too.

"Of course." Her voice was almost a whisper.

"Take care, Christmas Joy." Too bad he couldn't give her a quick hug.

"Thanks so much. You take care of yourself, too, Junior Caldwell."

9

J oy walked up the steps to her front door with a bag of
groceries in each hand. Mom had a longer commute
home from her job, so Joy never minded making a stop
after her last class of the day. Nothing in the bags sounded
exciting for supper, but she couldn't be choosy.

Leaves swirled around her on the porch as she pushed her
way in. December was up to its tricks again, warm as autumn
one day, followed by a bitter wind the next.

"Grandpa? What's up?" She placed the groceries on the
kitchen table and followed the sound of the television. She
found him in their family room, watching a game show.

"Nothing." He turned the television off. "Absolutely
nothing."

She sat in a high-back chair across from the couch. It was
lonesome for him when they were all gone. An advantage of
the assisted living center would be that there were more
people to talk to during the day.

"Mom and Dad will be home soon. I think we're having

your favorite chili for supper." She patted his hand, and he smiled up at her.

What's up?

Funny that Junior used the exact same phrase she'd greeted Grandpa with.

Just walked in.

Can I call?

Sure.

She was glad they wouldn't keep up the texting much longer. It was more fun to hear his voice.

"I'll be right back, Grandpa." She walked toward her bedroom as her phone rang.

"Hi!" She plopped down on the end of her bed.

"No more school till next year!" Junior said. "How about you?"

"I'm done too." Joy smiled, bringing a throw pillow to her lap.

"I thought I might come out and get the lay of the land before the first performance of the live nativity this weekend. Today's Tuesday, so there are only a few days left. Want to go somewhere to eat afterward?"

"Sure. I'm glad you mentioned that. I need to talk to Lisa's mom to be sure the costumes are ready. But, believe it or not, since you agreed to be a shepherd, I now have all of the parts covered." Joy stood and ran her hand across the rough roof of the nativity's stable on her dresser.

"Great. Looks like it may be pretty cold tonight, so I might come early So, maybe around five?" Junior asked.

"Sure. It will be almost dark, but there are floodlights out there. I'll see you soon." She opened her closet door, looking for warm layers for Junior's little "walkabout". The wind would be the biggest problem. She would put her hair up and find a knit cap for her head. Her heart raced as she thought about his mischievous grin. She'd better help Mom get supper started, so she could skip out when her new friend arrived.

JUNIOR STOPPED in front of Joy's house. Just to the left of her front porch, he caught a glimpse of the tree house he'd seen the last time he was here. She'd promised to let him have a closer look. Probably silly, but he was fascinated by Brannon's creation.

"Hi!" Joy stepped out onto the porch. "Mom's almost got the chili ready for our supper. Want to stay here?"

"Oh, I don't know." Family meals were fine, but he was looking forward to having dinner with Joy alone. "I passed an Italian place on the way over here. Do you know if it's any good?"

"Mrs. Gino's? It's great. And probably not too busy on a Tuesday night." Joy pushed her hair up inside her cap.

"I want to see where the live nativity will be, but you also promised to let me check out Brannon's tree house." Junior reached for her hand.

"Sure." Joy trotted behind the house to the massive tree at the edge of the clearing. "I don't think anyone has been up there since Brannon's last treasure hunt. I guess that's been right at two years."

"I'm game if you are." Junior smiled.

"Brannon always started the treasure hunt in the treehouse. I don't think he ever really grew up." Joy stepped up on the bottom rung of the ladder nailed to the tree's trunk. "Let's go."

Junior clambered up after her, waiting while she pushed the trap door up to enter the makeshift structure. She disappeared above him, and he pulled himself up. A musty, dusty smell greeted him, and he sat beside Joy, legs crossed. There might be room to stand, but he didn't want to risk it.

"This is pretty neat." Junior crawled on his knees to a window that looked away from the house. He could see the rooftop where he'd first met her on Thanksgiving afternoon. Beyond that, the old schoolhouse was visible on the town's highest hill.

"Hey! Look what I found." Joy crept over next to him. "The last clue."

Junior took a scrap of wrapping paper from her and read the words written there. "No one expected to find the Son of a King in a lowly manger. He's always with us, even in the oiliest, grimiest spot in the town."

"*Ooh.* I would have been so mad if I'd read that." Joy bumped her head as she stood up. "Why didn't he hide the baby in a cleaner, safer spot?"

"Someone has not moved on." Junior reached up and guided her to sit beside him.

"I guess not." She stared out the window. "Hey, who's that?"

Junior followed her pointed finger. Two figures emerged from the shadows on the highway in front of Ed's Diner.

"I think she's carrying a baby in one of those sling things." Joy scrambled to the trap door and quickly moved down the ladder.

Junior clambered behind her. The surprises in this place wouldn't quit.

～

315

JOY REACHED the road just a few steps ahead of her mother, who had been watching the approaching visitors from their front porch.

"Are y'all okay?" Joy stopped in front of the young woman, whose left hand pressed firmly against her sleeping baby, while her right held a bottle of water.

"Yes. Thanks." Tears glistened in gray eyes as the visitor smiled.

"We're glad to see friendly faces. Our car broke down about a mile down the road." The man who had been walking a few steps behind the lady spoke up. "The car won't even start, so we couldn't run the heater. It's too cold to wait back there with the baby for the tow truck, so we followed the GPS here."

"You're safe now. I'm Joy Fredericks. This is my mother, Terri, and my friend, Junior Caldwell." Joy stepped back as the man embraced the woman and the baby.

"We're Susan and Marty Smith." The woman reached to shake Joy's hand. "And this is baby Carrie."

"I'll go get my husband. He should be able to help with your car." Mom took the man's arm, led them to up the steps and opened the front door. "Please come inside."

"I'll be glad to go out there with your dad," Junior whispered as he walked beside her. Somehow, she wasn't surprised.

"This is Snowville, right?" Susan adjusted the baby as she stepped into the entryway.

"Yes. It's not much of a town, but we like it." Joy winced. She needed to lose the habit of cutting her own town like that.

"We had hoped to at least drive past here on our way to our motel tonight. It looks charming." The baby wiggled on her mother's hip.

Mom came out of the kitchen with Dad close on her heels.

"If you'd like, we can look at your car." Dad shook Marty's

hand. "I'm Jason Fredericks."

"Marty Smith." He pulled a cellphone from his pocket. "But we can call a wrecker to take it into town. I just needed to get my family somewhere warmer to wait."

"We might not need a wrecker." Dad walked down the steps toward his truck. "Let's just see what's up."

"Mr. Fredericks, I've done minor repairs on my family's vehicles. Is it okay if I tag along?" Junior squeezed Joy's hand.

"Of course. My mechanic son is just a phone call away, but it will help if we have a diagnosis to give him." Dad turned to the visitor as the screen door slapped behind him. "What kind of vehicle are we dealing with, young man?"

"It's an older model imported station wagon. It's been a good car, but it's at the point where things are falling off. I was trying to make it to our motel for the night." He removed his baseball cap and ran his fingers through his hair. "Do you have room for me to come along too?"

"Sure. Let's go, guys." Dad led the way to his four-door pickup. Marty took the front passenger seat, and Junior climbed into the back.

Joy waved as Dad's truck left the driveway. Helping stranded motorists was nothing new around here. Folks from out of town didn't realize how long it took for help to arrive. She walked through the screen and the big wooden door into the house. The idea of sharing an Italian dinner with Junior had sounded good. Did exciting surprises follow him everywhere?

"Joy, dear." Mom approached her quietly at the front entryway. "Could you help get Mrs. Smith's baby settled in your bedroom? We can make a pallet of blankets on your floor and keep her safe while her mommy freshens up."

"Of course." Joy waved at the lady seated in Dad's favorite rocking chair with her sleeping baby on her lap. "Follow me."

"Y'all are so incredibly kind," Susan whispered as she followed Joy down the hall. "I knew Snowville would feel like home, but this is above and beyond."

"This was really your destination? That never happens." Joy opened the door to her room. "Let me get some quilts out of the blanket chest over here, and we'll get that little one fixed up." She opened the lid of the wooden box her dad had built and found one of her grandma's quilts. Folded in half, this would be soft enough for the Smith baby.

"Oh, my." The young mother was frozen in place near Joy's dresser. "I can't believe this."

"What?" Joy stood up from smoothing the quilt on the floor in a spot where they could quickly peek in to check on the baby.

"This nativity scene. Except for the stable and the baby Jesus, it's almost exactly like mine. I've never seen one that even comes close." She leaned over, placing the sleeping baby carefully on Joy's quilt. "Where did you get it?"

"I found it here in Snowville. It belonged to the first preacher who served our church from the 1950s to the 1970s." Joy stood near Mrs. Smith. "My Grandpa built the stable, and we lost the baby Jesus. And you have one that looks like it, Mrs. Smith?"

"Please call me Susan." The lady took Joy's hand. "We should probably talk in the living room. But first, could you show me where your bathroom is?"

"Of course. Please make yourself at home." Joy led her down the hall. So, Susan owned a nativity scene like this one? How odd. And why did she and her husband and baby come to Snowville? This evening was getting stranger and stranger.

"Did you get the baby settled?" Mom came out of the kitchen, wiping her hands on a towel.

"Yes, I think she's fine. Susan is in the restroom." Joy

peeked into the dining room, where Grandpa sat eating his chili. "Mom, do you have enough chili for me? Junior and I had planned to go out for supper, but now he's helping to fix the Smith's car, and I don't know when he'll be back. Maybe I can get Susan some too."

"You know I always make enough to last for days and days." Mom led the way to the kitchen. "Let's get some more bowls and silverware out."

Joy brought bowls and spoons to the table. Mom followed with a tray of celery and carrot sticks.

"Cornbread's delicious, as usual, Terri." Grandpa raised his muffin in a toast to Mom.

"Thanks, Freddie. Not too much jalapeño for you?" Mom settled beside him.

"Nah. Never too much for me." Grandpa smiled and continued to eat his chili.

Joy carried her bowl to the kitchen island where Mom's crockpot kept their supper warm. She ladled hot chili and spooned on some shredded cheese and diced onions. A handful of corn chips topped off the meal.

Susan emerged from the hallway, and Joy waved her to the table. "There's plenty to eat. Please join us."

"This is such a blessing. I knew we were headed to the right place when we heard about Snowville." Susan walked from the table to the island with her bowl.

Joy sat down across from Grandpa and Mom. "What made you want to visit here?"

"My Great-grandma Harris used to tell me stories about her family in Missouri. She lived there until she married my great-grandpa. Then, he moved them to Oklahoma, where he worked in the oilfields." Susan sat down next to Joy. "Grandma loved talking about her family's trips to Snowville to visit her distant cousin. I think he was the pastor of your church."

"Are you talking about Orly Schumacher?" Grandpa laid his spoon next to his bowl.

"Yes. I believe his name was Orly." Susan wiped her mouth with a napkin. "Did you know him?"

"I took over for him as pastor in Nineteen seventy-five." Grandpa's eyes brightened. "He had retired a few years before and went to live with his son in Little Rock. When he died, they buried him next to his wife here in Snowville. This place gets under your skin like that."

"Amazing! Isn't God good to bring us so close to this place before our car broke down?" Susan laughed. "I'd love to hear anything else you remember. Grandma Carrie loved that couple and this place so much. And I loved her. We even named our little girl after her."

"Grandpa, where is the family Bible you found? I'm sure Susan would love to see that." Joy poured Susan some lemonade. How would she steer the conversation back to the nativity scene?

"Excuse me. I am getting a phone call from Marty." Susan walked away from the table with her phone.

Joy felt a buzz in her pocket, notifying her of a text from Junior.

> Coming back. Smith's car needs a serpentine belt.

> Mom's got plenty of chili. You can eat when you get here.

> Thanks. I'm always up for a good bowl of chili.

> You okay with jalapeño cornbread?

He might not be as fond of it as Grandpa.

100 percent!

One more reason Junior was a good fit with this family.

"They're headed back," Susan said after peeking in to check on her sleeping baby. "I need to try to find a rideshare to get us to the motel in Fort Smith."

"What? You need to find what?" Grandpa asked.

"They want to get a taxi to take them to town," Joy explained.

"No taxis come out here," Grandpa said.

"Besides, by the time your husband finishes eating, it will be late." Mom stood to take her bowl back to the kitchen. "We have plenty of room here. Y'all can stay with us."

"That's beyond sweet. But our Carrie may be waking up through the night. We wouldn't want to disturb you." Susan folded her napkin and scrolled through several screens on her phone.

"There's a whole empty house next door," Grandpa said. "Your munchkin is not loud enough to bother us from over there."

"Great idea, Grandpa!" Joy clapped her hands. "They can be the first guests at the Fredericks B and B."

"You have a bed and breakfast?" Susan asked Joy.

"Not officially. But Grandpa is staying with us now, so he's right about the empty house. You'll have everything you need over there." The wheels in Joy's head were turning again. How wonderful to be able to spend more time with these new friends.

"*Mmm.* Supper smells great." Dad entered through the front door.

Susan stood to meet her husband as he entered the dining room.

Joy waved at Junior and set his place at the table.

"Did you get the car fixed?" Mom asked.

"No. Brannon said he'd come out tomorrow. He needs to find a serpentine belt to fit their car." Dad washed his hands at the kitchen sink.

～

WIND WHISTLED through the pines as they stood at the top of the stairs on Joy's front porch. Junior's cheeks stung as tiny drops of sleet pelted him.

"Thanks again for supper." He reached for Joy's hand. "I need to go home to help Dad make sure the critters are okay. If only my sisters could take care of their animals themselves." He made a big show of rolling his eyes in disgust.

"You don't mind that much, do you?" Joy smiled.

"No. I love the horses. The goats are annoying as everything, but they are growing on me. The dog and the barn cats take care of themselves." He laughed. "But Dad still expects me to be responsible for them."

"You're a good man, Junior Caldwell." She pulled him closer and pecked his cheek.

"Glad I've got you fooled, anyway." He looked down into her eyes and kissed her forehead. "I still want to take a closer look at the location of the live nativity. Maybe I can come back tomorrow?"

"I guess you can do anything you put your mind to." Joy grinned. "See you soon."

He bounced down the steps and turned to wave before starting his truck. Too bad it took so long to drive out here and back. He still owed her an actual dinner date.

He smiled as he turned around and headed back to the narrow highway. So far, the time he spent with Joy always left him looking forward to more.

10

J oy settled on the end of her bed as the battery-operated lights twinkled around the nativity scene figures in front of her dresser mirror. The family was still buzzing about car repairs, fan belts, and travel plans. It was a little bit selfish of her to take this quiet moment now. She needed some time to gather her thoughts.

Little Carrie's eyes popped open, and Joy lifted her from the pallet before she could realize she was in a strange place. She snuggled the baby next to her and headed to join the conversation in the living room.

"So, it's settled. The three of you will stay next door in my house tonight." Grandpa was addressing the Smiths when she came out of her bedroom. "Joy, will you go over there with me to be sure they can find everything? You and your grandma didn't always inform me when something got moved."

"Of course." Joy walked closer to Susan and smiled as baby Carrie reached for her mama. "I'm just not sure where this little one will sleep. Unless we get the crib that Brannon and

Ashley used when Shelby was little." She transferred the baby to the safety of Susan's arms.

"No worries," Marty spoke up. "I got the portable crib out of the car when we returned. Mr. Fredericks said he didn't think we needed to try to get into town tonight."

"You got that right. Snowville may not have a hotel, but we can provide hospitality when necessary." Dad hugged Mom's shoulders.

Joy couldn't remember when these two had been so excited.

"I thought we might convince your friend, Junior, to stay too," Mom said, coming close to Joy.

"No, he was concerned about the weather. I don't think his dad would be excited about him being out here if we have a storm tonight." Joy peered out the window. The lights in the yard illuminated clouds that were hanging very low and boiling menacingly.

If only they had normal, peaceful snow, like other places enjoyed at Christmas. Instead, thunder and lightning might precede sleet and freezing rain. Then, as the ground temperatures dropped, they could wake up to a thick coating of ice over everything.

Did you make it home?

Joy sent a quick text to her new friend. No answer. He must still be driving.

"Whenever you're ready, I'll walk to Grandpa's with you," Joy said to Susan. "We keep the bedrooms clean, and I'll help you find extra quilts in case it gets cold tonight."

"Sounds wonderful." Susan shifted the baby into her other arm. "Are you ready to go, Marty?"

"Yeah. We probably should get out of the way of these nice folks." Marty reached to shake Dad's hand again. "It's so good to make new friends. We're looking for a place to live around here, and I plan to tell the real estate agent not to get too far from Snowville if possible."

"It's a bit of a drive to town, but we like it," Dad said.

"I do most of my work from home, so I might only have to drive to town once in a great while for meetings." Marty picked up the diaper bag and walked toward the door. "It seems like you have a strong cell signal out here, so that's good."

"Joy here has helped us make sure we take advantage of the government offers to get good Wi-Fi out here." Mom smiled at her. "She's studying community development in college, and I think she plans to start with this community."

"Hey, that's great" Susan followed Marty and Joy out the front door.

"God is good!" Joy bounced down the steps and headed toward Grandpa's house.

Joy unlocked Grandpa's front door and turned on all the living room lights with one switch.

"The place could use updating, but it's clean, and everything you need is here." She walked toward the kitchen.

"Yeah. I even do some cooking here when my watchdogs turn their heads." Grandpa entered the house behind the Smiths. "So, the fridge is stocked with basics, milk, eggs, bacon. Help yourself."

"Wonderful." Susan sat at the kitchen table, bouncing the fussy baby on her knee.

"If you don't mind, show us where the bedroom and bathroom are. I think all of us are about ready to crash." Marty still held the portable crib in its zippered case.

"Of course." Joy exited the kitchen, but Grandpa was already halfway down the hall.

"This is my room, and there is the guest room across the hall." He stood in the doorway of his bedroom.

"We're guests." Marty stepped into the room across the hall and set down the crib.

"There are plenty of towels in the bathroom." Joy led the way to the door just beyond the guest bedroom. "Grandma collected samples of every kind of shampoo and soap imaginable under the vanity so you can take your pick."

"Awesome." Marty ran his hand through his hair.

"Well, we should say *goodnight* then." Joy grabbed Grandpa's arm and steered him back towards the front door. Susan was settled in a rocking chair with a blanket covering herself and the nursing baby.

"Goodnight. Thanks again for being above and beyond gracious." She used her free hand to blow a kiss in Joy's direction.

"You're welcome." Joy smiled.

"More than welcome." Grandpa teetered a bit before finding his footing and opening the massive front door. "Sleep well, friends."

Sleet pelted Joy's head as she helped Grandpa back to her house. They had both been too excited to bundle up appropriately. Good thing their houses were mere steps apart.

"Well, we never thought we'd have our first guests so soon, Christmas Joy." Grandpa squeezed her arm just before they started up the steps to the porch.

"God had a big surprise for us, didn't He?" She held Grandpa's arm as he took slow, halting steps up. They might need to install a ramp to make things easier for him. She'd talk to Dad about that.

THE WIND HOWLED in Junior's ear as he walked through the back door into the mud room of the Caldwell house.

"I'm home, Dad." He sat on the bench to remove his boots and plopped his car keys into the basket marked with *J* that Mom had made many years ago. Her voice rang in his ear with the familiar admonition, *"It only keeps you organized if you remember to use it."*

"Okay, son," Dad called from his post in front of the television. "Is the weather getting worse between here and Snowville?"

"Worse than what?" Even though their rodeo had been over for almost a year, every response to his dad seemed to sound like a smart-aleck retort. "It's nasty, all right. Cold sleet. I was glad my defroster and wipers worked."

"Me too," Dad walked to the cabinet to get down two mugs. "How about some hot chocolate to warm those bones?"

"Won't turn that down. I'll take a quick shower and put on my PJ's while you get it ready." He padded down the hallway, past his sisters' empty bedrooms.

This house seemed so big for just two guys. At least Mom's housekeeping habits had been burned into them. They kept it cleaner than most bachelor pads. Turning the corner into his room, he grabbed his flannel pants and a sweatshirt and headed back to the bathroom.

A notification buzzed in his blue-jean pocket.

> Have you seen the weather forecast for this weekend?

Of course, a worried text from Joy.

> Not yet.

He could imagine what she was thinking.

> They're talking snow and ice between now and Friday night. I don't think we'll be kicking off our live nativity.

One day at a time.

Should he call instead of texting?

I know. Thanks for listening.

She immediately sent another text.

Goodnight.

'Night.

Being the one to provide reassurance was a new role for him. He liked this feeling. He placed the phone on the dresser and left his jeans in a heap on the floor. Mom's housekeeping habits only went so far.

Joy's eyes widened as the pellets hitting her window became more frequent. She reached for her robe and walked to the window, looking out over her front yard. Earlier, tiny balls of white sleet had bounced off the ground. The rain was coming down harder and harder, but now it was freezing and sticking rather than bouncing.

Wind rattled her window, and she reached up to touch the cold pane. Instead of harmless sleet or peaceful snow, this freezing rain would soon coat everything. By morning, the grass in the yard and the gravel on the road would be like concrete. Driving would be difficult, and walking would be dangerous for everyone.

"Wow. Can we please have a break?" Who was she talking to? Did she think God would halt this storm so they could have their live nativity scene Friday night?

We would be doing it to honor You, You know. That prayer sounded disrespectful, even to her ears.

The flickering lights in her nativity scene caught her eye. The birth of that precious little baby had certainly not been smooth and uneventful.

"Lord, forgive me for second-guessing Your plans. If we can't do our live nativity scene this weekend, help me be sure we properly honor the birth of Your Son. Amen."

She dropped her robe and slid back under the blanket and two quilts Mom had placed on her bed. How selfish and immature she was. She sighed and closed her eyes. Junior's text popped into her head. "One day at a time." He was pretty wise for a rodeo clown.

"Joy, Joy, honey. Wake up." Mom was standing in the doorway of her bedroom.

"Huh?" She poked her nose and mouth out from the thick layer of quilts. The room was slightly colder than it had been when she finally went to sleep.

"The power is out. We need to go check on our guests at Grandpa's house." Mom walked to the window, raising the blinds to let light in.

"Wow. Did it snow?" She rolled out of bed and quickly tied her bathrobe around her flannel pajamas. Yes. It was definitely cold.

"If you can call it that." Mom found her slippers on the floor and tossed them to her. "There's a solid layer of ice covering everything. I guess that's what took the power lines down."

"Not a great first impression for our new bed and breakfast." Joy went to the closet to find blue jeans and a

---

sweatshirt. Pajamas would not be warm enough for this errand of mercy.

"I'm still not convinced about that crazy idea you and your grandpa have. But regardless, we have a tiny baby over there who needs to be warm." Mom closed the bedroom door on her way out.

"Mom, do we still have Brannon's old hunting boots somewhere?" Joy came out of the bedroom in her stocking feet. "I think my cowboy boots will be too slick on the bottom."

"I think so." Mom came back upstairs and opened the door to Joy's brother's old room.

Did it snow?

Joy laughed as she spotted a text from Junior on her cellphone.

Sort of.

She sent her reply as Mom made lots of racket during her search of Brannon's closet.

We don't have any power out here.

Ours is out too. I guess I will have to go out and start my truck in a bit to keep this phone charged.

Good idea.

Joy's cell phone was okay now, but it wouldn't last much longer. Her little car might not have much gas, but Dad's truck did.

We need to check on Mr. and Mrs. Smith and the baby.

She sent another quick text. There would probably be more time to talk to him later.

> Yeah. Let me know if y'all need anything. My dad's headed out to our deer lease to see how many trees came down. I told him I'd stay around home while he's gone, but I might come out to your place in a day or two.

He probably would enjoy driving in this weather, and coming to her aid would be a good excuse. She certainly didn't plan to take her car anywhere. Grandma had always said the only difference between boys and men was the size of their toys. She stifled a laugh. It would be good to see him anyway.

> We're fine for now. Let me know if you plan to come out.

> See ya!

"Here you go. They'll be a little big on you." Mom pushed her bedroom door open with Brannon's big lace-up boots.

"Thanks!" Joy pulled on another pair of warm socks before sliding her feet into the boots and lacing them as tightly as she could. These should give enough traction to make it over to Grandpa's house.

"So, are you planning to bring our guests back with you?" Dad asked as he added a log to the fire he had blazing in their fireplace. "I'll have this house toasty warm in just a bit."

"We'll see what they want to do," Mom said, pulling a knit cap down around her ears.

"We should have exchanged numbers with them," Joy said, checking the battery level on her phone. "Let's just get over there, Mom."

"Right behind you."

331

On the front porch, the sunlight reflecting off the icy front yard blinded her. Overhead, the branches of the trees tinkled like a set of wind chimes. She took a deep breath, and her lungs filled with cold air. With her bright red scarf across her nose and mouth, she made her way down the front steps. Only a couple of slick spots caught her foot, but she probably needed to come out to scrape the steps when they returned. She wouldn't want Grandpa falling if he ventured outside.

Mom crunched through the layer of snow on top of the ice and reached Grandpa's house a few steps ahead of Joy.

"Susan, Marty, are y'all okay?" Mom rapped on the front door.

Joy shoved her hands in her pocket. These one-size fits all gloves were not helping her fingers stay warm.

"Come in, come in." Marty opened the front door, ushering Joy and Mom inside.

"I'm so sorry the power went off," Joy said.

"I don't think you had any control over that, now, did you?" Marty laughed. "We're all fine. Susan is in the living room."

"How's Miss Carrie?" Joy walked closer to Susan, peeking under the blanket that covered the little face.

"As my Granny would say, she's snug as a bug in a rug." Susan laughed. "She has a great blanket sleeper that works exactly the way it was intended."

"My husband has a fire going at our house if you'd like to come over." Mom stood near the front door.

"Grandpa has a fireplace too." Joy crouched down to peer into the firebox at the edge of the living room. "There's even some wood in there."

"Yes, I noticed that." Marty said, "But I didn't want to start a fire without asking."

"Of course. Do whatever you like." Mom said. "That might

be better than getting the baby out on the ice to come to our house."

"I'll bring some more firewood in. Grandpa has quite a bit out there." Joy peered out the window at the pile she and Brannon had helped stack a few weeks ago.

"Yes. That would probably be better anyway. We have intruded enough on y'all." Susan agreed. We found plenty of food in the kitchen, and I noticed it's a gas stove, so we should be fine out here."

Little Carrie squirmed in her mother's arms.

"May I hold her?" Joy reached to retrieve the baby. With all the extra layers of clothes, she was soft and warm.

"Of course." Susan handed little Carrie over. "And come in here. I want to show you something." She walked toward the guest room.

"Marty brought the rest of our luggage on the last trip to our car. I'm so glad I packed this with my clothes. I thought it would be safer than in a moving box." She unzipped the suitcase next to the bed and squatted down beside it.

"Look" She held a carved figure up to Joy.

"Wow. This looks so much like the angel from my nativity scene." Joy balanced Carrie on her left hip and took the wooden figure from Susan. "So, you think the same man carved both of our sets?"

"The way my Granny talks, my great-great-grandpa carved nativity sets for several members of the family right around the Civil War. He replaced some pieces in her aunt's old set and then made a new one for my great-great-grandma. You must have the original set that was rescued from the riverboat down here in Arkansas. So, the pieces will be similar but not identical. When our power comes back on, we'll set them side by side to see how they compare." Susan reached for the baby, and Joy gladly transferred her to her mother.

Joy squatted next to the suitcase and carefully unwrapped another figure.

"Rescued from a riverboat? Now I'm really curious." She ran her finger across the carved woodgrain of the shepherd she held. "You and Marty were certainly meant to end up here. Is it bad to say I'm glad your car broke down?" She stood, wrapping Susan and the baby in a hug.

"I don't think it's bad, because I agree," Susan whispered. "But let's don't tell Marty. I don't think he's super happy about that right now."

"Probably not." Joy laughed. "When I come back with more firewood, I might want to look at the rest of your set if that's okay."

"It's much too good to keep under wraps," Susan said.

"That's the way I feel about mine." Joy winked at her new friend and walked out into the living room. "On my way to get some firewood, Mom." Zipping up her coat, she opened the front door.

She stomped across Grandpa's yard to the woodpile. Too bad she hadn't looked for his leather gloves inside. Maybe her little knit gloves would hold up long enough to lug enough logs into the house for Marty and Susan to use.

"Hey, girl!" Joy looked up to see Lisa's mom waving at her from the house on the other side of Grandpa's. "Y'all doing okay?"

"Yes, ma'am. Do you have enough firewood?" Joy knew this incredible lady could take care of herself.

"Malcolm—I mean Big Ed—has me fixed up. Come see me in a little bit. I'll show you the costumes."

"Yes, ma'am. I will." Joy crunched back across the yard with her arms full of wood. Who knew she'd be so busy on a day when the world had come to a standstill?

"I KNOW YOU EXPECTED THIS." Junior told the stock contractor on the other end of the phone call. "The live nativity out at Snowville has been canceled for Friday and Saturday. We might still need your camel next weekend if the weather is better."

He nodded, checking his list for the next call he needed to make about the sheep.

"Sure. I'll let you know." He disconnected, looking at the text from Joy again.

No live nativity this weekend. Stay warm!

He had expected her to be a lot more upset about this cancellation. It was a good thing her attitude was staying positive. Tomorrow, the roads would be clear enough that he could drive out to see how she was holding up.

He remembered the shine in her eyes when they viewed the nativity scene here in Crossroads. This was one girl who knew what was important about Christmas. He was fortunate he'd run into her on top of her grandpa's house that day.

"Son, are you ready to help me check on the horses and goats in the barn?" Dad opened his bedroom door.

"Sure." He disconnected the call he had been making. Maybe he'd add a sweatshirt under his warmest coat. The temperatures today were extreme. After they fed the animals to keep them warm from the inside, he hoped Dad could come up with some human food. Unfortunately, the roads wouldn't permit a hamburger or pizza run anytime soon.

He followed Dad out to the barn. On the other side of the pasture, a bright green cedar stood out against the white landscape. That would make a great Christmas tree. With less than two weeks until the big day, live greenery wouldn't have time to dry out. Yeah. This was a good idea. Cutting down a tree would generate some energy. Sounded like an excellent way to stay warm. Besides, wouldn't Mom be happy if she knew he was trying to bring back some Christmas spirit to the house?

"Hey, where are you?" Dad hollered from the open door of the barn.

"Coming." He jogged the last few steps and grabbed a feed bucket when he stepped into the warmth of the barn.

"Dad, do you know where Mom's Christmas decorations are?" He scooped some feed into the goats' bucket.

"Yeah. Why?" Dad checked the controls on the overhead heater.

"With this new snow, we need a little Christmas inside the house." Junior faced his dad with his hands on his hips.

"You are probably right. Your sisters borrowed some things just after Thanksgiving to fix up their new places. But, yeah. Even a couple of bachelors need to be festive this time of year." Dad found a brush and worked on Belle's flank.

"Oh, and I will need to know where we keep the Christmas tree stand." Junior filled the feed bin for the goats.

"It's in the box with the artificial tree, I guess." Dad removed his cowboy hat and stepped back.

"Won't need the tree, just the stand." Junior sealed the feed container to head off stray varmints and buttoned up his jacket before slipping his hands into his leather gloves. "Don't worry. I'll take care of everything."

Ax in hand, Junior tromped across the pasture behind the barn. Funny that he'd never noticed this tree until today. A line of scrubby evergreens along the edge of the field just below the rise led up to the hill where Hope and O.D.'s house stood.

He could have called on them for help with this little project. His brother-in-law might be working at the truck dealership, but his sister would have liked to help him decorate. No, it felt good to be doing this on his own. Dad had gone inside to stoke the fire in the fireplace and maybe even start supper on the gas stove.

How long did it take a cedar tree to grow? This one had probably been here since before Mom passed away. They'd had a couple of rough Christmases even before then. Uncertainty about whether the treatment was helping had led to Mom's reluctance to keep going through the ordeal. Toward the end, Mom had been at peace, but her illness cast a pall over the house.

That first Christmas after Mom died, no one was in the mood to decorate. O.D. and Hope got engaged and started fixing up his grandparents' old house. Then, the next fall, Faith and John K. got married and moved to Fayetteville. Junior's childhood home had been neglected. That was about to change.

Junior stood in front of the tree that was just an inch or two taller than his six feet. He snapped a picture and texted it to Joy.

> Guess what this is.

She didn't answer right away, so he texted again.

> My new Christmas tree. Not as big as
> the one I helped cut down in Snowville.

Enough of that. Junior gave the trunk a couple of good hard chops, then stood back to decide which way the tree would fall. A couple more whacks, and it fell away from him.

He stood up and removed his knit cap. Working out here was definitely keeping him warm. Maybe there was something else he could do outside. No, he'd better get this tree into the house. The clouds above him had darkened since he came out. They might be in for more precipitation.

"Okay, little tree. Let's get you into the warm house." He picked up the trunk and tried to shake off some stray ice collected on the branches. Yes, one job at a time. It would take the rest of the evening to get this thing set up and decorated anyway.

Joy's text popped onto his phone.

> Cool! I can't wait to see what it looks like after you decorate it.

He sent a thumbs-up symbol and a smiley face. Once again, he wished she didn't live so far away.

11

"Yes, they're being very nice about it." Joy stretched the cord of Grandpa's old wall phone so that she could see out the kitchen window of his house. "But, really. They're stranded here. They'd like to move on now that the roads are clearer."

"Joy, it's just not possible. You realize we have the same weather to deal with here in town, right?"

She should be used to his excuses by now.

Outside the window, Big Ed packed some more snow around the bottom of the snowman he'd built for his son. Unfortunately, there hadn't been enough snow to do much building, but Eddie was enjoying the novelty of the cold, white wonderland.

"It boils down to money, doesn't it?" Joy tapped the kitchen cabinet with a pencil.

"Don't be ridiculous." Brannon replied.

"Yes. It does. You are making more money pulling cars out of ditches than you would helping one stranded family. Thanks for nothing, brother." She slammed the receiver into its cradle near the refrigerator. Now, to tell Marty and Susan that Brannon wasn't on his way out to Snowville to fix their car.

She stepped out the back door and closed it carefully before picking her way across the backyard toward her house. As thankful as she was that Grandpa still had a telephone that worked and that his house had stayed relatively warm for the last few days, Susan and Marty were probably ready to move on, and Brannon wasn't being helpful.

"Hi!" Susan waved at her from the front porch. "Your mom has grilled cheese sandwiches ready for lunch."

"Thanks, I'm coming in. How's little Carrie?" Joy jogged the last few feet along the path her dad had cleared.

"She loves all of the extra attention. Marty and I won't be able to set her down after we leave here."

"Yeah. About that." Joy grimaced.

She turned toward the road to find the source of wheels crunching on gravel.

Junior's truck moved slowly to a stop in front of her.

"Tell Mom to save me a sandwich. And make another one." Her cheeks warmed as she walked toward the grimy white truck.

"I guess your cell phone lost its charge?" He waved and walked toward her.

"Yeah. Dad drove down the road to check on the guys restoring the power. I don't think my little car has enough gas. It wouldn't keep running long enough to charge anything." She found her blue knit gloves in her coat pocket and pulled them on.

"Our lights came back on late last night. I thought I'd take a drive today. The roads are still pretty rough, but my four-wheel drive made it okay." He stood next to her, his blond curls catching the sunlight.

"Aren't you supposed to be working on a research paper?"

Joy didn't want him to leave, but she hated to be the source of problems at his house.

"Believe it or not, I have a really good outline going. I did some research on financing a restoration project with grants. I'm forming a plan for your old high school gym. I'll have a week after we get back to school to do the writing and get it turned in. Dad was impressed enough to let me break out of 'ice jail' for the day."

She followed his glance up the hill to the school. His dad wasn't the only one who was impressed. Marty Smith waved at her from in front of Grandpa's house. Too bad her brother wasn't as motivated to come out here as Junior was.

"Come on in. Mom's got sandwiches ready." She attempted to keep her voice cheerful. Brannon's selfish behavior shouldn't ruin this happy surprise.

"Something wrong?"

She should have known her new friend would sense her mood.

"Oh, I'm just grumpy. Brannon's not coming to fix Susan and Marty's car. At least not today." She reached for Junior's hand. "We've enjoyed having them here, but I know they didn't intend to stay this long."

"And you feel responsible." Junior laughed. "You realize there is at least one big Act of God involved here, right?" He bumped her shoulder. "I tell you what, if your dad can help me tow it up to the old service station, maybe we can at least get the repairs started."

"Really? You'd do that?" Joy squeezed his gloved hand.

"Why not? As my Granny would say, 'Can't dance, and it's too wet to plow.'" Junior laughed.

"I've got to meet this Granny of yours." Joy opened the front door and led him inside.

Mom's kitchen buzzed with conversation as hot grilled

cheese sandwiches arrived on the kitchen table. Joy found bowls and ladled tomato soup for each person seated there.

"Thank you, sweetheart." Grandpa smiled as he settled himself at the table.

"Got some for me?" Dad stomped his feet inside the back door. "I told the power crew that Big Ed planned to cook supper for them this evening. They didn't officially confirm, but this might move downtown Snowville up on their list."

"Here, Dad. You sit next to Junior." Joy brought a sandwich and a bowl for his soup.

"So, Ed and Lisa are able to cook at the diner?" Mom asked.

"The smoker still works, and they have some beans cooking on the gas stove," Dad said between bites. "They might need some help serving."

"If we can get someone to watch Carrie, I'll be glad to help," Susan said.

"I can be your babysitter!" Mom brought some more napkins to the table.

"Just let me know how I can help too. The power crews deserve anything we can do for them." Marty agreed.

Chatter continued until Joy stole a sideways glance at Junior.

"Marty, I talked to my brother a while ago." Joy cleared her throat. "He's not going to be able to come out to work on your car today."

"What?" Dad laid his spoon down with a clatter.

"That's understandable," Marty said. "We're not in a hurry to leave, anyway."

Susan smiled at him and hugged little Carrie closer on her lap.

"Mr. Fredericks, if you'll help me pull their car up to the old gas station, I'd be glad to take another look." Junior wiped his chin with a napkin. "If we just had a serpentine belt."

"Dad, aren't some belts hanging on the back wall of the service bay? You know, the wall that didn't get knocked down?" Joy pictured the workbench in her mind.

"Hey. I think you're right." Dad reached for a glass of water. "And since Marty's car is an older model, there's a good chance we might be able to find the right one."

"Always thinking." Junior smiled at Joy.

JUNIOR PRESSED extra hard on the brakes in the Smith's car as Joy's dad's truck slowed to a stop in front of the boarded-up building. It had been a while since he'd steered a disabled vehicle towed with a strap. Thankfully, there hadn't been a big hill to come down just before the final curve. This car wasn't picking up any speed for sure.

"There. Stopped," Junior whispered aloud. He hoped he could live up to his promise to Joy. Replacing a serpentine belt wouldn't be hard, but with cold fingers, it wouldn't be fun.

"Okay. Good steering, young man." Mr. Fredericks shook his hand. "I'm going to check on Big Ed at the diner. You'll find the tools you need inside the old gas station. Brannon just boarded up and left everything where it was."

"Mom and Grandpa have quite a little daycare with Eddie and baby Carrie. They might need help bringing in some more firewood." Joy stood nearby with a ring of keys.

"I'm on it." Mr. Fredericks waved from the driver's side of the heavy dual-wheeled truck as it lumbered toward Joy's house.

Junior waited while she removed a Master lock on an old wooden door. The front reception area of the old gas station was covered with plywood, and the big overhead door leading to the former garage bay didn't look operational. At least the area outside the old place was neat and clean. Obviously, Brannon wanted to keep things presentable. He was probably hoping for a possible buyer for the station.

"I wish there were lights in here." Joy's flashlight swept the crowded room.

An oily, grimy odor greeted them. No doubt it smelled like every other back room of a gas station all over the country. Junior used the light Joy's dad had loaned him to illuminate the area in front of his feet before he took another step.

"What does your brother plan to do with this place?" Junior walked around a case of motor oil and spotted some old rubber belts hanging on the wall.

"He's talked to some folks about buying it, but it would take so much work to get it back to any kind of functional business." Joy walked toward the same parts he had seen. "I think it could be cleaned out and transformed into something else. Maybe a little café or even a market of some kind."

"Great idea." Junior shined his light on the cardboard label surrounding a large belt. "This one just might work."

"Really?" Joy stood next to him.

"Yeah. Looking closer, I don't think it's quite right." Junior climbed over an old stepstool and some metal that must have been on the part of the building that took the hit by the semi-truck. "But what about this one?" He reached behind the bench to grab the top of another rubber belt pinned behind the wooden structure.

"Be careful. There may be some broken glass down there. That front window went flying during the wreck." Joy angled her light onto the belt he was reaching for.

"*Oomph.*" Junior gave the rubber belt a good yank, and it came up to the top of the bench, sending something clattering to the floor at his feet.

"What's that?" Joy bent down, picking up a round ball of bubble wrap secured in duct tape.

"I don't have a clue." Junior supplemented her flashlight with his.

"I don't believe it." Joy handed him her flashlight and held the object in both hands. She carefully peeled the gray tape from the plastic bubbles and opened the package.

Junior aimed his light toward her trembling fingers and wrapped her shoulders in a hug.

"It's the baby from the nativity set!" She whispered.

"Huh! And your no-good big brother took better care of it than you expected, didn't he?" Junior laughed.

Joy smiled at him, holding the highly polished wooden figurine close to her chest.

"It's been here all along. I never thought I'd see it again."

"Our dads would turn this into some sort of lesson, I'm sure," Junior said. "Jesus is always with us. If there's distance between us, we put it there."

"Well said." Joy stood on tiptoe to kiss his cheek. "I'm just so happy right now."

"Me too." Junior agreed. "And I'm pretty sure this is what I need to fix the Smith's car. Today turned out pretty well, didn't it?"

"For sure." Joy took her flashlight back from him, placing the unwrapped baby Jesus in her coat pocket. "You know what? God has been sending us some good gifts this year."

"Yes, he has." Junior pulled her against him, tenderly kissing her lips. Maybe the gift of Joy was the best one.

"I think we have a table for you right over here." Joy greeted Junior as he walked into the diner, with Marty trailing behind.

"I'll need to clean up first." Junior wiped his hands with a red shop rag.

"How's the car?" Susan pecked her husband's grimy cheek.

"Running. I learned a lot as a mechanic's assistant today." Marty stepped to the side. "But I need to clean up too. Don't want to contaminate Big Ed's diner."

The two tromped through the crowded tables to the hallway leading to the restrooms. Joy grabbed a pitcher of iced tea to refill the glasses of the power company workers enjoying a meal. Then, she guided a struggling Lisa to an empty table near the door.

"Here, you'd better get off your feet." It was getting tougher and tougher for her friend to walk around.

"Yeah. I need to respond to the texts that keep coming into my phone." Lisa pulled her cell phone out of her apron pocket. "I already know what they say."

"Your Mom?" Joy moved the little table to give Lisa some more room.

"Worse than that. My OB nurse." Lisa frowned as she typed. "The doctor has just about had it with me being out here so far from the hospital. Especially with more winter weather in the forecast."

Joy's mind churned with visions of Big Ed trying to drive his pregnant wife to town on icy roads.

"Joy, I'm afraid I won't be here for the live nativity this weekend." Lisa replaced her phone in her apron pocket.

"Oh, honey. Don't worry about that." Joy pasted on a smile. After the event was canceled for weather last weekend, she'd almost given up on making it happen this year.

"The doctor wants me to stay in a motel near the hospital until the baby gets here, which may be sooner rather than later." Lisa massaged her stomach.

"What about Little Eddie?" Joy waved at Ed, who had plates of barbecue pork in the window for Junior and Marty.

"My mom will keep him here until we rent another room for them too. I can't say I like the timing of all this. The baby is not actually due until after Christmas, and the weather this time of year is usually warm, so I just didn't have any idea." Lisa mopped her forehead with a napkin.

"Hey, you just do what you need to do. I love you like a sister, so this little one will be my niece." Joy sat down across from her, patting her hands.

"Thanks."

"You okay?" Big Ed stood at Joy's elbow with the two plates of food.

"Here, sit down with your wife." Joy took the plates from him. "And thanks for doing this. I'm sure these workers appreciate it. You two are the best." No way to hug the big guy until she set the food down. Snowville was blessed to have this hardworking couple.

"Here you go," She found an empty spot for Junior and Marty and placed their plates next to the rolled-up silverware.

"That looks great!" Junior smiled at her. "Can you sit down with us?"

"Maybe in a minute." Joy stopped beside him. "I think the workers are about to leave. Then, there will be plenty of clean up." She used her forearm to push back her hair so she wouldn't get her hands dirty.

"Okay, what's wrong?" Junior reached for her hand.

Somehow, she needed to learn to hide her worries a little better. But maybe that was impossible with this guy.

"I just learned we're losing our Mary and Joseph for the live nativity," Joy whispered. "I don't know if this thing will happen."

"Hey. You said you played Mary last year. I was planning to

be dressed as a shepherd to keep an eye on the stock, but I could fill in as the concerned daddy." Junior picked up the bundle of silverware and unwrapped a fork.

"Thanks. I appreciate your positive attitude." She bent down to give him an awkward hug. "Talk to you soon."

Joy and Susan bustled around the diner, clearing plates and carrying them to the kitchen. The bright sunshine reflecting off the ice outside almost made Joy forget they had no power in the building.

She heard Susan whistling as she passed near the big sink in the kitchen.

"We wish you a Merry Christmas?" Joy laughed. "Better be careful. These hungry guys will be looking for figgy pudding."

"I don't remember when I've had so much fun." Susan laughed. "After sitting around looking at each other for a few days, this hard work feels good."

"Now that your car is fixed, I guess you'll be leaving. I'm sure there is a motel in town that has power by now." Joy used the sprayer to clean a dish.

"We won't go far," Susan said. "Marty and I have been talking. With my family connection, we've decided to find a place to live nearby. I have my eye on that old gas station, too. It would be a great place to sell locally made honey, jelly, and that kind of thing. We might even have fresh vegetables and eggs if we find a spot that would support a garden and a chicken coop."

"Really? You're staying?" Joy placed the plate she was holding in the other side of the sink and turned to hug Susan.

"Marty's job can be done almost totally from home. So, our home might as well be somewhere we love." Susan laughed.

"That's the best news ever!" Joy wiped her hands with a towel. "God just keeps giving us the greatest gifts this year!"

"Great job, ladies." Ed pushed the kitchen door open. "I

think the power crew has decided to move Snowville up on their schedule. Not that I asked them..."

"The way to a workman's schedule is through his stomach." Joy laughed. "You did a wonderful thing here, Ed."

"That's for sure." Susan agreed.

"Why don't you ladies join those last two customers? I'll finish up in here." Ed hung a skillet on the pot rack over their heads.

Joy held the door for Susan as they walked into the almost empty diner. The sunlight coming through the front window seemed to be dimming a little.

"Is that what I think it is?" She moved closer to the cold plate glass.

"Snow! Not ice this time, just good old-fashioned flakes of snow!" Susan stood beside her, looping her right arm with her elbow.

Lisa stood up and walked toward them.

"Thanks for your help, Joy." She waved as she passed them. "I guess I'd better go help my mom get all our stuff packed up. Now that it's snowing, my nurse just might come out here to get me."

"Take care of that precious little one. She might just share my Christmas birthday." Joy hugged Lisa the best she could with the baby in the way.

"Hi, Ladies. Where's your food?" Junior pulled out a chair for Joy.

"Right here." Ed set two plates full of food down on the table. "For my servers extraordinaire. Lisa, I'm right behind you. Just getting things locked up here."

Susan and Joy settled at the table and unwrapped their silverware.

"This is delicious. Reinforces our decision about settling in this community." Marty smiled.

"Susan was just telling me." Joy picked up her fork.

"Oh, and by the way. Suz, what would you think about playing important roles in the community's Christmas celebration? That is, assuming the weather clears up by next weekend." Marty winked at Joy.

"What are you talking about?" Susan asked.

"It was his idea!" Junior held his hands out in front of him.

12

"Do you think they've missed an angel and a shepherd down there?" Junior held Joy's hands as they looked over the brightly lit town below them.

"Most of the visitors are gone." Joy smiled up at him. "I think we can take a short break."

"Are you sorry it's the last night of the live nativity?" His thumb made little circles in her palm.

"No. Even though we only did it for three nights, we had a good crowd. I'm so glad the weather was nice this weekend." She leaned on the window ledge in the tower room of the church building.

"Hey—there's Cody, rounding the curve just past the manger scene." Junior pointed. "Imagine if that path wasn't paved. He could never have enjoyed this."

"I knew that was a good idea when we did it a few years ago. I wanted everyone to be able to come and see." Joy moved closer to his side.

"Susan and Marty were great as Mary and Joseph. And

when little Carrie was sleeping in the manger, well ..." Junior swallowed to keep the tears out of his voice. Standing next to the stable in his shepherd's costume, he'd felt closer to Bethlehem than ever in his eighteen years.

"Yes. It has been good." Joy looked up at him.

"I know your family will want you around for the next few days but remember you're coming to see my Christmas tree. I'll even make you a birthday cake a day late."

"You're making the cake?" She laughed.

"Yeah. My big sister said she didn't think I could do it alone. Challenge accepted."

He had asked his dad the other night how he would know when he'd met 'the one.' Dad's answer—"When all you can think about is the next time you see her."

"I will be more than happy to eat the first cake you've ever made yourself." Joy shook his hand.

"It may not be the first. I plan to practice on Christmas. Granny will be there, and ..."

"Thank goodness for grandparents." She looked at her hands. "I wasn't dressed this way when I found the nativity scene up here, but my grandma was the first one I showed it to."

"And now, it's finally complete again." Junior brushed back a stray lock of hair from her forehead. Many things seemed complete these days.

"Hey, maybe I will even be so good at cooking, I can fix some killer meals for you next year at college." He grinned, remembering how happy Dad had been when he'd firmed up his college plans.

"You're not majoring in culinary arts. Just concentrate on your physical education courses, so you can be the coach or activity director when we reopen the Snowville gym." Joy smiled.

"That's the plan." He pulled her close for a quick kiss.

"I guess we'd better go back downstairs. Your sheep may have run away by now." She held his fingers as she started down the winding staircase.

Junior followed, careful not to step on the hem of his shepherd's robe. There weren't many girls who could make him wear a costume like this.

Joy stopped at the bottom of the stairs and turned toward the entryway of the church building.

"It belongs here." She turned on a spotlight above the table her dad had built for the old nativity scene. "Grandpa helped me understand that. Susan said the family story was that a blacksmith named Snow rescued it from a riverboat wreck and returned it to her family in the Eighteen hundreds. Grandpa said this town was named after a man named Snow, who ran a blacksmith's shop on the edge of town. I don't think God makes mistakes."

"You are so right about that." Junior hugged her as close as he could, with her angel wings interfering.

"Now, the whole community can enjoy it. Brannon can do scavenger hunts for his son if he wants to, but he is not allowed to mess with this nativity scene ever again." She touched the baby in the manger, then reached for Junior's hand again.

"I don't think he would dare." Junior agreed. "I'm glad you decided to move it over here."

"Some gifts are too good to keep to yourself." Joy stood on tiptoes to kiss his cheek.

Junior's face warmed. Yes. He'd have to agree. This year, he'd received some of the best gifts ever, and it wasn't even Christmas yet.

THE END

About the Author

Raised by a single mom in Southeast Kansas, Jenny moved to Arkansas as a senior in high school. There she found an instant connection with her new classmates, especially her prom date, whom she married in 1976. Writing took a backseat to a full-time job with the State of Arkansas while they raised their children. The stories in her head wouldn't let her alone, so she found kindred spirits in the Fiction Writers of Central Arkansas, and American Christian Fiction Writers-Arkansas Chapter. She served in various offices in each of these groups, attending conferences and placing in contests along the way.

She was a monthly columnist for Ouachita Life magazine for many years, and self-published two collections of her observations about life with the help of Britta Meadows at Peas in a Pod Publishing.

After retiring twice from the State, she found a publishing home with Scrivenings Press when her first novel, Hope Takes the Reins, was published in 2022. It was followed by Faith

Moves Mountains in 2023, and will be joined by Love Never Fails in January of 2024.

Now that she and her husband are both retired, they look forward to visits with three married children and eight grands. One of their favorite activities is driving the backroads of Arkansas. James indulges her love for history when she is especially drawn to old, abandoned towns and dreams of bringing them back to life.

This story was inspired by the only real collection she owns, a set of Department Fifty-six Original Christmas Village houses and businesses, which come out of storage to be displayed during the holiday season, and sometimes for Christmas in July.

Also by Jenny Carlisle

Hope Takes the Reins

Crossroads Series—Book One

O.D. Billings has lived in the shadow of his brothers all his life. Even his name brings him down, so he has used only initials for years. Now, his older brother has returned home from the army, rejecting the role his family expects him to assume in their pickup truck dealership, and the younger brother is intent on risking his life on the back of a bucking bull. O.D.'s fans at the rodeo love his confident swagger during tie-down roping competitions, but every trail he heads down on his own seems to wind up going nowhere.

Hope Caldwell's world is still reeling after her mom's recent death from cancer. She thrives on keeping the family's rodeo business going. Getting back to normal seems impossible when she overhears her uncle's plans to sell out. How can she continue without the only way of life she has known for all of her nineteen years? Can she rely on the help of a big-talking cowboy? Or does he have too many problems of his own?

Get your copy here:

scrivenings.link/hopetakesthereins

~

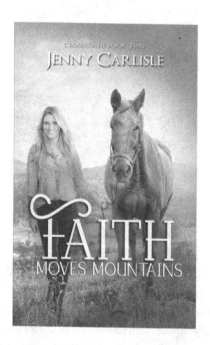

Faith Moves Mountains by Jenny Carlisle

Book Two in the Crossroads Series

John Kennedy (John K.) Billings has spent his whole life living up to his hero inspired name. Now, back from a traumatic incident in the military, he finds himself running from the fact that he is only human, with real-life struggles to overcome.

Faith Caldwell feels free to pursue her own dreams now that her family's regularly scheduled rodeo has ended. After helping care for her cancer-stricken mother she is determined to bring big city medical expertise to small-town Arkansas. While trying to prove she can fulfill her dream on her own, a new admirer seems determined to pull her down.

Both enjoy the idea of seeing more of the world, but find their hearts are still tied to the mountains of Arkansas, and the people who live there.

Can these lifelong neighbors help each other face their weaknesses while following God's plan for their lives?

Get your copy here:

https://scrivenings.link/faithmovesmountains

More Christmas Books from Scrivenings Press

Chiseled on the Heart

by Elaine Marie Cooper, Kelly Goshorn,

Cynthia Roemer, and Candace West

A Christmas Legacy Novella Collection

The Gift of a Lamb by Elaine Cooper

Orphaned and forced to move hundreds of miles to a new home, 9-year-old Elias and 12-year-old Charlotte cling to each other for security as war brews between the colonies and Mother England. Facing fear and adversity, Elias is filled with anger as he and his sister journey to the unfamiliar north to live with their uncle. But Uncle Silas has much to teach young Elias about faith and trust in God. And even more lessons about love and forgiveness that will nurture the young boy towards becoming the man his parents always wanted him to be.

A Lasting Legacy by Cynthia Roemer

Loudoun County, Virginia, 1814

When a disabling injury sends Daniel Hawkins home from war, he's at a loss how to provide for his young wife, Maggie or the child she's carrying. As Christmas approaches, he finds a sheep his father carved as a boy and decides to bide his time whittling a Nativity as a gift for Maggie. When she goes into labor during a Christmas Eve blizzard, Daniel is forced to face his feelings of inadequacy. And perhaps learn that God has a plan for his life after all.

Healing within the Pieces by Candace West

Prison shackles haunt Nathaniel Hawkins upon his return home only to discover it occupied by a woman in hiding.

Bad men are no strangers to Delia Evans, but the intruder who barged into the farmhouse shrinks from her.

With no other refuge, they must endure each other. But have they misjudged? When the past shadows their doorstep, is a grudge worth the price of a man's life?

The Christmas Carving by Kelly Goshorn

Wyatt Hawkins, dreads Christmas. Memories from the fatal shooting of his childhood friend and fellow Union soldier at the hands of Confederates on Christmas Eve, 1864, has left a bitter taste in Wyatt's mouth toward God, the holiday season, and his former fiancée, Madelyn Cunningham. As Christmas draws near, can the Christmas star he's carving for his family's heirloom Nativity point Wyatt back to the woman he's never forgotten and the faith he's left behind?

Release date: October 3, 2023

https://scrivenings.link/chiseledontheheart

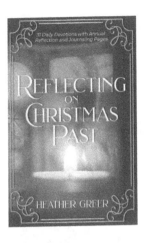

Reflecting on Christmas Past:

31 Daily Devotions with Annual Reflection and Journaling Pages

by Heather Greer

Each December starts with hope. This year the peace and joy promised in every Christmas song will finally be ours throughout the season.

By mid-December, we're worn out, weighed down by our to-do lists. Decorating the tree was rushed, crammed between baking and visiting relatives. Our card list grew. So did the gift list. Now that the kids (or grandkids) are all in school, we have more than one Christmas program to attend. We can't skip the office party. Oh, and did we forget caroling again?

Wouldn't it be wonderful to slow down and focus on the traditions that make Christmas meaningful to us? Wouldn't it be nice if we could remember what those are?

With thirty-one devotions and ample space for reflection and memories, we can enter each Christmas season with renewed focus on what matters most to us and leave behind the extras that usher in disappointment and fatigue. Ending this holiday season with the same hope, love, and joy we entered it with is what Reflecting on Christmas Past is all about.

Release date: October 10, 2023

https://scrivenings.link/reflectingonchristmaspast

~

Mama Dated Santa

Contemporary Romance by Amy R. Anguish

Trudy McNamara doesn't do Christmas anymore. But she will do anything for her nephew Mark, even take him to visit Santa. After Dad died and the holiday bucket lists stopped, December hasn't been the same. But Trudy finds herself tangled up with the toy store Santa and Christmas when she discovers her mom ... dated Santa.

Nick Russo, manager of Russos' Toy Emporium, is at a loss as to how to save his family's store. When Uncle Paul, the Santa and part-owner, hires Trudy to revamp their store, Nick's life turns upside down. He's been so focused on the numbers, the Christmas season has become nothing more than one last drive for sales. But Trudy makes him re-evaluate his attitude as well as want to help hers.

Release date: October 17, 2023

https://scrivenings.link/mamadatedsanta

True Blue Christmas

Mystery by Susan Page Davis

New neighbors, cryptic Christmas cards, and jury duty. What next? Campbell McBride is juggling her new role as a private investigator with her slightly wacky personal life. Can she and her dad figure out who stashed a valuable painting in their client's attic? And is the murder of an egocentric landlord somehow connected?

Release date: November 7, 2023

https://scrivenings.link/truebluechristmas

❧

12 Days of Mandy Reno

Contemporary Romance Novella by Regina Rudd Merrick

Law student Amanda Reno is stuck in her tiny hometown in
Kentucky to complete her studies virtually and work part-time at the
Clementville Café. Her parents are stuck in Brazil, leaving Mandy to
celebrate Christmas without them.

Young Sheriff Clay Lacey takes matters into his own hands, devising
a plan to take Mandy's mind off her crushed expectations. She is no
longer his classmate's tagalong kid sister, but a young woman he is
increasingly attracted to.

How will Mandy react when she finds out Clay is the one working to
make sure she has a memorable Christmas? Will she be pleased? Or

will she cringe as she thanks the man who may be falling in love with her?

Release date: November 14, 2023

https://scrivenings.link/12daysofmandyreno

Scrivenings
PRESS
Quench your thirst for story.
www.ScriveningsPress.com

Stay up-to-date on your favorite books and authors with our free e-newsletters.

ScriveningsPress.com